UNEARTHED

UNEARTHED

LARA STAUFFER

HORIZON PUBLISHERS
AN IMPRINT OF CEDAR FORT, INC.
SPRINGVILLE, UTAH

This is a work of fiction. The characters, names, incidents, places, and dialogue are products of the author's imagination, and are not to be construed as real. The opinions and views expressed herein belong solely to the author and do not necessarily represent the opinions or views of Cedar Fort, Inc., Permission for the use of sources, graphics, and photos is also solely the responsibility of the author.

ISBN 13: 978-0-88290-981-3

Published by Horizon Publishers, an imprint of Cedar Fort, Inc., 2373 W. 700 S., Springville, UT 84663
Distributed by Cedar Fort, Inc., www.cedarfort.com

LIBRARY OF CONGRESS CATALOGING-IN-PUBLICATION DATA

Stauffer, Lara, 1972- , author.
Unearthed / Lara Stauffer.
pages cm.
Summary: Matt resents his father and boycotts everything he stands for until Matt becomes involved in an archeological dig in Mexico.
ISBN 978-0-88290-981-3
1. Excavations (Archaeology)--Mexico--Fiction. 2. Father and child--Fiction. 3. Book of Mormon stories. I. Title.

PS3619.T384U54 2012
813'.6--dc23

2012009716

Cover design by Brian Halley
Cover design © 2012 by Lyle Mortimer
Edited and typeset by Whitney A. Lindsley

Printed in the United States of America

10 9 8 7 6 5 4 3 2 1

Printed on acid-free paper

For Chad,
for encouraging me to
get here, and
For Rich and Ana, who
always believed I could.

ACKNOWLEDGMENTS

AN AUTHOR IS NOTHING WITHOUT THE PEOPLE AND resources around her, and for them I am grateful. This book would never have been realized without the talents and time of the following people:

My wonderful kids—Emilie, Jared, Zach, and Carson—for understanding when Mommy had to "sit and stare at her computer"; Michelle Miles, the best crit partner ever; and my dear writing friends Eva Schegulla, Brenda Birch, and Colin Galbraith. My sister (and most enthusiastic cheerleader) Cassaundra Kover, and my brother Chris Roney for his encouragement. Also my lifelong friend Aimee Eliason, who read my first novel in high school (and was very *kind* about it!) and who is still my first choice for beta reader today. Also a HUGE thank-you to Shersta Gatica; my editor, Whitney Lindsley; and all the folks at Cedar Fort.

Joseph L. Allen, John L. Sorenson, John Welch, and Brant Gardner, from which I drew my inspiration and research, and Dan McKinlay of The Neal A. Maxwell Institute (formerly The Foundation for Ancient Religious and Mormon Studies), for patiently and helpfully answering my inquiries.

Finally my parents, Rich and Ana Roney, whose unwavering belief in me has kept me strong, and my wonderful husband, Chad Stauffer, who has loved and supported me through the process.

You guys rock!

Lara

PROLOGUE

"And it was about the sixth hour, and there was a darkness over all the earth until the ninth hour. And the sun was darkened, and the veil of the temple was rent in the midst. And when Jesus had cried with a loud voice, he said, Father, into thy hands I commend my spirit: and having said thus, he gave up the ghost." (Luke 23:44–46)

*   *   *

"And it came to pass in the thirty and fourth year, in the first month, on the fourth day of the month, there arose a great storm, such an one as never had been known in all the land. And there was also a great and terrible tempest; and there was terrible thunder, insomuch that it did shake the whole earth as if it was about to divide asunder. And there were exceedingly sharp lightnings, such as never had been known in all the land. . . . But behold, there was a more great and terrible destruction in the land northward; for behold, the whole face of the land was changed, because of the tempest and the whirlwinds, and the thunderings and the lightnings, and the exceedingly great quaking of the whole earth. . . .

And many great and notable cities were sunk, and many were burned, and many were shaken till the buildings thereof had fallen to the earth, and the inhabitants thereof were slain, and the places were left desolate." (3 Nephi 8:5–7, 12, 14)

*   *   *

Mexico City was eerily quiet.

And rightfully so—it was just before 4:00 a.m., and the revelry from the night before diminished to a few solitary club patrons drowning their sorrows as muted chords of music drifted out into the quiet streets.

At the stroke of four, the earthquake started innocently enough—with mild groanings and shifting beneath the earth's crust. Within seconds, knickknacks rattled on table-tops and shelves, and warning sirens shrieked long and high. After fifteen seconds, it was in full force, a 5.5 on the Richter scale, and was felt by everyone in the city.

It was a surprisingly short quake—the main phase lasted about twenty seconds, just enough to set off car alarms, to down a few power lines, and to frighten a lot of people—especially the ones old enough to remember the devastating Quake of '85.

When it was over, no buildings had fallen, but there were a few casualties. A large chunk of Catedral Metropolitana, Mexico City's famous cathedral, had fallen to the ground and smashed an empty tour bus parked nearby, and the Zócalo, a prominent square in the middle of the city, now had jagged, unsightly cracks in several places.

There were no major injuries, only severe jitters, and as soon as the sun rose, cleanup would begin. Mostly there would be relief—relief it hadn't been a "big one." In fact, a large portion of the city's population turned over in their beds and went back to sleep.

*   *   *

Ninety miles away in Cholula, tourists in the local hotels slept right through the quake, barely feeling anything as the ground shuddered beneath them.

One elderly lady, who'd had trouble sleeping anyway, sat up in her hotel room and held tightly to a rosary, repeating a prayer over and over. She had felt her bed move and a gentle rocking motion that lasted only a moment, but nothing more than that.

Outside her window, she could see the outline of the ancient church that sat on the great pyramid Tipanipa, its windows lit, sitting ghostly silent in the silvery moonlight.

Little did she know that something in Cholula *had* happened during the quake, which had now been over for several minutes.

She sighed softly and lay back onto her pillow, clutching the rosary to her bony chest and muttering to herself.

Within three minutes, she was asleep, along with everyone else.

1

SOMEONE IS IN MY ROOM.

Matt could sense it, even though layers of sheets and blankets were cocooned around his head. He hadn't been able to sleep until the early morning hours, and now sleep was impossible. Sunlight filtered annoyingly through the slats in the closed blinds. He lifted up the corner of his comforter and snuck a peek to see who had invaded his room. His mom stood in front of the bed, hands on her hips, surveying the untidy clutter with a frown. *What does she want?*

She was probably thinking his room looked like an earthquake had hit it. Then again, it had looked this way for the past eighteen years, so she was used to it. Matt peeked at her again. She was staring at the floor, no doubt studying the balled-up shirts, socks, and shorts, not to mention old, smelly shoes and stacked-up sports equipment, strewn everywhere on the blue Saxony carpet. The walls were just as untidy, plastered with posters of famous athletes and painted wood shelves sagging under the weight of multiple trophies and medals. Matt pulled the comforter back over his face and pretended to be a large, shapeless lump snoring loudly underneath the thick plaid coverlet until he heard the dreaded noise.

Whoosh!

"Wake up, sleepyhead!"

Matt groaned within his covers as bright sunlight assaulted the room.

Whoosh. More sunlight.

"C'mon, Matt! 'Rise and shout, the Cougars are out!'" Karen Staubach sang as she reached over him and finished pulling the blinds up with another *whoosh*. Clouds of dust puffed out over the bed, and Matt rolled over, covering his head with both arms to shut out the blinding light. "*Mommm . . . what are you doing?* I'm sleeping."

"Look, just because you're a high school graduate now doesn't mean you get to sleep in the rest of your life," she chided, patting Matt's legs to give her room to sit. He obliged, and she sat on the bed, resting her hand on his shoulder.

"Your dad needs your help. He's only with us this weekend—and then he's gone the rest of the summer until you leave."

Matt squinted at her. "Same old story. What does he need from me?"

"Just knowing you want to help him would be *nice*," she replied in an exasperated-mother tone.

Matt sighed heavily and pulled the covers over his face again. "But I don't want to help him. You could've waited to tell me this later instead of the crack of dawn," came his muffled voice.

"It's *eleven fifteen*!" Karen retorted, slapping the covers.

"Yeah," Matt groaned. "The crack of dawn."

"Get up before I beat you," Karen joked dryly, rising from the bed. "I have Krispy Kreme downstairs, in case you were wondering." She threw the shameless bribe over her shoulder and headed for the door.

Doughnuts. And not just any doughnuts—*Krispy Kreme.*

"Okay, Mom, you win," Matt muttered as he rolled out of bed to find a shirt.

*   *   *

"So what *exactly* does Dad need help with?" Matt sat at the large oak kitchen table downstairs, wolfing down doughnuts and milk. Karen stood at one of the white-tiled counters, eyes glued to the tiny TV set by the microwave. The news was on, as it was every morning.

"Uh-oh—an earthquake in Mexico. I hope your Dad's site wasn't affected." Karen stopped squeezing the oranges to watch. "*Oooh*, good thing that bus was empty. . . . I'm sorry, did you say something, honey?"

"What does Dad need my help with?" Matt repeated thickly through a mouthful of doughnut.

"Oh—he's in the garage . . . he needs help loading the supplies, and later on he's going to pick up some more equipment from the lab." Karen kept her eyes on the TV screen as she spoke, squeezing the already-limp orange in her hand. "I have to get Beth to swimming lessons, then I've got two haircuts, and then I have to run and pick up groceries for tonight, otherwise I'd help too."

"What's tonight?" Matt asked, draining his glass.

"Dinner," Karen replied with a smirk. "You promised to eat dinner with us tonight, remember? And Taryn Gilley is coming over. You need to be nice to her."

Matt snorted. "Why did you have to invite her? She's . . . weird."

"Because," Karen began, turning the TV off and sitting down with a full glass of orange juice next to her son, "she's one of your dad's students this year, as you already know, and your dad wants to go over things before they leave." She paused and lifted an arm to run her fingers through Matt's silky, dark hair. "Your hair is getting so long. Maybe I could just trim it a little . . ."

Matt shook his head. "Not in a million years, Mom."

Karen Staubach had a beautician's license and ran a business out of their gray, split-level house, where she had a steady clientele. Matt couldn't remember a time when anyone but his mom had cut his hair. But she always cut it so . . . *short*.

"I'm trying to grow it out this time," he told her so he wouldn't hurt her feelings.

Karen sighed. "And I bet you haven't shaved in a week."

Matt smiled his thousand-watt grin, the grin that had been voted "Best Smile" of his high school graduating class. It was a smile that could melt any female heart within close range. Karen looked at her only son, the all-star basketball player. He'd gotten a scholarship to play ball, and he was leaving in two and a half short months. She would miss him.

"I'm not shaving before *she* comes over, if that's what you're getting at," Matt muttered.

"She's a nice girl," Karen commented, sipping her juice.

"Yeah, and she'll find some *nice guy* who loves wasting his time digging up dead things just like she does," Matt finished.

Now it was Karen's turn to roll her eyes. "I don't know what's a bigger waste of time—digging up pieces of history, or shooting a rubber ball through a hoop all day long . . ."

Matt's smile faded, and Karen was instantly sorry. "Oh, Matt . . . you know I didn't mean it that way," she began as he shoved an entire doughnut in his mouth and rose from the table. "I'm proud of your talent. You're a great ball player," she added, her voice growing louder as he walked away.

"Yeah, I know," Matt grumbled, grabbing his car keys. "I'm gonna go wash my truck."

"WHAT ABOUT HELPING YOUR FATHER?" Karen yelled as the screen door slammed shut behind him.

She sank back down at the table. "Nice, Karen," she mumbled to herself, running a hand through her short brown hair and sipping her juice. She grabbed the remote from the top stack of newspapers on the table and turned the TV back on.

*　　*　　*

At dinnertime, Karen found herself in the kitchen yet again getting ready.

"Mmm, pot roast. Hold me back."

She smirked at Matt, who entered through the back door, tossing his keys on the counter. "Don't be smart," she snapped back. "Pot roast is good for you. Did you get everything moved?"

Matt nodded. "Dad is gonna kill me one of these days."

"Well, in my defense, about a hundred and eighty pounds of it was sun block and bug spray," came a voice from behind him. Ben Staubach, a tall, reedy man with tanned skin and thinning cornsilk hair, entered behind his son. "Smells great, honey," he complimented, walking over to the sink to wash up. "Taryn here yet?"

"She called and said she was running a few minutes late." Karen turned her cheek so Ben could give her a kiss. "She's such a nice, *thoughtful* girl." She gave her son a pointed look.

"Any calls for me?" Matt asked, deliberately ignoring her and checking the message board.

"Not that I know of," Karen replied. "Why don't you wash up? You and Beth can set the table—unless you want to make the rolls."

She saw Matt roll his eyes and skulk out of the kitchen. She motioned silently at the door swinging in his wake. "He okay?" she whispered to her husband.

"Seems to be." Ben sighed, taking a bag of frozen instant rolls out of the freezer. "He didn't talk much this afternoon, but he's been keeping to himself a lot lately."

"He's been keeping to himself the last two years," said Karen, sniffing, watching her husband dump the rolls onto a silver baking sheet. "He still doesn't want to go, does he?"

"Nope. Hasn't changed his mind," Ben replied, sounding more than a little sad. "I didn't press him either."

Karen exhaled in frustration as she arranged the meat and vegetables on a platter. She couldn't understand why Matt didn't want to go to Mexico with his father, especially right before he went away to college. This would be the only time they'd be able to spend together, but Matt wanted no part of it. It broke her heart that her only son seemed to want nothing to do with Ben's work, but he'd never opened up about it, and Karen had stopped prying.

There were a lot of mysteries to Matt. But the most upsetting was that Matt hadn't been to church since his sophomore year in high school. One day, he just announced he needed to "take a break" from church for a while. And after that, he'd refused to go. All the pleading and force in the world (pleading from Karen, force from Ben) didn't change his mind, even when Ben threatened to turn him out of the house if he didn't go to church. Karen had pleaded with Ben to relent, and after a while, he'd given up. Ben was too busy with his teaching and his projects anyway—which Karen suspected was a part of Matt's strange behavior.

It had been a sore subject in the Staubach family since—one to avoid bringing up. Matt was the "one who didn't go to church," and Karen was tired, tired of the Relief Society ladies attempting to comfort her, tired of the home teachers showing up and Matt storming out, tired of explaining that Matt didn't go to church or wasn't active, and so on.

And now this strange attitude about Mexico—Matt was trying to isolate himself from everything his father did. Or so it seemed to Karen.

She listened to Matt tease Beth in the dining room as they noisily set the table. She'd had to practically beg him to eat dinner with them tonight. She wanted her son back—the old Matt, the boy who went to church and actually *liked* to be around his family. Where had he gone these past few years?

Her thoughts were interrupted by the doorbell. *Taryn.* That poor girl. For as smart as Taryn Gilley was, she was pretty clueless. Karen shook her head and smiled as she finished putting the rolls in the oven.

*   *   *

"You get the door," Matt said to his sister, Beth.

"No, *you* get the door!"

"I'm older than you."

"You're a dork, Matt. It's just Taryn."

"I'm busy setting the table."

"Fine, you can set the rest of it by yourself!"

Beth Staubach huffed out all her breath and thumped the silverware down in a clatter on the tablecloth. Her brother could be a real pain sometimes.

She walked to the front door and opened it. Taryn Gilley stood on the doormat, carrying a mess of papers and looking sweaty and breathless, which was how she usually looked. Taryn was Matt's age, and she had just graduated from high school too. Beth was a little sad that Taryn wouldn't be in Young Women anymore. And she had always been nicer to Beth than the other Laurels at church were.

"Hiya, Beth, am I too late?" Taryn asked, tucking a stray strand of dark hair behind one ear.

"No, we're just setting the table," Beth replied, grinning at her. "Come on in."

*   *   *

Matt listened as his sister welcomed Taryn inside. *Why does she have to have dinner with us? Isn't it enough that she lives down the street and works for Dad?*

There was something about Taryn Gilley that always made his skin crawl—it wasn't the unibrow, or her huge ears. Okay, maybe that was part of it, but it was the way she *talked*. Taryn was bold to a fault and said whatever was on her mind, which bugged Matt. Especially when she would look at him pointedly and ask him why he didn't go to church anymore—which she'd done frequently over the years.

Taryn made him uncomfortable. And tonight would be no different, he was sure. At least she was going away with his dad, and he'd probably never see her again. *Maybe she'll fall into a sinkhole in Mexico. . . .*

"You done with the table?" Karen poked her nose out of the kitchen.

"Just finished," Matt griped, dropping the last fork in its place.

"Good. You're not letting Taryn stand out there on the doorstep, are you?"

"No, Beth got the door."

"Just checking." Karen smiled and disappeared back into the kitchen, while Beth entered the dining room with Taryn behind her.

"Hi, Matt!" Taryn greeted brightly, and Matt tried not to flinch as he said a quick "Hey, Taryn" back.

Taryn looked the same as she always did: erratic dark hair pulled into a messy ponytail, huge ears and hairy eyebrows, and skin far too pale. Her nickname had been "Dumbo" in middle school, and in high school, where the kids were more cruel, she'd been called by a different name (which Matt had started and after a while felt kind of bad about): the Gilley Monster.

"Hello, Taryn. How's your family?" Karen asked as she came out of the kitchen, holding the pot roast. Ben followed closely behind her, balancing large bowls of vegetables and mashed potatoes.

"They're fine. They're all off to Tumtum the next few days. Mmm, that smells really good, Sister Staubach," Taryn replied, pulling out an oak chair and sitting down next to Beth and across the table from Matt. "Thanks for inviting me."

"Oh, *please*, you're welcome any time," Karen replied sweetly.

Matt resisted the urge to snort and roll his eyes.

"You didn't want to go rock climbing?" Beth asked, spreading her napkin on her lap.

"Well, I have a date with some rocks in Mexico on Monday, so I couldn't," Taryn answered, winking at her.

"Me too," Ben agreed, setting the mashed potatoes down. "And this time, we brought enough bug spray!"

Matt tried hard not to scoff at this last statement and observed the food on the table, calculating how quickly he could eat and leave without seeming too rude.

It's going to be a long night . . .

2

INNER ENDED UP BEING FAR TOO LONG FOR MATT. THE conversation was mostly between his parents and Taryn, with periodic interjections from Beth, but he kept to himself and silently ate. It was the same old topics, anyway, like at every other dinner.

Mostly they talked about DIG, which stood for Dyson International Gems. Sam Dyson was a family friend—he'd been roommates with Matt's dad in college. He also shared his dad's passion for archaeology. A successful diamond broker, Sam fully funded all the summer class digs Ben had taught since Matt could remember. This summer, DIG was sponsoring a dig in Cholula, Mexico. Taryn and his dad couldn't stop yapping the whole meal about how *this time* they were smack dab in the Book of Mormon lands, the new instruments they had, and *blah blah blah*.

After dinner, his mom brought out a chocolate cream pie for dessert, which Matt wolfed down to avoid having to hear any more about DIG, and afterward he went up to his room, while Taryn and his parents sat in the living room to continue discussing details of . . . *naturally* . . . the dig.

Matt folded his pillow in half and lay back on his bed, wishing Taryn would just go home.

*   *   *

Matt snapped awake. The sun had gone down, and the red numbers on his clock glared 9:15 in the semidarkness. He could still hear Taryn's laughter downstairs. *Good grief, is she ever going to leave?*

His room was stuffy, so he stumbled down the stairs and out into the backyard, where it was quiet and cool and where he could think. He sat down on the back porch steps and leaned forward on his knees, watching the stars winking at him in the sky.

All of his friends had gone to Moses Lake that morning— to the dunes—and he wished he'd gone with them. But this was the last weekend he'd see his dad all summer, and his mom had pleaded with him to stay. It was the least he could do, especially since he'd turned down his father's invitation to "hang out" in Mexico together. *As if that would happen in a million years.* His dad's idea of "hanging out" mostly meant sitting in a dirt hole with a brush and tweezers, poking at rubble while Matt watched, bored out of his mind. *No thank you.*

Matt heard his parents and Taryn break into loud laughter, and his eyes narrowed. He could be sitting by a campfire at the dunes right now. All the guys from his old team had invited him the day before. But he'd promised his mom he'd do dinner with the family. Now he was regretting it. *And of course all the cheerleaders are probably there too*, he thought, shaking his head. *Including Crystal.* Crystal Lessner, the cute blonde cheer captain who always smiled at him from the sidelines . . .

But he was here, sitting by himself, no cheer captain and no campfire, listening to the Gilley Monster entertain his parents in his house.

Could this night be more lame?

Matt folded his arms and sat thinking rude thoughts until he felt someone steal up and sit next to him. He turned his head and jumped at what he saw.

It was Taryn. She was looking at him earnestly, and he involuntarily scooted a good twelve inches away from her.

"Looks like I found the prodigal son," she observed, smiling, and Matt sighed, exasperated.

"And you actually wonder why I never talked to you in school." The words were out of his mouth before he had a chance to stop them.

Taryn seemed unfazed. "No, I knew why. You were just too cool. But it's okay. I forgive your immaturity. So, why aren't you going to Mexico?"

Matt hated it when she asked questions point blank. *Man, she is infuriating.*

"It's none of your business," he snapped, refusing to look at her.

"Forthcoming, as always." She sighed softly and was silent.

After a minute of silence, Matt was thinking of getting up and leaving, when she spoke.

"You know, I've always been jealous of you," she admitted, drawing her knees up and putting her skinny, white arms around them. "Your dad is the coolest guy I know. He's knows so much, and he's done *so* many great things." She looked out at the yard. "But what I've never understood is—you don't seem to care about any of it."

Matt didn't reply, so she kept going. "I'd kill to have my dad care even a little about what I love to do. But he's too infatuated with my brothers and their careers as 'potential pro football players.'"

"What, are we *sharing* now?" Matt asked, sarcastic. He wanted her to leave him alone. She was annoying. Everything about her was annoying.

"Yeah, I guess," Taryn replied, shrugging. "Why are you so against what your dad does? I don't get it."

"Of course you don't," Matt spat back. "All your dad thinks about is football? Well, *my* dad doesn't even know the rules of basketball. He only came to one of my games all last season. Archaeology is his life. There isn't room for me."

"Wow, you have it just as bad as me," Taryn mused quietly, surprised by the outburst of emotion.

Matt immediately felt dumb. He liked to give the impression he was made of stone. *Clearly this latest admission isn't helping with the illusion.*

"I'm sure both our dads care about us," Taryn offered, staring off into the backyard. "They just have their priorities screwed up. Work before kids . . . that sort of thing."

Matt snorted and smiled bitterly. "Yeah, whatever."

"But I'm serious about not understanding," Taryn repeated. "I mean, your dad is teaching kids like me valuable skills they'll use the rest of their lives—you could try and cut him a break."

Matt pressed his lips together and stared ahead. *I'm not going to tell her any more,* he thought. He was sick of his dad's obsession with dead things and with the past. Especially since his obsession had proven to be more important to him than his own family.

"He's too busy to care," Matt muttered. Taryn chuckled at this last statement, causing him to turn and look at her.

"Busy doing good for others," she corrected. "I guess I never understood why you've always had such a bad attitude about it."

Matt glared at her. "Look, it's nice that you *care* and everything, but I don't want to talk to you right now. Have a fun summer."

He patted the top of her head and stormed off, leaving Taryn sitting by herself, her mouth gaping open after him.

*   *   *

Matt felt a twinge of regret as he raced up the stairs to his room. He really shouldn't have been so mean to her. But the Gilley Monster was far too nosy for her own good. He wasn't going to let her dissect him like one of her pet projects. She was just a nerdy bookworm who loved digging around in the dirt like his father did.

But what had upset him most was how close she'd come to the truth.

All Matt's life, he'd been different from his father. Athletic, good-looking, and smart enough to get by in school, Matt was popular and well liked by everyone. But he was an exceptionally good basketball player too and his father never seemed to acknowledge his talent. Sure, his mom had made it a point to attend all of his games over the years. She'd even cheered him on when his team had traveled to the state tournament—and won. But his dad claimed to not understand the game or sports in general. Ben Staubach's life was archaeology—and teaching other students about archaeology. End of story.

Matt's mom had always been full of excuses: "Your Dad

loves you, sweetie; he just doesn't understand basketball," or "Your Dad wanted to be here, but he discovered something and had to stay to supervise the project." These excuses got old very quickly to Matt, who keenly felt his father's absence at his games.

The final straw came during a game Matt's sophomore year, when Matt ran into a player from the opposing team and was knocked unconscious, and he had spent the night in the hospital with a concussion. His father wouldn't even leave Guatemala because he was on the brink of a "major" discovery.

Of course the "major discovery" ended up being nothing. Matt couldn't forgive his dad, and the next Sunday, he stopped going to church. At the time, it seemed the only way he could strike against his father. And for two years, he'd stayed away. This summer would be no different. He was going to do his own thing, and as soon as he graduated, he was out of here.

And Matt had done well for himself. After his accident, with a renewed determination to be the best basketball player around, Matt practiced day and night—drills, weight training, aerobic conditioning, anything he could think of to become the best he could be. And it had paid off. All the hard work combined with his natural talent had caught the eye of a college recruiter at the state tournament, and Matt and one of his teammates, Ronnie Clemp, had been offered full-ride scholarships to play for Duke University.

His mom had been ecstatic, and his dad seemed happy for him, but not in the way Matt wanted.

It didn't matter. In two and a half months, he'd be in North Carolina, fulfilling his dream. At six foot three, he certainly wasn't as tall as Ronnie (six foot six), but he was the best.

Matt put his arms behind his head on the bed and closed

his eyes, reliving the highlights of the state championship game. Then the phone rang loudly, rudely interrupting his daydreams. Matt reached over and answered it on the second ring.

The line was crackly, and on the other end a panicked-sounding man's voice rambled in Spanish: "*Ben? Estas tú? No vas a creer esto! Nos pego el terremoto—*"

"Um, no comprendo . . . let me get him," Matt interrupted quickly. He didn't know much Spanish (he'd been sucked into taking French with a high school girlfriend), but it sounded like Manny, his father's counterpart in Mexico.

Matt took the cordless extension with him and left the room, taking the stairs two at a time down the staircase. "Dad? Phone's for you. I think its Manny."

Ben appeared at the foot of the stairs, joined by Karen and Taryn. He took the phone from Matt, who shrugged as he handed it to him.

"Hello? Manny, *Hola—*" He got no more out, because Manny had started speaking again, very loudly. Ben's eyebrows furrowed into a frown as he listened. Instead of running back up to his room, Matt sat down on the carpeted steps and watched his father. Ben's eyes widened in surprise.

"*Que sucedio? En serio? Que tan hondo es?*" he rattled off quickly.

"Something happened to the dig site during the earthquake," Taryn whispered to them all as Ben continued to listen and respond in hurried Spanish. "A big crack opened up in the earth, and it's really deep, and Manny says he can see something down there," she continued to translate.

Karen brought both hands up to her mouth. "Did he find something?"

Ben had walked away from them into the sitting room and was still conversing with Manny, but his voice was tinged with excitement as he spoke quickly, apparently giving orders.

Taryn was listening intently, absentmindedly twisting a fat lock of hair that had escaped her ponytail around her finger. "Wow. I guess we're leaving first thing tomorrow now," she translated for Karen, who gasped.

"So soon? But the . . . and the . . . well, I guess we'd better get packing!"

Beth, who had joined them a moment before, groaned. "But Dad was going to have some daddy/daughter time with me tomorrow! He promised!"

Matt had heard enough. It was probably just another stupid false alarm, like that time in Guatemala a couple years back. All his father's excitement had produced nothing then, and it was probably nothing now. Matt got up and walked silently up the stairs to his room. They probably wouldn't notice he'd left.

MATT COLLAPSED ONTO HIS BED AND FLIPPED THE TV ON to ESPN. He could still hear muffled voices below, and he turned the volume up.

A few minutes later, there was a loud knock on his door. He turned off the TV. "*What?*"

"Matt, it's Taryn. Do you mind if I come in for a sec?"

Matt was about to retort that yes, he *did* mind if she came in (not to mention the grief he'd get from his friends if they found out the Gilley Monster had been in his room), but he bit his tongue. He wasn't *that* mean.

"No," he said tiredly. "What is it, Taryn?" This was the most she'd ever spoken to him since that Saturday activity he'd been forced to go to at the church their sophomore year. It was a little too much to handle all at once.

The door opened, and Taryn entered. Her eyes were

unusually bright. It was obvious she was excited about the phone call. She walked inside a few steps and glanced uncertainly around the room, pausing.

"What's up?" Matt asked impatiently from his bed. He had the remote pointed lazily at the TV and was ready to turn it back on.

"Were you even listening just now?" Taryn asked, incredulous. "The earthquake opened up a fissure at the dig site—and *something's down there!*"

Matt looked at Taryn. "Obviously *you* weren't listening earlier. I don't care, remember?"

Taryn's mouth fell open, and she looked at him as if he were the dumbest guy in the world. Then she must have realized her mouth was open, because she shut it quickly and nodded her head. "All right, then," she said, marching over to sit on the foot of his bed.

It was too much for Matt. "What do you think you're doing?" he asked rudely, pulling his legs up as she sat down.

"Listen, *stupid*," she began. "I've got a deal for you. One you won't be able to resist."

Matt looked at her pointedly. "Try me." He meant it. *She is so annoying. Did she really just call me stupid?* But before he had time to get angry, she started talking again.

"This is what I propose. You give your dad a month." She held up a finger. "*One* month in Mexico."

Matt narrowed his eyes at her. "You've got to be kidding."

"No, I'm actually quite serious," Taryn replied. Her eyes blazed at Matt, stopping a retort dead in his throat. "You need to go to Mexico because, honestly, you don't appreciate what your dad does, and you need to." She paused, and took a deep breath. "And in return, I'll do something for you."

Matt looked at her, utterly nonplussed. *What is she talking about?*

"You're going to Duke, right?" she continued.

Matt nodded. "Right."

"Well, what if I offered to tutor you next year?"

"What?"

"Tutor you. You know, for different classes. I'm assuming a sports scholarship isn't excusing you from doing actual *schoolwork* in college."

"Are you saying I'm dumb?"

"No, I'm sure you're a whiz."

"That's sarcasm, isn't it?"

"It doesn't matter. We could set up a schedule on Skype. You would have your own personal tutor whenever you need, for any class. The entire year."

"That's not worth it to me."

Taryn looked at him, surprised. "Please!" She put her fingers in the air, making air quotes. "Hi, I'm Matt the superstar. I barely passed calculus and almost didn't graduate high school, but who cares? My super basketball-playing powers will get me through *college* . . ."

She'd hit the nail on the head. Now he was mad.

"Look, Gilley M—" He stopped himself, tossing the TV remote down. "I don't need your help. I'm not going. I have important stuff to do here this summer."

She narrowed her eyes at him. "Like what? *Sleep?*"

They both glared at each other across the bed.

Taryn obviously wasn't backing down. In fact, she didn't seem intimidated at all by Matt's show of temper. She folded her arms, and when she spoke, her tone was quiet and pleading. "It's *one month*, Matt. Four weeks. Thirty days. You can do anything for thirty days. I'm offering to tutor you for a *whole year of college*. Take it or leave it."

Matt looked at her. She had guts—that was for sure. And he did hate school sometimes. It wasn't exactly his strong point . . .

Taryn studied him, the corners of her mouth turning up smugly. "You're considering it, aren't you?"

Matt bit his lip. "And all I have to do is go on this stupid dig for a month?"

"Right. And just one other little thing . . ." Taryn trailed off, clearly embarrassed.

"I'm *not* taking you on a date," Matt blurted out.

Taryn wrinkled her nose at him. "No! I just need you to explain to me . . . in minute detail . . . the rules of football."

Matt snorted. "Really."

Taryn looked miserable. "I don't understand football. And my dad thinks I'm slow because I don't get it. I think it's some sort of . . . *affront* to him or something. Especially since he coaches. It's like how you don't understand *your* dad's work."

She had him there. Matt looked at her, a little more kindly. "You want me to explain football to you," he repeated.

"I mean, what's the big deal?" Taryn retorted. "Football, basketball, *foosball*—they all have a ball and two teams. They're all the same, aren't they?"

"Actually, they're very different," Matt began gently but caught himself.

Taryn grinned up at him in triumph. Her teeth were a lot whiter than he remembered.

"You're gonna take me up on it, aren't you?"

*   *   *

"Oh, honey, I haven't seen you this excited in a while," Karen mused as her husband ran out from the bathroom and stuffed toiletries into the open suitcase on their bed. She sat in an overstuffed chair by the heavily curtained window, watching him. "But you really have to leave tomorrow?"

Ben looked at her. "Things have changed, Karen. How can I stay here?"

Karen nodded. "I get it. I just wish I had you around for a little while longer, that's all. But I'm used to it now."

Ben walked over and swiftly kissed his wife on her forehead. "We'll Skype every night."

"*Liar*," she retorted with a smile. "But at least promise me every few days."

"Where's Taryn? Did she go home?" Ben asked absently as he grabbed all the clean socks out of his dresser drawer and dumped them into the suitcase. "I'll have to call Sam to make sure the jet is ready for us at 10:00 a.m."

"Oh, I don't know if she left. You want me to call?" Karen offered.

"Mom? Dad?" It was Matt. He was standing in the doorway, his hands shoved deep in the pockets of his cargo shorts. Karen noticed Taryn was standing just behind him.

Ben actually stopped packing. "What is it, son?" he asked.

Matt looked down at his feet. "Well, I was thinking about . . . things . . ." He paused, and Taryn cleared her throat quietly. Karen stared at them both.

"It sounds like you really wanted me to go on this dig, and if you haven't changed your mind . . . I think . . . I think I'd like to go. But just for a month. To see what you do. On digs," he finished awkwardly.

This was met with silence. Karen felt her eyes grow as big as dinner plates. Ben's mouth dropped open.

"Are you sure, son? You *want* to go to Mexico?"

Matt grinned at his father. "Why not? I don't have much else to do right now. Unless you don't want me to go . . ."

Ben immediately stepped forward and shook Matt's hand enthusiastically. "No, son, I would love for you to go!" He stopped shaking his hand and folded Matt in his arms in an awkward embrace, and patted him heartily on the back. Matt looked sheepish as they broke apart.

"This is a day for great news!" Ben exclaimed happily. "What made you decide . . . ? You know what? I don't want to know. You've just made me so happy, son. I promise you won't regret it."

Karen fought the tears that welled up in her eyes. Matt had never expressed any interest in Ben's work, and she had all but given up hope for any father/son reconciliation before Matt left for college. But now it seemed there was *some* hope after all.

She stood up and blinked away her tears. "Well, it's late, and you guys are leaving tomorrow, so I'll help you get packed. You going home to pack, Taryn?"

Taryn didn't seem to hear her. She was standing behind the duo of father and son with a strangely victorious look on her face.

I don't know what Taryn said to Matt to convince him to go, but thank heaven for her, Karen thought happily. And she had an idea of how she could pay Taryn back for her kindness.

"Well, it's late," Karen repeated. "You'd better get home and pack, Taryn, 'cause I need you here at six o'clock sharp tomorrow."

"Six in the morning? *Why?*" Taryn asked.

"You'll see," Karen replied, grinning.

Ben was right. Today was certainly a day for good news!

4

THE NEXT MORNING WAS CHAOTIC. MATT FOUND HIMSELF acting the part of the glorified pack mule after being unceremoniously woken up by Beth shining a million-watt flashlight directly in his face at five thirty.

"Mom told me to!" she screeched as she ran out of the room, dodging pillows that were flying at her like missiles.

Taryn had arrived at six with two duffel bags and only one eye open, and had been whisked by Karen into her "salon," which was really a back office Ben had converted for her to work in. By nine o'clock, they still hadn't emerged. Matt kept glancing at the doors of the salon as he worked, wondering what his mom was up to.

Ben spent most of the morning with his ear glued to his worldphone, speaking in rapid Spanish as he ran around making last-minute plans and directing Matt in his pack mule duties. Finally, all the luggage was loaded into the shiny, black DIG van.

Beth was a sobbing mess because she was losing her dad and her brother in one fell swoop. She wouldn't stop giving Matt random hugs.

"C'mon, Beth, it's just a month!" Matt protested when Beth came up behind him and hugged him for the umpteenth time that morning.

"That's not what Mom said," Beth retorted. Her voice was muffled because she had her face buried in the back of Matt's T-shirt. "She said you might be gone all summer."

Matt snorted. "Well, Mom's wrong, so don't worry." He dropped the duffel bag he was holding and turned to give her a gruff hug. "Thirty days, and I'm out of there. Then I'll be back to giving you a hard time again, squirt."

He ruffled her bangs, and she giggled and ran off. She could be irritating sometimes, but Matt would definitely miss her. He slung his bag over his shoulder as Ben walked into the kitchen and snapped his phone shut.

"I think we're all ready to go. You have your passport, son?"

Matt nodded and patted his shorts pocket. His dad always made sure everyone in the family had passports, even though he was the only one who ever used one.

"Good. The jet is ready. What *are* Taryn and your mother up to?"

Matt shrugged his shoulders. "Don't know. They haven't come out all morning."

Suddenly the doors to the salon opened, and Karen came out wearing a large smile on her face. "You guys all ready, then?" she asked, walking over to give her husband a hug.

"Yep, we've got stuff wrapped up at both ends," Ben replied. "I was just trying to expedite the robot shipping— they said ten days, and I need it in about *ten hours*. Luckily

Sam was able to pull some strings for me."

Karen laughed, releasing him. "Sam always comes through, doesn't he?"

Suddenly a blurry shape bolted out of the salon and whizzed by Matt, and all he caught was the back of a glossy brown head as Taryn disappeared out the kitchen door.

"Was that . . . *Taryn?*" Ben said to his wife, who winked at him and nodded.

"I had to help her out. Just a little," Karen said happily. "Now, here's where we do the group hug thing."

She reached out toward Matt as Beth materialized out of nowhere, hugging him tightly again. The four of them held each other close (a little too close for Matt, but he was good and didn't flinch) while Karen offered up a quick prayer, asking for protection for them all while they were away from each other.

Then there was another round of hugs, during which Ben's cell phone rang again, and he answered it, motioning for Matt to go out through the garage and wait in the van.

Matt hugged his mom once more and peeled Beth's arms from around his waist and chucked her gently under the chin. Then he trudged out through the dim garage and slid into the front seat of the van idling at the curb. The leather seat was warm from the sun, and the inside smelled brand new.

He looked back at Taryn, who was huddled in the back with her face turned toward the window. She clearly didn't feel like talking, and Matt wasn't going to pry. He welcomed the silence as he turned back around and stuck his earbuds into his ears. The music was loud, and he bobbed his chin to the beat, closing his eyes and erasing everything from his mind.

Ben came out a few minutes later and slid into the driver's seat, grinning and yanking the earbud out of Matt's left ear after buckling himself in.

"*Ow!* What the heck?" Matt sputtered, surprised.

"You kids ready for the adventure of your lives?" Ben asked as he put the van in reverse and backed away from the curb.

"Yeah, sure, Dad," Matt said evenly, smirking and putting the earbud back in.

Karen and Beth stood by the family minivan in the garage and waved after them as they drove down the street. Matt was surprised at the sudden feeling of sadness that gripped him. He'd never been away from home for more than a week. He would miss them. *But I'll be back in a month,* he thought, waving back.

Once they were out of sight, Matt leaned back into the seat and closed his eyes again. It was a forty-five-minute drive to the airfield where the DIG company jet was waiting for them, so it was as good a time as any to catch up on his sleep.

*   *   *

A few moments later, it seemed, someone tapped Matt roughly on the shoulder. "Wake up, son, we're here."

Matt jolted awake. Had he been out the whole time? He got out of the van, stretching as he went around to the back.

They were on the tarmac of the airfield, and the black and tan DIG jet stood waiting for them fifty feet away. A worker had already wheeled a trolley around to the back of the van, and Matt joined Taryn and Ben as they pulled the luggage out and piled it onto the trolley.

They worked quickly, and Taryn kept her head down and stayed quiet the entire time, which Matt found strange. He couldn't help but notice Taryn's hair was sleek and straight for once. Normally it was unruly and untidily kept in a ponytail.

"So, my Mom did your hair?" Matt asked as he took a

big piece of luggage from her and tossed it onto the heap on the trolley.

Taryn looked up at him for the first time that morning, and Matt did a double take.

She was looking at him with an annoyed scowl on her face, but *her face* . . . it looked so . . . *different*.

Her eyebrows were nicely shaped, and there were actually *two* of them. She was wearing eye makeup and lip gloss, which was something Matt had never seen her wear, not even at church.

Her shiny hair fell into her face as she glared at him, and she brushed it back behind her ear. Her fingernails were even and polished a pale pink. *Wow, Mom really went to town on her.*

"Yes, your mother did this to me; it wasn't my choice," she said through gritted teeth. "And if you tease me about it, I'll . . . *kill you*," she added and stalked off.

Halfway between Matt and the plane, Taryn bumped into the luggage trolley with her hip and knocked most of the bags off onto the tarmac. Matt stifled a laugh. *Yep, that's the Taryn I know.* Some things couldn't be changed, no matter how much hairspray and polish you put on them. The workers motioned her away, rolling their eyes, and piled the luggage back up, while Taryn set her shoulders with as much dignity as possible and marched up the portable stairway into the plane.

Matt chuckled after her and jumped when his dad poked his head out of the plane. "You coming, son?"

The inside of the plane smelled like new leather, just like the van, and the rich smell of baked goods wafting out from the back cabin made Matt's mouth water. There were six over-sized leather seats, and it was surprisingly plush and roomy. Taryn had already taken up the back row and had her laptop open with her head buried behind it.

Matt chose the seat across the aisle from his dad and buckled himself in.

A slight, red-haired woman in her forties came out of the serving area to greet them. She was dressed in a sharp black suit jacket with a tan skirt. "Hello, Mr. Staubach. Can I get you folks anything before we take off? Some pastries? Juice?"

"Sounds great, Sharon, I'll have one of those raspberry Danishes," Ben replied. "Matt? You want something?"

Matt shrugged. "I'll have a few of those too. And milk if you have it."

"Of course, Mr. Staubach," Sharon replied, smiling crisply. "And for you, miss?" she asked, turning to Taryn.

"Just orange juice for me, thanks," Taryn muttered, keeping her head out of sight behind the laptop. Sharon nodded and disappeared into the back.

"Flight's about seven hours," Ben said to Matt as his worldphone started ringing again. It sounded annoyingly loud in the small cabin. "You bring a book like I suggested?"

Matt shook his head. "Nope. I'm gonna sleep," he replied and put the earbuds back into his ears. Ben shook his head as he flipped open his phone and answered the call in Spanish.

*   *   *

Matt started awake, unsure of where he was, and suddenly remembered. He felt warm and unsteady, and he sat up and pulled his earbuds out. His iPod had shut off, and his ear canals were sore. He glanced around the cabin. Ben was asleep and reclining with his mouth open, and Taryn was still buried behind her laptop.

"Can I get you anything, Mr. Staubach?" whispered a voice. It was Sharon again. Something was weird about her. She was too cheerful. "Something to drink? Some lunch?"

Matt smiled at her gratefully, nonetheless. He was starving, and his mouth felt fuzzy. "Are we there yet?"

She smiled at him and checked her watch. "Only about three hours to go."

Two sub sandwiches and three glasses of milk later, Matt decided he was bored. It was the first day in a long time he hadn't been to the basketball court to practice. He was itching to feel the smoothness of the court under his feet, to smell the varnish of the wood. He loved to hear the swishing sound the net made when he nailed a perfect shot. He especially loved the feel of the ball between his fingers. He'd brought his lucky ball in his duffel bag. He knew there wouldn't be basketball courts where he was going, but maybe there'd be some packed dirt or a hard surface somewhere, so he could at least get some drills in.

He glanced around the cabin. His dad was still asleep, and Taryn was still typing away on her laptop, her forehead creased with concentration. She really seemed mad his mom made her look halfway decent, which didn't make sense to Matt. Girls were strange, complicated creatures.

Sharon had retreated back to the serving area and out of sight. There didn't seem to be any reading material on the plane, so Matt grabbed the pillow and neatly folded blanket next to him, and squished down until he was comfortable again, tucking his long legs under the seat.

It had been a really bad idea to come. What was he thinking? Right now, he could be in bed sleeping or at the gym or at the lake. Anywhere but on a stuffy plane. If they wouldn't have basketball courts where he was going, they probably wouldn't have workout equipment either. *Heck, they probably don't even have running water.*

He closed his eyes and folded his arms grumpily, letting out a long sigh.

5

HE WAS A TOTAL DAREDEVIL SPEEDING ON A JET SKI OVER A *placid lake of shining water, cutting up the stillness with his wake and darting in and out.*

Then he saw it. Ahead in the distance, so far away it was practically a speck, an island appeared in the middle of the vast water. Something shiny from the island caught the rays of the sun and blinded Matt. He had to know what it was. He leaned forward and urged the Jet Ski on, splashing across the water as the waves suddenly became choppy and his way became difficult. As he got closer, something happened. The water became rougher and rougher, and soon it became violent, tossing him on the waves until his Jet Ski threatened to tip over . . . and it did, crashing him into black waves that weren't so friendly anymore. His mouth and eyes and ears filled with water as he struggled for breath, gasping as the surf tumbled over him like a rag doll . . .

Matt awoke with a jerk and nearly slid out of his seat. His ears were plugged, and the plane was shaking.

"It's just turbulence, son. We're about to land," Ben reassured him from the row across.

Matt tried to yawn, but his ears stayed stubbornly plugged. He glanced back at Taryn, who was looking out the plane window at the landscape as they descended. With white knuckles, she clutched the seat in front of her.

That's why she's so quiet. She hates flying, Matt concluded as another strong jolt shook the cabin.

The pilot's voice came over the loudspeaker. "Sorry, folks, it's a bit choppy this last part. We're slightly ahead of schedule, and the current time is 5:13 p.m. Temperature's a balmy eighty-nine degrees, and there's a nice wind from the east at about eight miles per hour. In other words, a perfect day for lying on a beach."

Except I won't be lying on a beach, Matt thought irritably. *I'm going to go stare into some big crack in the ground and pretend I'm enjoying myself.*

Things soon smoothed out, and the plane landed with only the slightest of jolts. They had arrived at Mexico City International Airport, where a van would be waiting for them, Ben informed Matt, to take them to the dig site and their permanent lodging.

A van was, indeed, waiting on the tarmac: a white cargo van with no windows. As Matt stepped off the plane behind his dad and Taryn, he noticed a tan jeep parked several yards away. A small man wearing a white linen shirt and pants was leaning against the jeep, speaking with a tall uniformed policeman as they approached. He stopped talking when they reached him and came forward, greeting Ben in Spanish. He had a mustache and jet-black hair slicked back from his darkly tanned forehead. He was small but quite muscular.

Matt wondered if he lifted weights.

"Manny, *mi amigo, como estas?*" Ben replied, giving the man a hearty hug. "Matt, this is Manuel Cardenas. Manny, *este es mi hijo,* Matt."

"Hola, Señor Matt, you can call me Manny," he greeted cheerfully, extending his small hand to Matt. Matt grinned and shook Manny's hand, which, for its small size, was surprisingly strong.

"Hola, Manny," Matt replied, feeling dumb.

"Hola, Manny," Taryn greeted as she materialized at Matt's side and shook Manny's hand. *"Coma estan tú esposa y niños?"*

Matt knew enough Spanish to realize she'd just asked Manny how his wife and kids were. Manny replied to her question, gesturing and speaking rapidly, and Matt smiled, pretending to know what Manny was saying and feeling like taking French instead of Spanish might not have been the *greatest* idea after all.

After a while, everyone burst out laughing, except Matt, and Ben cleared his throat. "Sorry, son, Manny's daughter lost her first tooth this morning. Manny, do you mind if we use English from here on out?"

"No problem, Ben," Manny replied in a nearly perfect American accent. He winked at Matt. Then he motioned toward the uniformed officer. "This is Señor Muldes," he explained. "He will guide you through customs quickly, so we can get going." They all stared at the formidable Señor Muldes, who had his arms folded and clearly wasn't the smiling type. He reminded Matt of Mr. Clean—only with hair.

Manny hopped into the jeep, grinning at them. "I'll wait right here for you. If they don't arrest you, I'll see you soon!"

Matt, missing the joke, gaped after him as Ben dragged him away by the arm.

*   *   *

Nearly forty-five minutes later, Ben, Matt, and Taryn were finished with the rigorous checking process by the Mexican customs officials. Señor Muldes had taken them to the front of the line, but it had still taken a long time for the officials to go through everything. Matt was thankful the crates and boxes full of Ben's archaeological equipment and contraptions had already been cleared and loaded onto the DIG van, otherwise they *might* have been arrested.

Once they had their bags back, Señor Muldes guided them out of the customs area, down a long hallway, and out to where Manny was waiting in the jeep. Ben shook Señor Muldes's hand and thanked him. Matt and Taryn thanked him as well. Manny greeted them cheerfully as Ben got into the front seat of the jeep. Matt had no choice but to sit in the back next to Taryn. The backseat was small and cramped, and he didn't seem to have a place to put his legs, until Ben moved the passenger seat up as far as it would go. "Sorry, Dad. A problem of being tall," he apologized as Manny started the car.

Matt was beginning to get annoyed again. Being stuffed into a small space with the Gilley Monster practically bulwarked up against him wasn't his idea of fun. To make things worse, Taryn kept leaning down to adjust her knapsack and her newly shiny hair kept whipping Matt in the face.

She'll probably start chattering my ear off once we get moving.
To Matt's dismay, she did.

"This is my first time here," she said excitedly as they drove off the tarmac with the white van following them closely.

Matt looked at her. "You've never been here?"

"Well, *duh*, I've been stuck in high school, just like you," she said. "I'm majoring in anthropology with an archaeology emphasis at BYU when I go this fall, and this little jaunt will give me extra course credit." She seemed pretty proud of herself.

"Not like you need much more," Ben mentioned over his shoulder. He looked at Matt. "Taryn's accumulated so much credit, she's starting at BYU as a *junior*. Isn't that right, Taryn?"

Taryn nodded, blushing at the praise. "Yep, that's right."

"Hooray for you," Matt said evenly as they left the airport. Taryn's smile immediately faded. She sniffed and pretended to be interested in the view out the plastic window. Matt did the same. He felt kind of bad for shutting her down like that, but he didn't need her talking his ear off the whole ride.

Manny cleared his throat and turned on the radio, blaring Mexican folk music as the jeep drove onto a modern-looking highway. There were signs everywhere in Spanish and English. "It's about an hour-and-a-half drive to the site," Manny told them over the noise of the radio. "But first, I think we'll stop in Puebla to eat, yes?"

"Sounds good," Ben replied.

"Oh, yes!" Taryn exclaimed. She turned to Matt and beamed at him. "You'll love the food. I've heard it's not like the Tex-Mex we're used to. It's the *real* stuff! Of course I wish I could stand the hot stuff like my brothers can . . ."

And she kept talking and talking and talking. Matt huffed out his breath in dismay. *Another hour and a half?* He was sitting way too close to Taryn, and she was obviously over her sour mood. *Not a good combination.* Maybe he could fake being asleep again? But part of him wanted to take in the sights. He hadn't been to Mexico either, after all. He looked at Taryn, and she smiled at him, her white teeth gleaming in the semidarkness of the jeep. It was strange, seeing her like this. She looked so *different*, with nice hair and makeup. Almost like she was a different girl entirely.

"So, are you glad I bribed you yet, Dum dum?" she whispered obnoxiously to Matt, who frowned at her.

And then there's that mouth. Nope, she was the same old Taryn, made up or not.

"Jury's still out," he said finally as the jeep turned off onto the 150 and picked up speed. "I think I need another nap."

*   *   *

"Matt! Wake up! *I swear, all you do is sleep!*"

Matt sat up quickly. "I'm awake, I'm awake." His legs were asleep and cramped from being stuffed in the backseat. He looked groggily at Taryn and rubbed his stinging jaw with his hand.

"Were you *slapping* me?"

"Well, yeah, 'cause nothing else was working," Taryn retorted. "You know, your interest level is *pathetic*. Can we have the top down, Manny?"

"That sounds good, Manny, let's let the kids have a clearer view of things," Ben chimed in, clearly aware of his son's discomfort.

Manny pulled over to the side of the road, and with Ben's help, they had the soft top of the jeep folded down within a few minutes.

"Wow," Matt said as he looked around. They were about to enter a vast city, where crayon-colored buildings rose up amidst cathedrals and colonial-era buildings.

"This is Puebla, a great city," Manny said as the jeep roared to life again. "I'll take you to Fonda de Santa Clara to eat. Very good food there."

Matt had to remember to keep his mouth from falling open as they drove through the main part of town. Everything was a riot of color and music. There were mariachi bands playing on every block. Their music echoed off the buildings as the jeep jumbled and bounced on the cobbled street, passing colorful shops and hotels, cafés and clubs with their blaring neon signs. The bass beat of the city thrummed a preternatural rhythm in Matt's chest as they drove.

"They're having Festival de Musica, right now!" Manny shouted back to them over the din. "You like the music?"

Taryn nodded a little too enthusiastically, moving her shoulders and arms to the beat of the music. Matt rolled his eyes and looked the other way.

The entire atmosphere was like one giant party. Matt saw beautiful women everywhere, walking in brightly colored shorts and tank tops. He sat up and made a low whistle at a group of girls as they passed by them on the wide street.

"So, decided you're finally awake?" Taryn commented wryly.

Matt rubbed his eyes. "I've decided how it's gonna be," he said, ogling a raven-haired beauty who smiled radiantly at him as they passed. "I'll stay *here*, and you guys can live at the dig site."

Taryn snorted. "*Funny*. Actually, we're just passing through. The dig site is still miles away."

Matt turned to look at her. "How far away, exactly?"

"Well, Cholula is twenty minutes out, and we're a few miles outside of that . . . so pretty far I'd say." Her eyes darted to Ben, and she lowered her voice so only Matt could hear. "Besides, if you turn into a big flake, our deal is null and void."

"*What?*" Matt ejected, and Ben turned around quickly.

"What's wrong, son?"

"Oh, I just informed Matt there won't be any local hotties where we're staying," Taryn volunteered, her voice tinged with mischief.

"Is that true?" Matt asked his father, unabashed.

"Afraid so, son," Ben grinned. "And it will be a good thing for all the other young men on the dig. I find it helps them focus on the work at hand."

Matt sighed like a petulant child and leaned back in his seat, disappointed. "That stinks."

"Sorry," Taryn said sweetly. She caught the eye of a handsome dark-haired boy as they passed. "But yeah, it *does* stink, now that you mention it."

*   *   *

They had a quick dinner at Fonda de Santa Clara, where Ben ordered some of the tastiest food Matt had ever eaten, including a dish made with *mole pablano*, a sauce that, Manny informed him, contained over fifty ingredients, including chocolate. Puebla was famous for it, apparently, and Matt discovered he liked its rich, piquant taste. Taryn, a self-proclaimed "spicy stuff lightweight," drank about ten bottles of water during the meal.

"My lips are burning," she complained as they walked out of the crowded restaurant to the jeep. Matt's lips and throat were burning a little too, but he was too proud to admit it.

The sun was beginning to set, and Matt, full and sleepy, settled back uncomfortably into the small backseat with Taryn again. His legs were tired from being drawn up practically to his ears, and he was sure he looked ridiculous with them that way, anyway. His lower back started protesting immediately as Manny drove them out of town. Matt expelled a wistful sigh as the last of the lights from the big city twinkled out of sight.

By the time they reached Cholula, Taryn had fallen asleep

against the hard vinyl seat, and a few times Matt had to push her gently away to keep her from resting her head against his arm.

Cholula seemed to be a miniature copy of Puebla, and Matt could hear soft music and laughter drifting from the brightly lit mass of buildings that radiated out from the darkness. But they didn't drive through the city this time. They drove around it.

"Only a little way now, kids," Ben reassured as they passed through the outskirts of Cholula and turned onto a darkened road swallowed up by dense trees.

Matt kept nodding off (*What did they put in the food to make me so sleepy?*), and Ben and Manny spoke in quiet undertones the rest of the trip. Matt noticed Manny had reverted to speaking Spanish.

Suddenly the trees were gone, and they were on a rough road that cut through the brush. The jolting was unbearable to Matt's already cramped legs. Taryn snorted awake and mumbled a complaint as the jeep lurched on the road, ejecting dust into the hot, heavy air.

The road seemed to go on forever—Matt was glad when they finally arrived at a tall chain-link fence with locked gates. Manny put the jeep in neutral and hopped out to unlock them. The dust was so thick that Matt couldn't help but start coughing. Taryn had her shirt neck pulled up over her nose and mouth, and she glanced over at him as he leaned forward, coughing to clear his lungs.

"Sorry, son, we can't help the dust," Ben's muffled voice told him. Matt looked up and noticed his dad had a handkerchief pressed to his mouth and nose. Matt pulled the neck of his T-shirt up over his nose and felt much better.

He squinted through the dust and darkness and made out a cluster of small, white buildings in the distance that looked like the portable classrooms schools sometimes had. Manny, who seemed to be unaffected by the dust, jumped back into the jeep, and started the ignition. He drove about fifteen feet inside the gates and stopped the jeep again.

"Here we are!" Ben exclaimed through his handkerchief as Taryn sighed heavily, stretching and yawning.

"It's about time," she complained, rubbing her eyes. "I must have eaten too much or something. I'm beat."

"Is this . . . where we're staying?" Matt asked after the dust had settled, eyeing the nearby buildings skeptically. There were only two bright lights illuminating the camp; both had thick clouds of bugs buzzing furiously beneath them. It was too dark to see much else.

"It is," Ben replied, slinging his pack over his shoulder. "The other guys dropped off our gear already—they're DIG guards mostly—they bunk at the other end of the site, so we won't see them. And you'll be bunking here in the barracks for the duration of the trip."

"*Bunking*?" Matt repeated, forlorn. He certainly hadn't expected to be "roughing it." He'd always thought archae-ologists stayed in hotels and drove to the dig sites. He didn't know they *slept* at the dig sites . . .

"Aw, c'mon, Staubach, you afraid of a little camping out?" Taryn teased. "These are actually pretty posh, I've heard. We're lucky. Some archaeologists sleep in *tents* and don't have electricity or running water. DIG definitely spoils us."

"The one over there on the right is for girls, and boys are on the left," Ben said to both of them, indicating the white cabins. You can make yourself comfortable." He got out of the jeep and walked over to where Manny was shutting the gates and locking them in.

"For protection," he explained. Matt noticed the tall perimeter fence disappeared into the forest in either direction.

"Each barrack has its own showers inside," Ben continued as Manny pulled a small gadget out of his pocket and handed it to him. Ben pointed it at the fence. There was a blinking light, and the fence began to hum slightly. "You'll find they're actually pretty cozy. Oh, and a word of caution," he said as he walked back over and hoisted himself into the jeep. "Don't go near the fence. And, for heaven's sake, don't touch it."

Taryn uttered a small laugh that ended in an unbecoming snort.

"Why are you locking us in?" Matt asked.

"There's lots of expensive equipment at the site," Ben explained, checking his watch. "I'm not so much locking us in as locking *things* out."

"Where are *you* sleeping?" Matt asked.

Ben motioned ahead of them, as Manny put the jeep in gear and drove slowly toward the barracks. Matt saw a large trailer sitting at the side of another crop of small, white buildings he hadn't noticed before. "I'll be in there. We call it the command center. It has all the communication equipment, and it's close to the lab and storage units."

Manny pulled up neatly to the trailer and parked the jeep.

"Well, I'm going to have a shower and hit the hay," Taryn said, hopping out. "I want to see this fissure bright and early tomorrow!" She said good night and disappeared inside the cabin on the right.

Matt mumbled a halfhearted "good night" to his dad and slung his bag over his shoulder, entering the boys' barrack. He was greeted by a blast of cold air that felt wonderful on his hot, dusty skin.

Ben was right; the barracks *were* nice. Matt was surprised to find a nice Berber carpet beneath his feet. He snapped on the light. There were a dozen or so sturdy bunk beds in rows and ample closet space for belongings. There was a large flat-screen TV on one end and a hallway that led to the toilets and showers. Matt noticed Manny had followed him inside.

"This thing have cable?" Matt joked as he thumped his pack down on the nearest bed and gestured at the flat-screen.

"*Satellite*, actually," Manny said, smiling. "But you won't be watching much TV."

A "Yeah, right" was on the tip of Matt's tongue, but he thought it best to keep silent. He wasn't here as one of the work dogs. He was here to observe. *And if I feel like watching a little ESPN, who's going to stop me?*

"I know your type."

Matt looked over at Manny, who leaned casually against one of the bunks, arms folded, staring at him intently. "You aren't much interested in what your father does, are you?" Manny asked. He was smiling, but the smile didn't reach his eyes. His dark eyes glittered at Matt as he waited for an answer.

Matt sized him up for a moment and chose his words carefully. "No, I'm not."

"So, why are you here, exactly?" Manny asked. It was a direct question, and Matt didn't like direct questions, especially if they were nosy.

"I'm here because I want to see firsthand what Dad does," Matt lied. "And I'm going to Duke in a few months and wanted to spend some time with him, because, you know, I won't be seeing much of him after that . . ."

Why am I bothering telling this to a stranger? It almost seemed like he was trying to convince himself.

Manny nodded, a small smirk showing underneath his mustache. "I've got my eye on you, Mr. Matt. These boys who are coming on Monday, they are good boys. They work hard. And they don't need a corrupting influence."

Matt was so taken aback he didn't have a retort. Manny

took advantage of the silence and continued: "Your father is a good man and a hard worker. You need to see what he does, and you need to respect it. And there are rules," he motioned to a posted sign at the back of the barrack, "and you will follow them just like everyone else. *Comprende?*"

"Yeah, I get you," Matt said stonily. Clearly this Manny guy wasn't someone to cross.

"Just acquaint yourself with the rules, *por favor*," Manny continued, "and we'll see how things go. Who knows? You might actually learn some things, yes?"

"Yeah, wouldn't that be something," Matt replied evenly. "Now if you don't mind, I'm exhausted. I'd like to sleep."

"No problem, Mr. Matt," Manny replied, smiling at him. It wasn't an unfriendly smile, but it made Matt's blood run cold. The guy clearly meant what he said.

Manny turned and left without a sound. Matt collapsed onto the bunk, cursing Taryn for tricking him into coming and wishing he was back home in his own bed.

6

MATT AWOKE TO SUNLIGHT STREAMING INTO HIS BUNK and a strange crackling sound. He opened his eyes and realized someone had taped a piece of folded notebook paper to his forehead. Grunting, he sat up and tore the paper off and unfolded it. It was a note in writing he didn't recognize. He suspected it was Manny's, which was confirmed as he read:

Mr. Matt,

We hope you are enjoying your sleep. Breakfast was at 7:00 a.m., and since you were not outside to eat, we assumed you weren't hungry. We have gone to inspect the fissure at the southwest corner of the camp. You are welcome to join us, if you aren't too tired. Lunch will be at noon. We hope to see you there.

—Manny

Cursing, Matt crumpled up the paper and threw it at the wastebasket across the room. It sailed neatly inside. He *was* hungry. What was this place, anyway? *Boot camp?*

He dressed quickly in a T-shirt and shorts and stepped outside. The hot and heavy air pressed down on him, and he shielded his eyes against the unrelenting sun. He disappeared back inside the barrack and came out a few seconds later wearing his Duke Blue Devils baseball cap. *Much better.*

The camp seemed deserted. "Hello?" he called out. According to Manny's note, they were at the fissure in the southwest corner—*wherever that is.* Matt scanned his surroundings, from the small clump of nondescript white buildings, to the wall of dense trees a few hundred feet away. It was odd to see the jungle-like trees rising up in front of him, since the surrounding area was mostly low scrub and dense brush. He walked closer to the trees and saw a path cut through them. He followed it for a few minutes, slapping bugs off his skin, and came out into a large clearing that seemed to go on for miles. The hot sun beat down from a cloudless sky, and there were no more trees, only dust and cracked earth dotted with low shrubbery and rocks. He saw his dad, Taryn, and Manny about a football field away. He covered the distance to them easily, and when he got close, his dad welcomed him, clearly excited.

"Hey, look who's awake! Matt, come here, you need to see this!" Ben came forward and gestured for Matt to walk a little further. He was wearing his safari hat, and his nose was white with zinc oxide. Taryn was wearing a hat too. Manny wasn't.

Matt followed his father's lead to a large, jagged crevasse in the earth. It was at least eight feet wide and fifty feet long and tapered off at both edges.

"That's *some* crack," Matt remarked, looking down into it.

"Isn't it beautiful?" Ben asked. "It wasn't here two days ago."

Taryn was kneeling at the edge of it, drawing in a sketch-book with a pencil. Matt looked around and saw a large, blue-plastic tent about twenty feet away, crammed with boxes and long tables of computer equipment and monitors. He could hear the humming of a generator coming from a small shed next to it.

No outlets out here, he thought to himself.

"We weren't expecting this," Ben explained. "The earth-quake opened up two places in the ground. This fissure and a much smaller one, over there." He pointed toward a large clump of boulders about two hundred feet away. "We were actually going to start digging over there originally. But things have changed. Come look."

Matt followed his dad and Manny as they walked over to the large clump of boulders surrounding the small, grassy hill. Matt saw another crack in the ground, but it was much smaller than the big one. It was about a foot wide and eight feet long.

"So," he began, kicking a rock with his toe into the crack. "Are you going to esca . . . exa . . . ?"

"*Excavate*?" Taryn offered snottily.

"Yeah, thanks. Are you going to excavate this one too?" Matt asked, flushing a deep red and feeling stupid.

"Eventually," Ben replied. "This was our original dig site. But then *that* happened," he motioned toward the larger fis-sure, "and we figured it could wait. It's been very exciting."

Matt wasn't sure why a crack in the ground was *that* exciting, but he kept his mouth shut and scratched at his sweaty neck.

They walked back to the other site, and as they reached it, Matt stepped forward cautiously and peered into the chasm. He could see down about twenty feet or so, but then the rocks narrowed, and the rest was darkness.

"We've rigged a line, and after we've done a few more tests

to make sure it's safe, we'll scout the fissure to see what's down there," Ben continued. Matt saw the nearby rocks in which they had driven long stakes and secured a nylon line.

"Wow. What caused it?" Matt asked, stepping away from the edge, feeling queasy.

Taryn looked up from her sketchbook and glared at him. "Hello? The *quake*," she replied, annoyed. "Have you even been paying attention the past twenty-four hours?"

Matt frowned at her. *She doesn't look so good this morning,* he noted. She was paler than usual, there were dark smudges under her eyes as if she hadn't slept well, and her hair was pulled back into its usual ponytail under her hat.

"So, who's going down to check it out?" Matt asked casually. He was beginning to sweat profusely in the humid air, and his long hair felt heavy and hot on his neck. *Maybe I should have let Mom trim it after all . . .*

"We all are," Ben said, unlatching a large metal box. "You interested?"

Matt stared at his dad. "You want me to go too?"

"Why not?" Ben replied, smiling. "It's simple rappelling. You've done that tons of times."

He was right. One of Matt's favorite pastimes was rock climbing with his buddies. Only he'd never rappelled into a *dark, unfamiliar chasm.* Dark, tight spaces weren't his thing. He'd inherited that fear from his mom.

Matt looked at his dad. He noticed Manny was busy looking in another direction.

"Uh, okay. Sure," he conceded. "But why would we want to go down there? It could be dangerous."

"That's exactly what Buddy's going to find out for us," Ben replied, grinning at the contents of the crate next to him. "'Buddy' here is a robot. We will lower him down, and he'll survey the interior of the fissure and determine whether it's safe."

"You're letting a toy robot decide if it's safe?" Matt asked skeptically.

"It's a *robot archaeologist*," Taryn corrected, slamming her notebook shut. "Like the one they used in the Cheops Pyramid."

"The what pyramid?" Matt repeated, clearly lost.

"Ahem," Ben cleared his throat with a glance at Taryn. "We'll be a few hours, son, to get everything set up, so maybe now would be a good time to go take a look behind the boys' barrack." He dusted off his hands. "I've had DIG put together a little something for you."

Matt didn't need to be asked twice. He double-timed it back to the camp, happy to leave them to their work with their sketchpads and robots. *Boooring.* Besides, it was just a crack in the ground. What were they expecting to find? The Loch Ness Monster?

He went around behind the barracks and stopped suddenly at what he saw. He stood still for several minutes in shock, a lump forming in his throat.

It wasn't anything he'd been expecting. And it was so unlike his dad to do something like this that Matt found himself involuntarily choking up, which was something he never did.

It was a *basketball court.*

Granted, it wasn't perfect—the cement had clearly been poured as a foundation to hold another barrack, but instead there was a real hoop mounted at one end and a key painted on the asphalt around it. Clearly his dad had gone to a lot of effort to make him feel at home so far away from everything he knew.

The basketball court looked out of place in the middle of the scrub with a backdrop of mountains behind it, but it would do. Matt went back into the barrack, retrieved his lucky ball and basketball shoes, and hungrily gobbled down the last few granola bars he'd swiped from the jet. Then he warmed up and shot hoops and ran drills until lunchtime.

*   *   *

Lunch was a simple meal of warm beans and meat on tortillas. Ben explained that the cooks and supplies wouldn't be arriving until the next night and that the on-site kitchen was pretty much bare until then.

"I can drive into the city for supplies," Matt volunteered. *And maybe I can bump into some local babes*, he thought hopefully, but Manny smiled and shook his head.

"Thanks for the kind offer, Mr. Matt. But you can help your father here, and I will go."

Matt suppressed an angry retort. Was the little man in league with Taryn to completely ruin all his fun?

Matt gave the tiniest glance over at Taryn, who was eating a bean-filled tortilla as if nothing else existed. She caught his eye and grinned at him triumphantly, a large black bean husk stuck to her front teeth.

It's going to be a long thirty days, basketball court or not.

*   *   *

The process of configuring "Buddy" and equipping it with the right cameras and attachments took longer than Ben had anticipated. It was nearly dinnertime when the robot was finally ready.

"The price of having such wonderfully advanced technology," Ben joked as he, Manny, and Taryn surveyed the sinking sun in the western sky. "Getting it all set up can be . . . well . . . *advanced.*"

Ben had shown Taryn how to secure several work lights and lower them into strategic places inside the fissure while he and Manny prepared the equipment. But at this point, they only had a few hours of good light left.

Part of Ben wanted to proceed, but it would be a slow process and without the added benefit of full sunlight.

The three of them stood at the mouth of the fissure, arms folded, unsure of whether to proceed.

"Your call," Taryn said. She glanced over at the sun, which had sunk lower in the sky in the last half hour. "But I'm not gonna lie. As soon as we get started, it will be dark, and hard to make notes and see all the equipment."

"That settles it, then." Ben sighed. "We'll wait until Monday morning."

He glanced over at the trees concealing the camp. Ben hadn't seen Matt since he had gone inside to take a nap after lunch. Clearly he still wasn't very interested.

Taryn shrugged her shoulders. "It *is* disappointing, but it's a safety issue too."

"Agreed," Manny volunteered. "Let's go into Cholula for dinner, you think?

Ben nodded absentmindedly. "Yeah, I guess there's not much else to do."

They locked Buddy and the equipment up in the water-tight storage lockers and hiked back to the camp.

Matt was busy shooting hoops behind the barracks; Ben could hear the bouncing of the ball against the pavement as they broke out of the trees.

Manny grinned. "I think Mr. Matt will be glad to hear we're going into town."

Taryn snorted. "Poor guy. He's completely out of his element here."

"And we're *in* ours, let me remind you both of that," Ben

said quickly. "I don't want to completely alienate him. So, Taryn, please try and keep the 'techie speak' to a minimum. Layman's terms only around him, okay?"

Taryn nodded reluctantly. "Got it."

Ben looked at Manny, who held up both hands. "I'm bein' nice to Mr. Matt," he protested, grinning.

"Yes, I'm sure you are," Ben said, clapping him on the back. "Now let's eat. I'm starving!

7

THE NEXT DAY WAS SUNDAY. MATT OPTED OUT OF ATTEND-
ing sacrament service in town, which wasn't a surprise.

Out of respect for the Sabbath, no one went near the fissure. But the anticipation was thick in the air, almost palpable.
The students would be arriving that night, and on Monday
morning, excavations would begin.

Matt was busy . . . being bored out of his mind. He almost
asked his dad if he could have the jeep to go into town. But he
knew he'd be turned down. He went outside and shot hoops
instead.

Shooting hoops usually calmed him, but this was different. If only he were back home in Spokane, he'd be shooting hoops with Dave and Adam, his good friends. Afterward,
they would head to Adam's house to watch a game on TV.
Then maybe they'd play some poker or cruise around in

Dave's Mustang with the top down. Or head to a party, where no one cared what Matt did. With Dave and Adam, he could at least be . . . *himself.*

Here in the middle of nowhere, with the watchful eyes of his dad, the Gilley Monster, and Henchman Manny hovering over him, he felt stifled and caged.

Sunday ticked by agonizingly slow for Matt. He mostly slept and watched ESPN (he'd convinced Manny that he was going stark raving mad if he didn't get to watch some games and promised he'd turn the TV off before the other students arrived).

Taryn stayed in the girls' barrack most of the day. Matt hadn't seen much of her except from a distance earlier that morning. Wearing a white knee-length skirt and a green gauzy short-sleeved blouse, she had climbed into the jeep to go to church with Ben and Manny. She actually looked halfway decent, Matt had noticed grudgingly. Her hair was long and straight again, and she was wearing makeup. In fact, if he didn't know the real Taryn, he would actually have thought she was *pretty* . . . from a distance, of course.

But he did know her. And that *mouth*, and that *attitude*. No pretty face was worth putting up with those bad boys.

*   *   *

It was nearly five o'clock, and Matt was lying on the bed nearest the TV, arms behind his head, happily watching the Yankees beat the pants off the Red Sox. Suddenly, he heard a commotion outside, a mixture of loud voices and car engines. The other students had arrived. He watched TV for a few more minutes and then turned it off and headed outside to see what was going on.

Several white vans parked outside the barracks had already

been emptied of their occupants. A bunch of guys and girls stood chattering in a large group, and Ben was in the middle of them, shaking hands and greeting the newcomers as they greeted each other and found their luggage. Men in khaki pants and black T-shirts emblazoned with "DIG" in large, white letters on the back were busy unloading the remaining luggage and boxes.

Matt stood outside the barracks, watching the commotion, and saw his dad catch his eye and motion for him to join them. He reluctantly walked forward, self-conscious, and stood next to Ben, who whistled to get everyone's attention. The tumult of voices immediately died down as he held up an arm for silence.

"Hello, everyone, I'm glad to see you all made it here in one piece," Ben welcomed, talking loudly over the idling of the van engines. "As you may or may not know, I am Ben Staubach, head of this summer's 'Mexico Adventure' dig. I'd like to introduce you to my right hand, Manuel 'Manny' Cardenas, head of operations." Manny, whose arms were folded, nodded to the crowd.

"Also, you're all acquainted with Miss Nan Mecham." Ben motioned to a woman standing at his left, who looked so much like an older version of pre-Mexico Taryn, scruffy ponytail, unibrow and all, Matt had to fight the urge to laugh out loud.

"Nan," Ben continued, "will be our artifact specialist, should we be lucky enough to find any." (A few laughs rippled through the crowd at this.) "And of course, the man who needs no introduction—Jared Ramsey."

Matt felt himself gasp along with the rest of the crowd, as it parted to reveal a tall, well-built man in his mid-thirties. He was dressed casually in shorts and a polo shirt, and he oozed charisma from every pore.

Jared Ramsey, aka "The Battering Ram"—a former wildly talented professional football player for the Rams, had retired from the sport prematurely. He had shocked and disappointed his fans by announcing he was through with football and was retiring to be a linguistics professor at Brigham Young University. The man had a freaking *Superbowl ring*, and now he was content to sit in a classroom all day and talk about extinct languages.

Some of the girls in the group giggled and put their hands up to their mouths in surprise, and Jared raised a large hand in greeting, the wind ruffling through his blond hair.

"Jared has been extremely helpful on past digs, and I'm sure he will be a great asset to our team here," Ben continued. "And I'm sorry to report, ladies, he is happily married with four children and very much taken."

Everyone laughed at this, and Jared grinned, shrugging his shoulders.

Matt still couldn't believe it. The *Battering Ram* was here, in the flesh, working for his dad! Ben's nearly nonexistent coolness factor actually blipped to life a little for Matt. But then, mortifyingly, Ben was stretching out his arm toward Matt, calling out his name. *No he isn't—is he really going to embarrass me like that?*

". . . for you to meet my son, Matt. He'll be with us for the next thirty days. He's not going to spend his life nosing around ruins like you people; he's just spending some time with his old dad before he goes off to Duke to play basketball," Ben explained with pride. "So, if you have any questions during the dig . . . *don't* ask Matt."

Matt felt himself blushing furiously as everyone laughed again, and he looked up to see their faces. One face stood out in particular. A girl with bright blonde hair and a pretty face was busy looking at him as if he intrigued her. Matt knew that look. It was an "I-think-you're-cute-and-I-might-do-something-about-it-later" look.

Suddenly it didn't matter that his father was teasing him in front of twenty dorky archaeologist wannabes. He smiled his famous smile at the girl and waved at her sheepishly. He unwillingly caught Taryn's eye; she clearly had seen the exchange between him and the pretty blonde. She rolled her eyes at him and blew a stray hair out of her face.

Matt didn't care. *Why should I care what Taryn thinks?* She was so disdainful of him anyway; it almost seemed normal to have her annoyed at him over one thing or another. But the blonde . . . certainly she would be more accommodating . . .

"And last, but certainly not least," Ben's voice broke through, interrupting Matt's lascivious thoughts, "we have Terrence, our cook. Terrence is highly valuable to us all, for without *him* . . . well, we'd all starve."

Terrence, a nondescript and nearly colorless balding man of fifty, lifted a thin arm and waved to everyone as the group cheered and whistled.

"And there are also Rosa, Walt, and Jim, Terrence's assistant cooks." The attention turned to a short, plump woman and two men, who waved, smiling widely, at the cheering crowd.

"Now, Nan and Jared," Ben continued, "as group leaders for the girls and boys, respectively, have some rules and procedures and protocols they need to go over with all of you once you've unpacked and settled into the barracks. You will be broken up into groups according to your specialized majors . . ."

Matt didn't hear the rest. His eyes glazed over as his dad droned on for a while, and then sudden cheers and applause startled him back to reality. Everyone was picking up bags, backpacks, and suitcases and trooping inside the barracks, including the pretty blonde. She turned and took a last lingering glance at Matt before disappearing inside, and Taryn, catching the look on Matt's face, took the opportunity to stick her tongue out at him before following the blonde inside.

Matt shook his head, irritated at Taryn, and joined his dad, who was talking with Jared Ramsey.

"Ah, Jared, this is Matt. Matt, Jared," Ben introduced as Matt walked up to them.

"Matt, nice to meet you." Jared shook Matt's hand, nearly enveloping it in his strong, meaty fingers. "Your dad tells me you're going to play ball for Duke."

Matt nodded. "Yes, sir, I am."

Jared smiled at him warmly. "Good for you. We'll have to talk at some point. Right now I've got ten antsy students to see to. Catch you later!" He raised his hand in farewell and hoisted his large duffel bag over his shoulder, disappearing inside the boys' barrack.

Matt turned to Ben. "He is *so cool*. You say he's been on digs with you before?"

Ben smiled. "Yep. Four of them."

"And you never mentioned it to me?" Matt asked, incredulous.

"Well, you never asked," Ben replied. "Why would you have cared anyway?"

"About the fact that *Jared Ramsey* was working with you?" Matt repeated, shocked. "Are you kidding? I would've liked to hear about that!"

Ben smiled at Matt and clapped him on the shoulder. "Well, now you can get his autograph in person, if that's what you want."

"Eh, I don't," Matt said, feeling stupid. "So, what am I supposed to do now that everyone is here?"

Ben looked at him. "Why don't you go meet the other

boys and get acquainted with them? You'll be hanging out with them for the next thirty days."

"Twenty-nine," Matt reminded him.

Ben shook his head and smiled. "Give or take twenty-four hours. Now get inside and say hi!"

8

MATT NORMALLY WOULD HAVE DONE THE OPPOSITE OF what Ben told him to do out of spite, but these were strange circumstances. And he didn't want to be branded the "petulant son" of the Fearless Dig Leader, so he trudged over to the boys' barrack and slid inside. All of the other boys were grouped together in the middle of the room, listening intently as Jared Ramsey read to them from a list of rules and protocols.

Matt stood at the back, arms folded, until Jared was finished.

"Now, you guys know what's going on. I expect there won't be any 'hanky panky' around here for the next forty-five days," Jared began, amid groans. "And yes, I am woefully old-fashioned, and I do say '*hanky panky*.' That means we focus on the tasks at hand, work hard, are cheerful, and for Pete's sake, keep the hanky panky for the weekends!"

All the boys cheered at this, including Matt, who couldn't help himself. He felt like he was in a locker room before a game. Jared Ramsey was *so cool*.

"I've got some things to take care of," Jared continued. "So, all of you pick a bunk, get to know each other, and meet outside in one hour. We're going to have dinner, and Ben has a surprise for us."

"What kind of surprise?" a guy with red hair asked.

"Beats me, but the way he was talking about it, it must be pretty exciting," Jared replied. "See you guys at six thirty sharp for chow!"

He walked outside, and Matt watched him go. He still couldn't believe his good fortune. He definitely intended to pick Jared Ramsey's brain as soon as he could.

"Well, you all heard him," the red-haired guy said. "Let's pick bunks. Then let's go around and say our names."

"And then we can rub each other's shoulders and sing the 'make new friends' song," a slight boy with buzz-cut black hair chimed in.

"Shut up, Jack," a tall guy with blond hair retorted. "Ross is just trying to break the ice."

"Yeah, yeah." Jack turned to his bunk to unpack his knapsack.

Matt watched all this with interest. The redhead named Ross picked the bunk next to Matt's already claimed one, so Matt stepped forward to introduce himself.

"Hey, Ross, is it? I think the name idea is a good plan," he said generously, extending his hand.

"Matt, right?" Ross said, taking his hand and shaking it firmly. "Ross West. This is Andy Hale—we're both from Boston."

"Beantown, cool," Matt replied. "I can tell by your accents."

"And Jack the Jerk is from Delaware," Andy chimed in. "What do they do in Delaware, Jacky? Make *jer-ky*?"

Jack scowled and threw a pair of socks at Andy's head. Andy caught them deftly and hurled them back at Jack, clipping his ear.

"Hey! Knock it off, will you!" Jack yelled.

"Hey, dude, it's all cool," Matt said, walking over to him. "One of my best buds is from Delaware." He stuck out his hand. "Matt Staubach."

Jack, who barely made it up to Matt's shoulder, looked at his hand skeptically, then took it. "Jack Dante. Sorry, man, I'm having a crappy week."

"You and me both," Matt replied, grinning. Jack seemed uncertain but finally grinned back.

Matt turned to another boy, who was unpacking his shoes and placing them in a perfect row underneath his bunk. "And you are?"

The boy stopped and smiled. He was a pudgy boy with brown hair and a weak chin. "Mitchell Spencer," he replied. "Very pleased to meet you."

"Pleased to meet you too, Mitch," Matt replied, suppressing a smile.

"Actually, it's *Mitchell*, not Mitch," he corrected evenly. "I don't believe in nicknames. And you look nothing like your father, except I believe you both share similarities in the lower mandible . . . and possibly the nasal structure."

Then he turned around and went back to arranging his clothes into neat piles on his bed.

Matt, at a loss for words, glanced at Ross and Andy, who both looked like they were about to burst out laughing.

*   *   *

A short while later, after they were all introduced and unpacked, the boys headed outside for the white dinner tent, newly erected in front of the kitchen building by the hired DIG muscle. There was a delicious smell wafting from the tent, where several long tables were set up, but Terrence, emerging beet-red and sweating from the kitchen, informed them that dinner wouldn't be ready for another twenty minutes, since "Alfred burned the lasagna." He then launched into a tirade concerning Alfred's lesser qualities, and Matt steered everyone out of the tent.

"Hey, let me show you guys something cool," he said, leading them to the back of the barracks. Ross and Andy both whooped when they saw the basketball court.

"Are ya *kiddin' me?*" Ross exclaimed, in awe. "Man, your dad went to all this trouble to do this for you? Way cool."

"Wanna shoot some hoops?" Matt invited cordially. Ross and Andy and a few other boys agreed enthusiastically, but Mitchell shook his head. "I've never been physically inclined. I'm more suited for 'cerebral athletics,'" he said, making an excuse. "But I will observe and cheer at the appropriate times."

He sat at the side of the court, cross-legged, and Jack, after staring at the taller boys for a minute, muttered, "I'm out," and joined Mitchell on the sidelines. Another boy named Carl sat out as well, claiming asthma.

Matt ran and got his ball, and the boys split up into teams of four. Ross and two other boys named Jeff and Dan were on Matt's team. They were skins, so they removed their shirts and left them in a pile next to Mitchell.

After ten minutes of play, it became apparent to Matt both Ross and Andy were extremely good at basketball. Not as good as *him*, of course, but they held their own. He found he was working pretty hard to stay ahead of Andy, who was a few inches taller than him and very quick.

Matt stole the ball easily from one of the other guys and shot it nicely into the hoop just as Taryn stepped into view.

"Hey, Matt, your dad wants a word with you," she said, smiling sweetly at him. "He's in the trailer." She was still dressed in her skirt and blouse from church, and her hair shined in the sunlight. All the other boys stopped and stared at her.

"Right now?" Matt panted, bending down and resting his hands on his knees.

"I believe so," she said and gave the other boys a once over, catching Ross's eye before she left.

"Who's that?" Ross asked, wiping his forehead with his arm. "She wasn't on the plane over."

Matt rolled his eyes. "That's the Gilley Monst ... um ... I mean, that's Taryn. She lives in my neighborhood," he said quickly. "She flew up early with me and my dad."

"Lucky you," Ross said, giving Taryn's retreating form an appraising glance, a large grin on his face.

"Yeah, lucky me," Matt retorted, shoving the ball into Ross's muscular chest. Ross muttered a small *"oomph!"* of surprise.

"I'll be back," Matt said, grabbing his shirt and pulling it back over his head.

The boys resumed playing behind him, and Matt walked past the food tent to the large trailer parked by the group of buildings. He knocked on the door and heard his dad yell a muffled, "Come on in!"

He opened the door and stepped into cool air-conditioned room. The inside of the trailer didn't match the outside—it seemed much larger and spacious. There were many computers and TV screens on tables running along both sides of the trailer amidst maps and stacks of books and delicate-looking instruments. Ben sat at one of the long tables, talking with Sam Dyson via Skype.

"Well, my son is here, Sam, so I'll let you go, but I'll give you a report tomorrow, after Buddy has time to sort out the fissure. Really, really exciting stuff," he said, motioning for Matt to wave to Sam. Matt moved behind his dad and waved at the computer screen.

"How's it going, Sam?" he said, grinning.

"Hey, kid, you keep your dad in line there, okay?" Sam replied in return.

"Will do. Thanks for letting me tag along for the ride," Matt said, unable to think of anything better to say.

"No problem. We'll catch you both later." Sam gave them a thumbs-up, and the connection was terminated.

Ben sighed and turned to Matt. "He's a good guy," he said as he stretched in his seat.

"You sent for me?" Matt asked, folding his arms.

"Yeah, I just wanted to ask how you're doing so far," Ben replied, leaning back in the computer chair. "I know you're bunking with a bunch of boys you don't know, and I tried to make you feel at home here, but it's just . . . well, it's not *home*, and I don't want you getting disenchanted before we really get into the swing of things. It really can get exciting."

Matt smiled. "Dad, it's okay. The guys are cool. And I wanted to thank you for the basketball court thing too . . . I mean . . ." He stopped, unsure of how to voice what he was feeling. "I mean, I really appreciate it."

Ben smiled. "Well, I'm glad you don't want to go home just yet. I'd really like to have you around tomorrow when we take a look down in that fissure. You up for it?"

"Of course." Matt grinned. "Why not?"

"Great," Ben said, the chair creaking as he stood up. "Let's eat before Terrence runs off one of the undercooks!"

9

AFTER DINNER, THE STUDENTS WERE ASKED TO REMAIN seated to get their assignments. They were broken up into two teams of ten each, with five girls and five boys on each team. Jack, ever facetious, raised his hand and asked if the teams were supposed to give themselves "cool names," and Andy told him to shut it.

Team One, which consisted of Ross, Andy, Mitchell, Jack, and Dan, found themselves matched up with Taryn, Jenna (the blonde girl Matt had been staring at), Claudia, who was a chubby female version of Mitchell, and two other girls named Candace and Libby.

Matt was pleased to know he could hang out with any team he liked, whenever he liked.

The rest of the students made up Team Two, which Ben informed them would be supervised by Jared Ramsey. Matt was disappointed to hear it; he seemed to get along best with the Team One members. Nan was to supervise Team One. Matt looked at her, and the urge to laugh out loud at her uncanny resemblance to Taryn overcame him again. He snorted, and he turned it into a cough. Ross pounded him on the back.

"Thanks, man," Matt said appreciatively, eyes watering.

Then Ben told them all what had happened over the weekend with the earthquake, and made the announcement about the fissure (very dramatically, Matt noted). The shock was almost palpable. It seemed like all the air had been sucked out of the tent.

"Are you kidding me?" someone in the group finally said loudly. Matt glanced around at all the students, and most of them had looks of stunned disbelief on their faces.

"You mean, the epicenter of the quake was fifty miles away, but the ground opened up *here*, at our dig site?" Ross asked, incredulous.

"It appears that way," Ben responded, eliciting a few *ooh*s and *ahh*s from the room. "Now, if you'll all follow me, I'd like to take you to see the main fissure."

They herded through the trees, slapping at bugs as they walked to the southwest corner of the camp. Matt fell easily in step beside Ross and Andy, who were expressing their desire to work on the fissure.

"I hope we're the team assigned to it," Andy commented as they made their way through the underbrush.

"Me too," Ross chimed in. "Think about it . . . all the places the quake could have torn the ground apart . . . and it just happens to neatly create a fissure right inside our government-sanctioned dig site?

"Mysterious ways, my friends, mysterious ways," Andy replied, glancing at the setting sun overhead. "INAH didn't know what they were getting into when they signed us up for this."

"INAH?" Matt repeated.

"It's the Instituto Nacional de Antropología y Historia," Ross answered. "Mexico's National Institute of Anthropology and History. You have to go through them to excavate anything here."

"Ah, I see," Matt said.

"Here we are," Ben announced, sounding a little out of breath when they reached the fissure. "Please be careful. We're not sure how stable the ground is yet. We've equipped a robot archaeologist to collect data and help us find out what's down there, and, if it's safe, the team assigned will stay to explore it. But don't worry," he said among disappointed groans, "you'll all get a chance to explore it, regardless of which team you're on."

The students cheered, and Ross glanced at Andy and Matt, grinning hopefully.

"We have decided Team One will have that responsibility first," Ben said. There were a few cheers and more than a few groans. "Team Two, if you will now follow Jared, he will explain the procedures for the other dig site. After four weeks, the teams will switch."

Jared waved his hand for Team Two to follow him, and they left, a few of them lingering and giving wistful glances at the fissure. Matt saw Ross give Andy a silent high five.

"Now, everyone, gather round," Ben said, motioning them to come closer. "We're all members of the Church, here, so I can tell you all that this year, I decided on this dig site because it seemed a logical place for finding artifacts from the Late Preclassic and Early Classic periods, also known as the time of the Nephites."

Matt resisted the urge to snort and roll his eyes. (Not that anyone would have noticed anyway, because they were all staring worshipfully at his dad.)

He wanted to go back to the barracks and shoot hoops. Anything but standing here in the hot sun, melting into a pool of sweat. But as Ben spoke, Matt discovered (a little reluctantly) that the palpable excitement the other students were giving off was affecting him—to the point where he actually found himself starting to become mildly interested in what was down in that fissure. But only *mildly* . . .

He caught the eye of the blonde, Jenna, who was looking at him too, and she quickly looked away, a small smile on her full lips.

Team One it is, Matt decided right then and there. It looked like he'd be hanging around the fissure for the next thirty days. *Or was it twenty-nine?* It didn't seem to matter so much anymore. He sneaked another look at Jenna, taking in her long, tanned legs, perfectly encased in her almost-too-short denim cutoffs.

Nope, not much at all.

*   *   *

Later that night, the boys were in the barrack, talking about the fissure. They had all crowded onto the bottom bunks, and Jack had opted for the top of Matt's bunk, since he was smaller. He'd confided earlier to Matt that his girlfriend had dumped him the day before he left for the dig, and it had really messed him up.

"Two years, we went out," he told Matt quietly as Andy pontificated to the rest of the crowd about the questionable reliability of the robot archaeologist. "And then the day before I leave, I go to her house with flowers and a new cell phone so she can text me on weekends, and she's in her living room with some guy I don't know. I walked in on them, and they weren't exactly picking out wallpaper." Jack's voice was bitter. "She never wanted to text me or email me, and I thought she was just a Luddite, but in truth, she just wasn't interested anymore."

"Who wasn't interested?" Ross asked, butting into the conversation.

"Nothing, West, don't worry about it," Jack said, getting defensive. He glanced at Matt. "I'm gonna brush my teeth." He slid down from the bed and padded off to the bathrooms.

Ross moved over to the spot Jack vacated by Matt. "He okay?"

"I hope so," Matt answered, not betraying Jack's secret. "So, what's your story?"

"I was wondering more about yours," Ross answered, making himself comfortable. "None of this is your thing, right? So, if you aren't here for course credit, why *are* you here?"

Matt snorted. "You're the umpteenth person who's asked me that. I'm beginning to wonder myself."

Ross chuckled and shook his head. "Sorry, man. You just seem a little . . ."

"Out of place?" Matt finished for him. "Out of my element?"

"Yeah, something like that," Ross answered honestly.

"Well, originally, I was dead set against coming," Matt confessed. "I've never been much of a fan of old stuff, and I wasn't going to come, until Taryn . . ." He trailed off, unsure whether he wanted to share with Ross that Taryn had tricked him into coming.

"You're here for her?" Ross asked, misunderstanding. "So you two are . . . *together* or something? I get it now."

"Whoa, whoa, no way," Matt corrected him quickly. "Taryn and I are *not* together. We aren't even friends."

Ross looked confused. "But you said you weren't going to come here, except for her."

"Except she *bribed me*," Matt clarified. "Taryn and I haven't spoken more than fifteen words to each other since we were five. We're not friends. We're just . . . different."

"How? It's not like you're a different *species*," Mitchell observed from the bunk across the way.

Matt resisted the urge to tell the boys about the Gilley Monster before she'd been all shellacked and plucked and polished by his mom. He knew it would be good for a laugh, but something inside him knew it would be mean. Taryn was different here. His mom had given her a new look, and Matt felt it would be mean to talk about the old Taryn. So he kept silent.

"She told me she'd tutor me my entire freshman year if I came here for thirty days. She said it would be important to my dad, or something," Matt confided. "Pretty lame of her, huh?"

"Actually, the contrary," Ross mused, clearly impressed. "In fact, I think I'm in love."

Matt laughed. "*Gilley?* You've got to be crazy, man!"

Ross shrugged his shoulders. "I think she's pretty. She seems . . . *sweet.*"

Matt choked on another laugh. "Go ahead, talk to her," he managed. "She'll dispel all that for you pretty quick."

Ross smirked at him. "I think I will."

"What can you tell me about the blonde, Jenna?" Matt asked suddenly, feeling curious. "You know her before here?"

"Nope," Ross answered, shaking his head. "But she's gorgeous, talented, and perfect."

"Really?"

Ross grinned. "Sure. Just ask her."

They both laughed. "That bad, eh?" Matt asked.

"Intolerable," Ross admitted. "I had to listen to her talk the whole plane ride over."

"So, what's *your* story?" Matt inquired, after he'd stopped chuckling.

"Not much to tell." Ross shrugged his shoulders. "I'm starting my major in anthropology and archaeology at Harvard. My counselor told me going on this dig with your dad would be a once-in-a-lifetime opportunity for my major, so I applied, and here I am."

"You're not going to BYU?" Matt asked incredulously. "Isn't that *sacrilege*, or something?"

Ross grinned, embarrassed. "Well, it's my family's legacy. My dad, his dad, and his dad went to Harvard. Plus, my mom doesn't want me out of the state. She wants me close. Which is fine with me, 'cause I can go home on weekends, and my laundry gets done." Matt grinned at him.

"But I'm the only son, and when I go on my mission, she'll have to get used to me not being around," Ross continued. "I can't wait to turn in my papers. I can do it a few months after my freshman year, in October."

"Cool," Matt said flatly. *Please don't ask, please don't ask . . .*

"I just hope I go somewhere Spanish-speaking. Just so all my agony in Spanish class wasn't wasted," Ross joked. "Where do you think you'll end up on your mission?"

Of course he had to ask. Matt folded his arms. "I don't know yet. I have a full-ride basketball scholarship to Duke, and I'm worried I'll lose it if I go."

"Full ride?" Ross asked, clearly impressed. "That's awesome. But I had a friend who had a full-ride to Pepperdine, and he didn't lose it. They held it for him while he served his two years."

Matt didn't want to talk about going on a mission any-more. It made him feel stupid, and frankly, he was probably the only one in the room who had no intention of going. And *that* made him feel even more stupid.

"Well, I'll have to see what they say. Different colleges might have different policies," he answered, quickly and finally. He stifled a fake yawn. "Man, I'm beat. I'm turning in."

Ross yawned as well. "Me too. I hope I can sleep."

"Why?" Matt asked, perplexed.

"Are you kidding? We get to see what's at the bottom of that fissure," Ross replied, as if Matt were crazy. "Aren't you curious?"

Matt shrugged his shoulders. "Yeah, I guess."

Ross laughed and shook his head. "You are a mystery, my man. Have a good night."

10

MATT . . . MATT WAKE UP. HEY, MAN, YOU COMING WITH us?"

Matt stirred in his sleep. He'd been having a great dream, but the memory of it faded as he jerked awake.

"*Wh-what?*" He opened his eyes to see Ross and Andy both staring down at him.

"We're heading to eat. You want us to wait?" Ross whispered.

"What time is it?" Matt asked groggily.

"Half past six," Andy replied. "We're supposed to be at the site at seven."

"*Outstanding,*" Matt muttered sarcastically, tearing off the covers. He looked around the barrack. It was completely empty except for Ross, Andy, and himself.

Part of him wanted to give them both another sarcastic

comment and pull the covers back up and go to sleep, but he didn't want them thinking badly of him.

"You guys go ahead to breakfast. I'll be there in five minutes," he said, jumping up to get dressed.

Ross and Andy exchanged grins and left.

Cursing, Matt pulled on a fresh pair of shorts and a shirt. He ran wet hands through his hair and brushed his teeth. *Can't neglect the pearly whites.*

When he entered the tent, everyone was already seated, eating and talking in hushed tones. Terrence had laid out a pretty good spread, and Matt's stomach rumbled as he picked up a tray and loaded up.

"Wow, I believe that really *was* five minutes," Mitchell commented as Matt sat down with his tray at the table. Ross, Andy, Mitchell, Jack, and Jeff were already halfway finished with their eggs, hash browns, and bacon.

"Where are the girls?" Matt asked, noticing there weren't any around.

"They ate earlier I think. Orange juice?" Mitchell offered, handing a full pitcher over to Matt. Matt thanked him, poured himself a large glass, and started eating. The food wasn't half bad. Not as good as his mom's, but pretty decent.

"Sorry, I guess we should have woken you up earlier," Jack said, breaking the silence. "But we weren't sure if you were . . ." he looked at the other boys, and Mitchell nodded, "following the same rules we are."

Matt finished chewing and swallowed. "I don't think I have any set rules, but I'll follow yours. Go ahead and wake me up next time."

Jack looked relieved. "You don't mind waking up at six?"

"Not if you don't," Matt replied thickly. *I'm not going to be shown up by a bunch of science geeks.* Not that Ross and Andy were, but Mitchell and Jack certainly fell into that category.

*   *   *

Breakfast seemed to wake everyone up, and by the time they arrived at the fissure, the boys discovered the girls had indeed beaten them to it. Apparently Buddy had already been lowered into the enormous crack a few hours before—Ben was standing at the precipice, holding a complicated-looking remote control with a screen. The other girls were huddled around the edge, peering in as closely as they dared. Matt noticed Jenna wore pink Bermudas and a clingy white top with pink trim that made her tanned skin look pretty darn nice. Taryn and Manny were in the blue tent some feet away, standing behind Nan, who was typing on a keyboard and focused intently on a computer screen.

"Good morning, ladies," Ross greeted as they came up on them.

One of the girls, Claudia, scowled at them and put a finger to her lips. "Shhh—we can't hear!"

"Hear what?" Matt asked in a whisper.

"Heck if I know," Ross answered dubiously.

"It's water!" Taryn suddenly shouted excitedly. "I can see it!"

"Water?" the boys repeated in unison.

"I see it too," Ben agreed, watching the little screen on his remote intently. "Scanning now."

"There's a ledge, Ben. It looks safe," Manny said, squinting at the screen. "About ten feet of clearance. After the entry, it looks like it widens up into a natural cavern."

"We need to drop more lights down there," Nan observed, squinting at the screen as well.

"Okay, I'm pulling up," Ben said, working the controls on the remote. Everyone made a collective relieved noise, as if they had been holding their breath.

The girls got up as a group and wandered over to the boys.

"We were wondering if you were ever going to get in on the action," Jenna told them sweetly, looking directly at Matt and smiling. *Dang, her teeth are perfect.*

"How early did you get here?" Matt asked.

"About an hour ago," Jenna said, rolling her eyes. "Taryn had a hunch Ben was already working with Buddy, and she was right. She dragged us *all* out here." She made a little disgusted noise. "We hardly had time to dress or comb our hair." She flipped her perfectly coifed mane of blonde hair over one shoulder, and Matt watched it gleam in the early morning sunlight, mesmerized.

"You sleeping with your eyes open, Staubach?" a snotty voice asked.

Taryn's face came into view beside Jenna's, and she was smirking with barely concealed glee.

"We're all pretty much the walking dead around here." Ross materialized at Matt's side before he could say anything rude. "I'm Ross. Ross West." He stuck his hand out, and Taryn looked at it. Then she took it and smiled at him. "Taryn Gilley."

"Okay, this is cute and all, but don't we have a fissure to explore?" Jenna cut in rudely. Taryn actually blushed, and Ross grinned and took a step back. Matt smiled at Jenna.

"So, what happens now?" he asked her. But before she could open her mouth to speak, Taryn was telling him.

"Someone needs to go down and place more lights. It's definitely safe; I saw it myself on the screen," she said excitedly, not seeing the glare Jenna was throwing in her direction. "And there's water there. It looks like a cenote. But a cenote with a bank around it."

"That's odd," Ross commented. "Most cenotes are just sinkholes. A cenote with a bank would be more like . . . a cenote that was *used* for something."

"Exactly," Taryn agreed. "Depending on how deep it is, Ben said he might have to hire divers to see what's in there."

"It could be a sacrificial cenote," Mitchell chimed in. "There might be human remains and artifacts."

Jenna wrinkled her nose. "Underwater caves creep me out. I don't think I'd like to go down. You go right ahead, Taryn."

"I already am," Taryn replied quickly. "I won the coin toss." As if on cue, Manny materialized at her side with a climbing harness.

"You ready, Miss Taryn?" He grinned.

Taryn looked at them. "Yep, I guess I am."

Matt and the others watched as she pulled the climbing harness up around her legs. Next were gloves and a hard hat with a light that reminded Matt of a miner's hat, and he watched as Taryn attached her carabiner to the climb line.

"Ready," she said, as she braced herself against the edge, facing them.

Ross leaned in toward Matt. "Does she know what she's doing?" he whispered, looking nervous.

Matt nodded and brushed him away as he watched Taryn back down the edge.

Ben moved forward. "Now, once you're down, we'll lower the lights, and you can stake them," he instructed. "If you run into any trouble, yell, and we'll haul you up."

Taryn grinned and gave them all a thumbs up. She lowered herself down until only her head and shoulders were visible. "All good?" Ben asked her. She nodded quickly as she got a good foothold. Her eyes met Matt's for the tiniest second . . . and then she was lowered out of sight.

Matt felt all the breath go out of his lungs at once. He walked forward and stood with his dad, watching the rope slowly give. "Is she really safe down there?" he asked.

"Perfectly," Ben replied. "As soon as we get the lights set

up, you and I are going down too. None of the other students get to go, not yet."

"Taryn said it was a . . . whatchamacalit-thingy," Matt said quietly.

"You heard," Ben said, grinning as he fed the line. "It's called a *cenote*. Cenotes are basically sinkholes where underground water comes up through the earth. Some of them are used as water sources, but some ancient civilizations sacrificed people in them. It was considered a great honor to get 'tossed into a cenote' in some cultures. It's exciting, isn't it?"

"Not so much for the victim, I bet," Matt commented, a chill running through him. He was about to ask his dad if there might be dead bodies floating around in the cenote, but he was interrupted by a faint yell from Taryn down below.

"I'm here! I'm ready!"

Matt backed away as Manny and Ben lowered down one, two, three, four lights attached to thick orange cords. Twenty minutes passed. Ben kept yelling down to Taryn, asking if she was okay, and every time she yelled back she was fine.

Everyone was getting restless waiting. Jenna had planted herself on the only faint patch of grass nearby, surrounded by Claudia, Candace, and Libby—like a queen bee among her subjects.

Ross kept glancing nervously at the fissure. "She's an expert climber," Matt reassured. "Her dad's a professional who's climbed pretty much anything, even a frozen waterfall once."

"Really? He must be pretty hard core," Ross mused.

"Yeah, he used to take a bunch of us climbing," Matt explained. "He taught her well."

"She doesn't seem like the athletic type," Ross said. "She seems . . . delicate."

Matt snorted. Taryn was anything but *delicate*. Well,

physically she was thin and pale—but her attitude more than made up for any physical "delicacies" as Ross put them.

Mitchell and Jack sat cross-legged a few feet away, deep in discussion about the physics of earthquakes, and Andy watched the other team, grouped around the rocks two hundred feet away, as they gridded off a large area with ropes.

"You want to be over with them, don't you?" Ross asked Andy, who smiled at him.

"Well, I *am* a geology major. I was sort of looking forward to studying the rocks too."

"*Double major*," Ross said to Matt, who had joined them. "geology and archaeology. We're all pretty much double majors around here."

"Can't decide which one we like best, so we just go for both of them," Andy replied, grinning. "Take Mitchell over there. Anthropology and quantum physics."

"Just dabbling on the side, is he?" Matt commented, impressed.

"Just a tad," Andy answered with a smirk. "What's *your* double major?"

"Basketball and basketball," replied Matt, not missing a beat.

They all snorted with laughter. Just as it was dying down, Ben appeared beside Matt with a climbing harness. "You ready, son?"

Matt took the gear from him. "Absolutely."

11

IT TOOK SOME TIME FOR MATT, BEN, MANNY, AND NAN TO all get down to the rocky floor of the cavern. Team Two had abandoned their work at the other site, and all the students were crowded around the fissure, peering down and giving shouts of encouragement.

The fissure did open up, as Taryn had said, and about thirty feet down, there was a ledge surrounding a pool of dark water about thirty feet in diameter. When Matt made it down, he stumbled, and Ben caught him. Everyone was there, and Taryn was crouched by the bank of the cenote, dirty and dusty, but elated.

The cavern, even lit by the bright lights, was dark and creepy to Matt. He eyeballed the water, hoping he wouldn't see anything *dead* floating in it.

"You guys, I think this was a watering place for a village

or a city," Taryn told them excitedly as everyone else crowded around the cenote, shining their flashlights into the water.

Matt didn't care for the water. He didn't mind water in general, but when it was dark (and contained who knows what), it creeped him out. He tried to hide it by making his voice sound gruffer. "Why do you think it was a watering place?" he asked.

"Because," Taryn said, "look at the ground beneath your feet!" They all looked down.

"Very good observation," Ben complimented, shining his flashlight along the ground.

"Good work, Miss Taryn," Manny said, looking at the ground in awe.

Matt looked at the dirt he was standing on. "What's so special about the ground?" he asked. "I don't get it."

"This ground is worn, son," Ben replied. "Worn down by many feet from many people. In fact, there's a trail, leading off here," he said, shining his flashlight to the left of the cenote, where Taryn was standing.

"I saw it," she agreed. "But it all ends in a cave-in." She shined her light at the crumbled boulders, walking toward them. "It all ends abruptly, here. Like it was buried, or . . . *oh my gosh*!"

A chorus of "whats" rang through the cave. Matt's heart thumped in his chest.

"Ben! Nan! Look at this!" Taryn squealed, shining her light on something Matt couldn't see.

Matt moved as Nan pushed by him and stopped beside Taryn.

"Is that what I think it is?" Taryn asked breathlessly, bouncing up and down.

"Oh my gosh," Nan echoed. "I believe it is."

"WHAT?" Matt exclaimed loudly, exasperated.

"Ben, come here," Nan said, her voice shaking. "It's a . . . it's a jar. A water jar, I think. Definitely Late Preclassic from the look of it. It's . . . it's completely *intact*, Ben."

"Huh?" Ben breathed. "Are you . . . are you *sure*, Nan?"

"I'd need to examine it up top, but yes, offhand, I'd say it is." Nan turned to him with a huge grin on her face.

Ben walked over and shined his flashlight at what Taryn and Nan were looking at. Matt walked forward and peered over Taryn's shoulder.

The object of their awe was a dusty jar lying on its side among the rubble. It was wide at the base and narrower at the neck. Matt thought it looked pretty average. Like something he could have made in elementary school. Okay, well, maybe *high school.*

"What's so special about a jar?" Matt asked.

Taryn turned and stared at him, her eyes huge. "Are you *kidding*?" she asked, her voice incredulous.

"Its okay, Taryn. He doesn't understand," Ben said quickly. He glanced over at Matt. "Son, I'll explain later. MANNY!" he barked.

"Already on it, Ben," Manny said, producing a walkie-talkie from his pocket and speaking Spanish into it.

Matt didn't understand what the big deal was. But he had a feeling he would find out soon.

*   *   *

Things happened quickly after that. Matt, Taryn, and Manny were hoisted up, but Ben and Nan remained behind. A black DIG van full of men arrived shortly afterward, and they unpacked some odd-looking equipment, including a large metal crate, which they proceeded to lower down into the fissure.

The students were told to back about twenty feet away, and they stood, mouths agape, watching the process as the men in DIG shirts did their work.

"Dang, what did they find down there? Where's Nan and your dad?" Ross asked as Matt went over and stood, arms folded, with the rest of them.

"They're babysitting the thingy," Matt said absent-mindedly.

"What thingy?" Mitchell asked loudly.

"Some water jar. They're totally freaking out over it," Matt said quickly.

"A water jar? Down there?" Andy repeated, awe in his voice.

"Yeah. What's so special about it?" Matt asked.

"Is it intact?" Jared Ramsey asked, pushing through the students to stand beside Ross.

"Yeah, Nan says it is," Matt answered, feeling important all of a sudden.

A low murmur of "oohs" and "wows" rippled through the students surrounding him.

"That's rare," Jared said. "Did she say anything else?"

"That it was a classic or something," Matt replied.

"That would be *Late Preclassic*," Taryn said, joining them. "And the reason it's so special, Matt, is because it's about two thousand years old."

"Oh," Matt said. "I didn't realize."

"Wicked!" Andy exclaimed. Ross looked mildly shocked.

"Who found it?" he asked.

Taryn blushed. "Well, I did, I guess."

"She totally did," Matt said, smiling at Ross. "And there's a . . . what did you say? Trail?"

"Well, before we found the jar, we saw a trail that disappeared into a cave-in," Taryn continued. "It looks like it was a watering place for either a village or a city."

Matt looked at the faces around him. They were listening intently to Taryn, wearing identical looks of shock and disbelief.

Suddenly a cheer erupted through the crowd, startling him. Everybody was clapping and yelling, and someone slapped him hard on the back.

"We're gonna find something *big*, baby!" Andy yelled, putting his arm around Matt's shoulders and shaking him.

"Now, now," Jared said, putting his hands up to shush everyone. "Let's not be too hasty. Let's not jump to conclusions. What's best for an archaeologist to have?"

"Patience and a level head," Mitchell regurgitated from memory.

"Exactly, Mr. Spencer," Jared said. "So let's weigh all the facts as we uncover them, and we'll see what deductions we can make as more information comes to light."

"Speaking of which," Mitchell said, pointing over their heads.

Everyone turned around to see the DIG men hoisting the metal crate up out of the fissure with a large pulley they had rigged near the edge.

"Efficient, aren't they?" Taryn muttered. More sounds of awe rippled through the crowd as Nan and Ben emerged shortly after the crate. It looked like the jar, padded to the max, had been packed inside the crate. The DIG men loaded the crate into the back of the van, and Nan jumped in just before the van drove away.

Ben walked toward them, a jubilant look on his face. He still wore his climbing harness. Matt realized he hadn't taken his off either.

"I think we're on to something big," he announced proudly to the perfectly silent crowd of students. "And I mean *big*."

*   *   *

Apparently, it *was* big. Big enough for Sam Dyson himself to arrive by helicopter to the site later that afternoon and meet for three hours with Ben and all the adult leaders in the trailer.

All the day's excavations had been called off, and the students milled around, uncertain of what to do. Matt, Ross, and Andy scraped together a few boys to play basketball, and Jenna and the girls sat around the perimeter of the court and cheered them on.

Taryn had opted to hang out in the lab with Nan, who was running tests on the jar.

After the fourth hour had come and gone with still no movement from the trailer, Matt abandoned the game. Pulling on his shirt, he meandered over to the lab.

He wasn't sure why he was going, but he was a little curious.

He knocked on the door and heard a muffled female voice say, "Come in." He opened the door and saw Taryn and Nan seated at a long, white table. Before them rested the jar. Taryn was wearing gloves, and Nan had removed hers to type something on the computer.

"You cleaned it." Matt walked up to them and sat across from Taryn. The jar was no longer dusty and muddy. It was a reddish-brown color, and plain. There was a pan of dirty water and several brushes lying on the table next to it.

"Isn't it beautiful?" Taryn breathed, beaming at it.

"Well, I guess." Matt tried to sound impressed. "So, it's really two thousand years old?"

"Give or take fifty years," Nan said from across the room, not looking up from what she was typing. "But that's just an educated guess. It will take longer to carbon date any material inside the jar and verify age."

"Matt, do you realize it's very possible a Nephite woman or girl carried this jar to that cenote, and drew water for her family?" Taryn marveled. "It could have been a girl my age. Just like me." She held her fingers out and made as if to touch the jar, but a sharp clearing-of-the-throat from Nan made her fingers stop in midair. "Whoever she was, she carried this same jar in her hands . . . *two thousand years ago.*"

"Wow," Matt said softly. *When she puts it that way, it does sound pretty incredible.*

"I wonder what she was like," Taryn sighed, lowering her chin onto her arms at the table. There was dirt on her face and in her hair, Matt noticed.

He looked at the jar. "I don't know, Taryn," he said. "I don't know."

12

NURIA DREW THE HEAVY JAR OUT OF THE COLD, CLEAR water and hoisted it onto her hip. She was slight for her fifteen years and liked to carry the jar on her hip rather than on her head, like some of the other women did.

"You leaving now, Nuria?" Izel asked from her side of the bank.

"Yes, Mother needs my help with the evening meal," Nuria made excuse. She smiled at her friends who were gathered around the water to gossip and talk, as was their daily ritual, and set off down the path toward her home, bare feet kicking up dust as she went. She was old enough to wear sandals now but still preferred to walk on the soft earth without them.

Suddenly, a low whistle startled her, and a tall, broad-shouldered boy stepped out from behind a tree, grinning at her. His skin was tanned darkly from the sun, and his warm brown eyes held a glint of mischief in them.

"Teom! You frightened me!" she chided. "What are you doing here? Spying on the other girls?"

Teom was her brother, older by three years. He folded his arms and looked at her. "Well, of course I was. But Mother wanted me to make sure you were safe. She worries."

Nuria rolled her eyes. "Mother worries too much."

Teom fell into step alongside her. "I worry too," he said quietly. "Here, let me take that for you."

"No!" she said, wrenching the jar away from his grasping hands so violently she almost spilled it. "It's a woman's work. I am honored to do it now."

"As you wish," Teom said as they came upon a large jumble of huts nestled at the gates of the Great City. These were the workers' huts where the workers of cement lived. Beyond the huts were the great fires that always burned, so they could make cement for the ever-growing city.

Trees were scarce, and precious few were to be found outside the city walls, since they had all been used to build the city. The few that were left had been spared to provide shade from the boiling sun, and the workers had to haul timber in from other lands. But the fields around the city were a patchwork of crops: corn, barley and sheum, and beans and squash.

Teom and Nuria scattered dust and chickens before them as they walked through the gates of the city to their home just inside. They walked through the wide street filled with people, and children ran about while their mothers spun cotton outside their houses in the cooler breeze. As Teom and Nuria went farther inside the city entrance, they heard familiar wailings and moaning: the sounds of mourning.

"Something has happened," Teom said darkly, putting his hand to the sheath he wore girded about his middle, where he kept his knife. "Let's hurry." He put his arms around the small shoulders of his sister as they arrived at their house and guided her quickly inside.

It was a good-sized stone house. Teom's father was a priest, so they had always lived within the city walls, unlike the farmers and builders, who lived in huts outside. Most recently, their father was a judge of the courts—a precarious position lately, if anything.

As they entered, a blur of color flashed by them. It was their mother putting the meal of tortillas and beans with peppers on the low table in the middle of the large room where they gathered to eat and sleep. Teom removed his sandals and laid them on the brightly colored braided rug by the door, where, to his surprise, his father's sandals rested as well.

"Father is home?" he asked. His mother appeared before them, her face wearing a strange expression. "Not for long. Something terrible has happened. The chief judge has been slain."

Nuria gasped. "Not *another* chief judge!"

Teom looked at his mother. "Murdered?" he asked quietly.

She nodded stiffly. "Now bring the water, Nuria," she snapped. "You certainly took your time with it."

"Sorry, Mother," Nuria said, bowing her head and pouring the water into the larger jar by the door.

Then a boy with dark, curly hair and inquisitive brown eyes appeared inside the doorway. "Is it time to eat yet, Mother?"

"Yes, Chemish, come inside. We must hurry."

Then Ammaron, their father, appeared from the only other room of the house. "I have been summoned," he announced. "Now let us all pray that we will be watched over during this time of danger."

They all gathered around and bowed their heads while Ammaron asked a blessing on the food and on their house. They ate in strained silence, except for Chemish's fidgeting. But all boys of seven years fidgeted, so he was ignored.

"What is to happen now?" Teom asked, breaking the silence.

Ammaron chewed and swallowed thoughtfully. "A meeting has been called. All the judges must go and discuss what is to be done. I will leave shortly." He looked at their mother. "Alba, whatever is God's will, will happen."

Alba wiped a tear from her cheek. "First, Nimrah murdered, and now, Gilgal. All in the space of two months. They have gotten so bold, Ammaron!"

By "them" they knew she meant the robbers. The city was overrun with them now. They had come over from Jacobugath, that great city to the west, and had gained the hearts of the people through secrets and promises of power . . . and murder. They had murdered the chief judges, one by one. Their goal was to overrun the government so their king, the murderous leader Jacob, might rule in the stead of the existing government.

"They *are* getting bolder," Ammaron agreed. "There are only three of us left now who are qualified to be chief judge." At this, Alba put her face in her hands and wept.

"Take comfort, Mother. Perhaps they will choose someone else to be chief judge," Nuria soothed, putting a hand on her mother's arm.

Teom remained silent, his food untouched. Finally, Ammaron wiped his mouth with his sleeve and stood.

"I must go. Pray for my safety. The robbers will be bold and have revelry tonight. You are all to stay inside until my return."

"Father, I want to go with you!" Teom protested, rising.

"No, Teom, you must stay and protect the family in my

absence," Ammaron said firmly. "I leave you with that charge."

Teom nodded once, somberly. Alba wrapped an arm around Nuria's shoulders.

Ammaron slipped on his sandals and wrapped his cloak about himself, glancing at them all with a hopeful smile before he stepped outside.

"We need to leave this place," Teom said angrily after he'd left. "We should have left a long time ago. The city has become so corrupt, and all the people who love God are either gone or are turning to the ways of the robbers."

"Is Father going to get hurt?" Chemish asked, his lip quivering.

Teom reached over and messed up his younger brother's black curls. "No, Chem. He'll be fine."

"We cannot leave," Alba said, wiping her eyes. "Your father is a *priest*—a man of spiritual importance. It is his duty to protect our laws and bring order. And guide our people in the way of righteousness."

"His duty is going to get him killed!" Nuria blurted. "Besides, Teom is right. No one listens to the priests anymore. They want our ways of government to end and make this evil Jacob to be a king over us!"

"That will do, Nuria," Alba said in a low warning voice. "Finish your meal, and you may help me sort the spinning for tomorrow."

Nuria sulked for the rest of the meal, and Teom stepped outside after he had finished eating.

*   *   *

The street had grown quiet, but Teom could see the lights farther in the city and hear drunken shouts and music coming from the heart of it.

They were celebrating. Didn't they realize that if there was a king instead of judges, they would be under his rule? Teom had heard stories from his friends about Jacob's city of Jacobugath—how they had forgotten God and worshipped idols and spirits, and participated in ceremonies and rituals of blood and lust.

Yet they grew in numbers, and many of Teom's neighbors and friends joined them daily. The robbers promised power and riches and a life of hedonism, free from guilt and restraint.

Teom had been raised to believe in one God, and in his son, Jesus Christ. Jesus had been born when Teom's parents were children—as the prophets had foretold. There was a day without a night, and everyone knew it had happened.

It seemed so long ago, and Teom wished this Jesus would come to them and stop the evil and the senseless murder. If he was truly the Son of God, and the Savior of the world, couldn't he do it?

Teom wanted to go find his friend Helam and talk to him. But Helam wasn't around much lately. They had grown up as boys together, only Helam had changed the last few months. He had started running with the wrong crowd—sons of robbers—and Teom had found himself alone more and more as Helam went with his "new friends."

Teom closed his eyes, feeling the hot night air press down on him. There wasn't even a whisper of breeze. He uttered a silent prayer to God that He would protect his father and make someone else chief judge. He knew it was wrong to pray for such a thing, but with the robbers trying to overthrow the government, no judge was safe anymore.

"Teom? Will you play a game with me before bed?" Chemish asked timidly behind him.

"Sure, Chem. Go on inside, and I'll be in," Teom replied,

grinning down at him. Chemish smiled back and danced into the house.

Teom looked to the lights of the city again, shining at the very top of the temple, and turned and disappeared inside.

*   *   *

Nuria glanced at her mother and brothers sleeping soundly on their mats. Her father still hadn't returned, but sometimes he stayed all night in the city. The priests would be up all night anyway, with the death of Gilgal. Certainly they would have much to discuss.

She slipped quietly out of the house, her bare feet making no sound as she drew a blanket tightly around her shoulders, her hair long and flowing down her back. She ran through the dusty deserted street, lit up by the moon, which tonight resembled a round ball of creamy light. Soon she was outside the gates of the city. The cement workers' fires were bright beacons in the darkness, and she passed by them to a stretch of flat huts, where he waited, impatiently, for her.

She ran to him, and he embraced her silently. They were together now. Everything was going to be safe and good.

"Helam," she said breathlessly as they broke apart. "Where have you been? It's been two days! I've come here every night, worrying when you weren't here!"

Helam, tall like her brother but lanky, gathered her to him again and kissed her hair. "I have been involved in some very important things."

"Are you going to come home now?" Nuria asked into the warmth of his chest. He smelled strongly of smoke and incense. The smells were foreign but comforting.

Helam broke apart from her. "No, I cannot come home. It

is no longer safe for me here. I have been . . . in the company of the robbers."

"What do you mean?" Nuria asked, incredulous. Her eyes grew wide. "You didn't have anything to do with the murder of the chief judge today, did you?"

Helam paused before answering her question. "That is not important. But I must leave and go to Jacobugath. I have friends there, and they will welcome me with open arms."

Nuria looked at him. "But Helam, the robbers . . . they are evil men who murder and steal and ruin lives! How can you be with them?"

Helam studied her for a moment before answering. "Nuria," he took her hands into his strong, steady ones. "I have *become* one of them."

Nuria tore her hands out of his and looked at him with horror. "*When?*" she whispered.

"A few nights ago, they performed the ceremony to welcome me," Helam confessed proudly, absentmindedly stroking his right hand, which was wrapped in a makeshift bandage. "And today, I proved my loyalty to them. I am one of them."

Nuria suddenly had a sick feeling that perhaps he *did* have something to do with Chief Judge Gilgal's death, after all. "What have you done?" she whispered.

"They have promised me so much, Nuria," Helam said, the reflected lights of the worker's fires dancing in his eyes. "I'll have my own house, and riches, and *power*—they are so powerful. King Jacob himself will welcome me when I go to the Great City." He paused, taking her hands again, crushing them gently with his intensity. "I want you to come with me, Nuria."

Nuria hesitated. "Come with you? To Jacobugath? But I can't leave my mother . . . and Chem . . . and what will Teom say?"

"What can he say?" Helam said, his voice suddenly bitter. "If we love each other, and we are joined in marriage, he can't say anything."

"You love me?" Nuria murmured, turning her face up to his. He bent his head down to hers and brushed her lips gently with his own.

"Yes, I always have. Since we were little children." He wasn't lying. Nuria had always been in his heart, even if she was the younger sister of his best friend. But Teom was no longer his best friend. Teom wouldn't understand the ways of the robbers; he thought he was better than them. *And Nuria was a woman now, no longer a child.* She could come away with him, and they would be happy together in Jacobugath. As long as he always did what the robbers exacted of him, he would have everything he wanted. It was a small price to pay.

His father had been killed in battle with the Lamanites when Helam was five. Since then he'd always been the "Widow's Son" growing up—the poor, unimportant one, especially next to Teom, the "Priest's Son." Teom, who was always stronger and faster . . . and better at everything.

Now it was Helam's time to be powerful. He was the "Widow's Son" no more. He was Helam Spear Thrower (or so the robbers had named him at his naming ceremony), and for the deed he had done today, he was going to Jacobugath to be welcomed with open arms by a king. And he would take the sister of Teom with him, to be his wife.

But something in Nuria's eyes changed after he kissed her. *Had she smelled the chief judge's blood on him? He had rubbed incense on himself to cover it up . . .*

"I can't go with you tonight, Helam," she said quietly. "It's too soon. Can you wait for me to think about it?"

"But . . . they expect me at Jacobugath," Helam protested, his voice becoming tense. "Can you not trust me?"

Nuria shook her head, tears springing to her eyes. "My family needs me. And I need some time to think . . . about you being one of *them*. And what of Teom?"

"What of him?" Helam demanded, impatient. "If he could only see how powerful the robbers are, then your brother would change his mind about being so self-righteous," he spat. "Things are different now, Nuria. Soon there will be great changes in this city. A hundred Teoms would be powerless to stop them."

Nuria drew away from him, pulling the blanket around her shoulders as if she were chilled, even though the air was hot and humid.

"Please give me some time, if you really love me," she pleaded, her voice barely above a whisper.

Helam narrowed his eyes at her. "I will. But first I will go to Jacobugath and get everything ready there for us to start our new life. I will be waiting here for you tomorrow night, but then I must go. I will be back in ten days."

Nuria nodded her head. "Thank you, my love."

Helam crushed her to him, pressing his lips to hers fiercely. He was feeling impatient and out of sorts tonight—and he wanted her to come with him now. But he didn't want to frighten her either. Even though she was a woman now, she was still very much a child in the ways of the world.

"Ten days," he repeated, releasing her gently. "And then we can be happy, *together*. Until tomorrow night?"

She nodded once and fled from him. He watched her go, her black hair flying out behind her in the glow of the fires.

She would agree to go with him. *She loved him*. He'd seen it in her eyes.

Turning, he departed into the night, full of new hope.

13

MATT AND TARYN EXITED THE ARTIFACT LAB, LEAVING NAN to her work.

"So, what happens next?" Matt asked as they trudged through the dirt-worn path back to camp.

Taryn grinned at him. "What's this? *Curiosity?*"

"Shut up," Matt said, looking straight ahead. "Okay." He stopped walking and turned toward her, hands shoved deep in his pockets. "I *might be* a little curious. What's the next step?"

"Well, knowing Sam Dyson, it'll be bulldozers and core drillers and dynamite," Taryn replied. "Or they'll widen the fissure and dig their way through to whatever they might find."

"What do *you* think they'll find?"

Taryn shrugged her shoulders. "It could be nothing. Or it could be . . ."

"Something big?" Matt finished for her.

Taryn nodded silently. "I had a funny feeling down in the cavern, when I was all alone placing those lights. I felt like I was in a cave full of ghosts—like they wanted their story to be uncovered and told." She shivered involuntarily and wrapped her arms around herself. "You see these mountains all around us?" She pointed at the tall peaks far in the distance, and Matt nodded. "They're all volcanoes. At one point or another they erupted, covering cities and towns and civilizations with ash and debris. Maybe this cenote was the water source for a city that was covered by a volcanic explosion—sort of like Pompeii."

"I've heard of Pompeii," Matt offered. "Dad told me about it once—the city that was perfectly preserved or something by the ash."

"Exactly," Taryn said with a pleased smile on her face. Then her smile faded, and Matt looked ahead to see Jenna and Claudia walking toward them, joined at the hip.

"So, what have you two been up to?" Jenna asked accusingly with a wide grin on her face as they stopped up short in front of them. "Oh my, Taryn, look at your hair! You'll need to shampoo at least five times to get all the grime out! And your face! You must be mortified!"

"I haven't really thought about it, actually," Taryn said, her voice confident. She produced a black band from her pocket and twisted her hair up into a ponytail. "I figured there were more important things to be concerned with other than the state of my hair." She looked sideways at Matt. "But I guess I'd better go and rectify it at once."

She smiled a little too sweetly at Jenna and left. Jenna elbowed Claudia in the ribs.

"You going to help her, Claudia?" Jenna asked, still smiling at Matt.

Claudia looked taken aback for a millisecond, but she nodded and obediently disappeared after Taryn, calling her name.

"So, Matt, is it?" Jenna continued, smiling at him in a very becoming way. "I've decided that of all the guys here, I'd like to get to know you best."

Matt grinned his thousand-watt grin. "I think I'm honored," he said, extending an elbow for her to take.

*   *   *

A while later, Matt and Jenna emerged from the other end of the camp. Both had told their life stories up to the present, and it had taken walking the entire perimeter of the camp to do it.

There was a hubbub around the barracks, and Jenna released her hold on Matt's arm as they reached the group of students. Ben was in the midst of them, both hands in the air, calling for order.

"It looks like things have taken an interesting turn," Ben said, grinning. Everyone laughed at the understatement. "Mr. Dyson and I have discussed at length how we feel we should proceed next, and this dig site is officially elevated to a much larger scale, with the new information we've discovered . . ."

Matt studied the faces of the students as his father talked—some wore expressions of awe, others of intense concentration. He spotted Taryn, freshly showered and standing between Ross and Andy, dwarfed by their stature. Maybe she was right about the volcanoes.

He looked sideways at Jenna, who smiled at him and leaned into his shoulder. *Man, she smells good.*

*   *   *

"So, I hear they're bringing in the big guns," Karen told Matt that night. Matt was in the main trailer, talking to his mom via Skype. Beth kept jumping into the webcam frame, waving and saying hi until Karen, exasperated, ordered her to go brush her teeth and get in bed.

"Yeah, they're arriving in a few days," Matt replied, scratching a mosquito bite on his arm. "You should see the cavern, Mom. It's pretty cool inside. But the water . . . you wouldn't like it."

Karen shuddered. "No, I can't handle dark water. It's not one of my things. Your dad thinks it's just a waterhole, but Sam wants to dredge it, I hear?"

Matt nodded, scratching his knee.

"I heard Taryn was brave, though. How is she doing?"

"Fine, I guess," Matt said, scratching at a bite on his other knee.

"That's not what I meant," Karen retorted.

"What do you mean, then?" Matt asked, stumped.

"Well, I gave her a makeover before you guys left, and frankly, I was astounded at how well she turned out," Karen said in her best "duh" voice. "Poor thing—she hadn't used tweezers *ever*, except to pick out splinters . . ."

"Hey, Mom, I need to go put some stuff on these bites," Matt said, interrupting her. "I'll catch you next time, okay?"

"Matt? Wait! You didn't answer my question!"

"What question?" Matt asked, scratching at his shoulder.

"About Taryn." His mom had an annoyed voice. "Have any young men taken notice of her, do you think?"

"Uh, yeah, there's this one guy who seems to like her," Matt answered. He was now scratching at his other arm.

"AND?" Karen prompted.

"Look, Mom, I'm not really interested in Taryn's love life," Matt said as kindly as he could.

Karen looked disappointed. "I'm sorry. I just feel . . . *invested* now. I mean, she turned out so cute. Who knew a brow wax job and a hair straightening could work such wonders? I just hope she keeps them up . . . I mean, if she lets them grow together again . . ."

"Good-bye, Mom, love you," Matt said, waving at the screen. "Tell Beth 'bye for me."

"'Bye, sweetie," Karen said, blowing a kiss at the screen. "Tell your dad I want to talk to him again for a quick minute, will you?"

Matt obediently went over to the other end of the trailer and tapped his dad on the shoulder. "Mom wants you again," he said. "Where do you keep the anti-itch cream?"

"Field box," Ben answered, motioning behind him to a large white box mounted on the wall.

"Thanks." Matt took out two tubes of cream and bid good night to his dad. He walked outside into the balmy, hot air and headed toward the boys' barrack. First, he was going to take a hot shower, and then he would smear the cream on all his bites and get a good night's sleep.

Taryn emerged from the girls' barrack just as he approached them. She was scratching at her neck. "Hey, Matt, do you know if they have anti-itch cream in the field box?" she asked him as he met her.

He handed her one of the tubes. "Courtesy of DIG," he said. "Oh, and my mom says hi, and to be sure you keep tweezing."

"Huh?" Taryn asked, flustered. Matt resisted the urge to laugh as she absentmindedly put a hand up to one of her eyebrows. "Oh, okay. Well, you can tell her I will."

Matt, feeling smug at her discomfort, grinned and started walking away.

"Hey, Matt, can I ask you something?" Taryn asked after him, her voice hesitant.

He turned around. "What is it, Gilley?"

"That Ross guy, is he okay?" she asked. "I mean, is he a nice guy?"

Matt felt awkward all of a sudden. "Um, yeah, he's a good guy."

"Okay, thanks," Taryn said quickly, clearly embarrassed. She darted back inside the barrack and Matt stood there for a moment, looking at the door.

"You look like a Greek statue," a familiar voice came out of the darkness. "Or I guess, considering the surroundings, a Mayan bas-relief?" It was Jenna. She had come from the direction of the boys' barrack.

"What are *you* doing out so late, little lady?" he asked, flirting.

"It's not even ten o'clock," she said enticingly. "I went by to see you, but the guys told me you were with your dad." She stepped closer to him, fiddling with the flashlight she held in her hands. "I heard the mountains by moonlight are quite a sight from Dig Site B. You game?"

Matt warred inwardly with himself for a moment—he didn't want to break the rules, and frankly, he was itching like mad and the thought of more mosquito bites was a major deterrent, but she was wearing a thin top and pajama shorts, and her hair shined in the moonlight like a halo around her head.

"Lead the way, ma'am," he said gallantly, tucking the tube of cream into his pocket and gesturing for her to start walking.

*   *   *

"You're using the wrong kind of repellent," Jenna told him conversationally as they sat on the largest rock together, staring at the nearly full moon. "I can't remember, is it waxing or waning?" she asked, tilting her head sideways to look at it.

"What kind of stuff should I be using, then?" Matt asked, anxious to know.

"The heavy stuff, with the most DEET," Jenna replied, turning and looking at him.

"I take it that's what you're wearing?" Matt asked lifting a finger and stroking the soft skin of her bare arm.

"Naturally," she said, smiling up at him. "I figured Clinique 'Happy' would be a tad over the top for the jungles of Mexico."

"Definitely," Matt agreed as she leaned over to kiss him.

*   *   *

"Dude, you are so busted," Ross whispered as Matt slipped quietly into his bed just after midnight. "I hope it was worth it."

"Waiting up for me, honey?" Matt asked in a high whisper, shedding his shirt and throwing it under the bunk.

Ross grinned in the moonlight that shone through the barrack windows. "And Jared is on to the two of you."

"He is?" Matt had the grace to look alarmed. He glanced over at the far wall, where Jared lay snoring lightly, his large feet poking out at the end of the bunk bed.

"Yeah, but I told him you were probably with your dad. Because you're special and all," Ross joked.

Matt snorted. "Thanks."

"She's dangerous, you know," Ross remarked, punching his pillow and laying his head down on it. "Consider yourself warned. Nighty night."

Matt grinned, remembering Jenna's kisses on the rocks of Dig Site B. *Dangerous isn't so bad . . .*

14

AD 33

TEOM TURNED OVER ON HIS MAT. SOMETHING HAD STAR-
tled him, a noise of some sort. He lifted his head from his
bare arms and looked at his sleeping family. His father was
noticeably absent, but his mother and brother slept soundly,
their deep, regular breathing reassured him.

Something was odd with Nuria, though. Her breathing was too quick. Like she had lain down quickly moments
before. What had she been doing? Had she left the safety of
the house?

Teom wasn't sure, but he was determined to find out. For
now, he was tired. He laid his head back down and drifted off
into a troubled sleep.

*   *   *

The next morning, Teom accompanied Nuria into the greater part of the city, armed with a basket of food for Ammaron. Chemish stayed home, sulking because he wasn't allowed to go.

Teom wasn't sure it was a good idea for Nuria to be here either. Because of the heat, a lot of people had taken to wearing very little clothing, and harlots called out to men in the streets in broad daylight. People staggered out in the open, drunken, and there were brawls and revelry and music everywhere. It made Teom ill, and the maize porridge he'd had that morning quickly soured in his stomach.

Teom kept his arm around Nuria's slim shoulders, keeping her close as they maneuvered their way through the filth and stink of the streets until they reached the great stone temple, where the priests had convened through the night.

A man and a woman were acting lewdly on the steps to the temple, and Teom turned away, disgusted. The whole atmosphere of the city had deteriorated—there seemed to be depravity at every turn.

Teom and Nuria practically ran up the steps into the safety of the temple; its elevation above the city mostly drowned out the chaos below.

Ammaron, dressed in his blue and ochre priest's robes, met them at the entrance. "My children, this is no place for your tender eyes," he protested as Nuria handed him the basket of still-warm food.

"Mother thought you would need nourishment after staying the night," she said quickly, looking nervous and shaken.

There was a large roar of voices and laughter from below, and Ammaron shook his head. "The entire city has become corrupt. They don't listen to their priests and holy men anymore." He looked at them. "I was named chief judge last night, in Gilgal's place."

The impact of his words hit Teom like a blow to the chest. "Father! How could they?" he exclaimed loudly. "They must know that such an act means your death!"

Nuria dropped the basket and threw herself into Ammaron's arms, and he stroked her smooth head as she wept. He looked up at his son, his eyes tired and wary. "Be of good cheer, Teom. If I die, I will die in the service of my God."

Teom scowled. "What sort of God would allow an entire city to live in such evil and corruption?" he demanded angrily. "What sort of God would allow his faithful servants to be slain by evil men?"

"That is enough, Teom," Ammaron cautioned with pleading eyes. "You and Nuria must leave, for I have much to do here. You will . . . tell your mother?"

"It will be a sad day for her," Teom muttered, taking Nuria's hands and drawing her away from their father.

"Teom, someday you will understand why I do this," Ammaron said, putting a strong hand on his son's shoulder. "Go with God's blessing, and please, hurry home. I will see you at the evening meal."

Teom dragged Nuria, still weeping, down the steps of the temple and through the tumult of drunken, boisterous people.

When they were safely away from the main part of the city, Teom stopped and put his hands on his sister's shoulders, making her face him. "Nuria, stop crying. It won't help Mother if you are like this when we tell her."

"I am not s-strong like you, Teom," Nuria hiccupped. "Father is going to be k-killed. It's what the robbers want. They want Jacob to be king over the city! There's no place for a chief judge anymore!" She collapsed, sobbing into Teom's chest.

Teom held her, silently asking God for strength. "Perhaps he won't be killed," Teom whispered into her hair. "Maybe God will protect him."

At this, Nuria pulled away from him, her tearstained face bright with hope. "Do you think so?" she asked.

"Come," Teom said, taking her hand. "Let's go home."

*   *   *

Alba shrieked into her apron when they told her. Chemish was absent, playing somewhere outside, and was spared the news.

"He seems confident, Mother," Teom reassured, as his mother stared at him with wide, horrified eyes. "He said he will be home tonight to eat."

Alba sank down to her knees and clasped her arms around herself. "I knew this would happen. I knew he would be next. They will kill him, and whoever comes after him, until the government is overthrown and the robbers place their king over this city."

"It's already their city, Mother," Teom countered softly. "Maybe the judges will see that the fight is lost and leave?"

Alba smiled bitterly. "Not your father. He is a religious man. He would never betray his calling. He would die for this cause." She turned her face up to her son. "And I would honor him, if he did." She put her face back into her apron and wept, and Nuria knelt beside her and put her arms around her.

Teom left them, and stepped outside. *He needed to find Helam.* He needed to find out if he knew the robbers' plan. But he didn't know where to look. He hadn't seen Helam for many days.

He walked out of the city, past the cement workers' huts and through fields of corn, until he reached the farmer's huts.

He walked to a hut with a bright rug that served as a door, where Helam's mother sat outside, spinning cotton.

"Good day, Mother Izel," he greeted, bowing to the woman. She was only a few years older than Teom's mother, but hard work and poverty had wizened and bent her into an old woman before her time.

"Ah, Teom, come, sit," she offered, patting the stool next to her. Teom sat and watched her hands as they expertly wove in and out, spinning a fine fabric.

"How is your health?" he asked conversationally.

"I get by," she replied, spitting on the spindle to cool it. "Helam was home last night, but only for a few moments. He is preparing to go live in Jacobugath."

Teom raised his eyebrows. "He is? Why would he go there?"

Izel shrugged. "He says he has work there. Work that pays him well. He gave me a bag of gold right before he left."

"What a good son to take care of his mother," Teom muttered, his mind on other things.

"You won't see him, I'm afraid; he left this morning. He told me he won't be back for many days." She spit again.

"I came here to speak to him, but if he has gone to Jacobugath, then I will see him another time. It has been too long," Teom said, rising from his stool. "God be with you, Mother Izel."

"And you too, young Teom," she said, grinning at him, her teeth completely absent.

*   *   *

Jacobugath? Teom wondered as he made his way back toward home. *Why would Helam go there? It's worse than here!*

He wandered in his confused thoughts and almost ran directly into a girl wearing a bright red robe.

"Forgive me," he muttered, and realized who it was. "*Jahza?*" He asked in disbelief.

Jahza had grown up with Teom and Helam. Her father had been Nimrah, one of the chief judges who was murdered. Teom remembered her as a girl who had always been modest and pretty. He had liked her a little, even.

Now, as she stood before him, he hardly recognized her. Her face was painted garishly, and her hair was pulled into the style of the women of the city. She had many bracelets and jewels that tinkled around her ankles and arms, and she seemed uncomfortable that he was seeing her in her immodest robe.

"Teom!" she greeted, her voice nervous. "I thought you had gone with Helam."

"To Jacobugath? Never!" Teom said with disgust. "What has happened to you, Jahza?"

"I was taken in by Hagoram," she admitted, her head down in shame. "He keeps me in his company."

Teom sighed heavily. "How could this have happened?"

A large, meaty man, richly adorned, walked up behind Jahza. "Who is this young man?" he demanded.

"It is only an old friend, Seantum," she said firmly. "He is no trouble to us."

"Then why does he not serve my master?" Seantum sneered, baring a mouthful of black, pitted teeth.

"Perhaps he will, in time," Jahza said quickly. She raised her eyes to Teom's only for an instant, mutely pleading with him to be silent. "There are many young men in this city who would serve Hagoram, are there not, Seantum?"

"Not so many as pretty as this one," Seantum leered, grinning at Teom. Teom's eyes widened in surprise.

"Give my greetings to your mother, Jahza. Farewell," Teom said, backing away quickly.

Seantum's raucous laughter rang out behind him as he hurried away.

15

THE NEXT DAY WAS BEDLAM. SAM DYSON HAD OUTDONE himself this time. By seven in the morning a diving team had arrived to explore the cenote and determine whether it was merely a water source or something else. Then bulldozers and a blasting company would arrive to widen the fissure.

There was nothing for Team One to work on until the diving, blasting, and bulldozing was complete, so Ben combined both teams to work on Dig Site B temporarily.

Matt opted to stay with his dad and the divers (which resulted in a major pouting session from Jenna) because he was bored out of his mind watching the students grid the site, sift and brush, and dig and document things they found. It was tedious, mundane work. The fissure was much more "exciting."

The divers reemerged at noon to report that the cenote

had once been part of an underground cave system, but a cave-in had closed it off from the other underwater tunnels. The lead diver, a gruff man named Dale, informed Ben they hadn't seen anything but broken pottery shards at the bottom, where women must have lost hold on their water vessels. No bones, no remains, no clothing remnants or jewels. They had recovered the pottery shards and sent them to Nan, who was now studying them in her lab.

As Ben was thanking the diving team and getting ready to report to Sam, a large rumbling sound was heard. It was three large bulldozers, four rock trucks, and a large truck with the word *Dyson* on the side, pulling into the camp.

Ben met with the team and drivers for over thirty minutes, and when he came out, he walked over to the court where Matt was shooting hoops.

"Hey, son, I have a question for you."

"What's that?" Matt replied, sailing the ball neatly through the hoop.

"I just radioed Jared to have him bring everyone back here for a powwow. These guys are going to need a minimum of three days to widen the fissure and clear out the rubble, and I don't think anyone will get any work done. So I'm sending everyone off for a tour of the dig sites at Palenque, for something to do while we're waiting."

"Okay," Matt muttered, wiping the sweat off his brow. "What do you want me to do?"

"Well, I'd like it if you stayed here, with me, if you don't mind," Ben continued. "I know you and . . . that Grayson girl are interested in each other . . ." Matt's eyebrows shot up, and he started to speak, but Ben waved him off. "And you will probably want to be with her, but she's here as a student, and I really don't want you to be a . . . well . . ."

"A distraction?" Matt finished for his dad.

"Yes, a distraction." Ben cleared his throat.

Matt was tempted to tell his dad it was *Jenna* who had made the first move and *Jenna* who had broken the rules to take him to the dig site the night before, but he didn't want to get her in trouble.

"Sure. Okay. Whatever," he said. "Are they really going to blow up stuff?"

"They are," Ben answered, grinning at his son. "Very, very *carefully*, of course."

"Cool," Matt said evenly and sank another perfect basket. *Swoosh.*

*   *   *

"But I don't *want* to go to Palenque," Jenna pouted, rolling off Matt a few hours later. She had taken him to a secluded spot in the trees to have lunch, instead of at the tent with everyone else. But food had been the last thing on both their minds. They'd spent the last hour cuddled up at the base of a large boulder, perfectly concealed from everyone.

"I want to hang out here with you and get to know," she said, crawling forward and kissing him on the nose, "*each other*," she kissed him again on the mouth, "*better*."

Matt groaned and sat up, brushing off his shirt with one hand and taking a large bite out of his turkey sandwich with the other. "Look, I really like you," he began, watching her pick dead leaves out of her hair. "And I like kissing you even more." He reached out and brushed a strand of hair behind her ear. "But my dad is right. I'm just a 'distraction' for you. I mean, you came here to learn something, right?"

Jenna made an unladylike noise and crossed her arms. "Not really. You want to know something really bad?"

"What?" Matt asked, intrigued.

"I'm not really into this stuff so much," she confessed. "My dad, he's an archaeology professor at Berkeley, and he told me if I applied for this dig and got in, he'd buy me a BMW when I was done."

"So, you don't want to be an archaeologist?" Matt asked, surprised.

Jenna shook her head, smiling like the devil. "Nope. Are you shocked?"

"Not really," Matt replied, grinning at her. "I kind of got that vibe from you."

"Well, I get the same vibe from *you*, you know," she countered, looking at him intently.

"Guilty," he said, raising both hands in the air. "But I have to admit, it *is* kind of interesting, down there. Wait till they open it up. You'll see. It's creepy."

"I don't like creepy," she said, taking a swig of her Diet Coke and swishing it around in her mouth, thinking. "So, are you going to miss me while I'm away?"

Matt smirked at her. "What do you think?"

Jenna leaned in to whisper in his ear. "Then maybe I should give you enough kisses for you to remember me by."

*   *   *

"It's gonna be awesome," Ross declared that afternoon, as the boys packed their bags. "We're flying on a DIG jet and spending three days at the ruins of Palenque! This is even better than vacation!"

"I've always held a keen interest in the Temple of Inscriptions," Mitchell chimed in. "But the Palace and Astronomical Observatory should be quite promising, as well."

"What for?" Matt asked, leaning against a bunk post with his arms folded.

"My novel," Mitchell replied simply. "It's a science fiction novel, where my protagonist gets sent back to the Mayan era, and Palenque seems appropriate—the historical parameters are an ideal fit."

Matt shrugged his shoulders. "Well, have fun."

"You're not going?" Andy asked, shoving shirts into his duffel bag.

"Nope, just staying here with Dad and keeping him company," Matt replied.

"Man, someone's going to take it hard," Ross assumed with a grin. "No *lovey dovey* stuff for you, Staubach!"

Matt grabbed one of the perfectly rolled shirts Mitchell had packed out of his bag and threw it at Ross. "She already knows," he countered. "So, you and Taryn will have to make up for the lack of lovey dovey stuff."

"You haven't heard, then?" Ross said, his face wearing an odd expression. "Taryn's not going with us either. She's staying here."

"*Huh?*" Matt said, blankly. "Why?"

"Don't know. Ask your dad," Ross muttered, dejected. "I guess I'll have to go solo. Or cozy up to Nan."

"That's not much of an option," Andy joked.

"Especially since . . . er . . . *ahem*, Claudia is taken," Mitchell said quickly, retrieving his shirt from the floor and rolling it up perfectly again.

"What? Who's claimed her? Wait . . . Mitchell . . . *you dog!*" Ross teased. "I didn't know you had it in you!"

"She's very much like me," Mitchell said, smiling a little. "And she's the first girl I can talk to who understands what I'm talking about. Most girls just look at me like I'm from another planet. It's always been their rudimentary reaction."

"I wouldn't know why," Matt muttered, grinning. "But good for you. So *you* and Claudia get to do the lovey dovey stuff, while we'll all be . . . deprived."

"I claim Candace," Andy spoke up and was immediately showered with an assortment of missiles: socks, shirts, flip-flops, and a roll of toilet paper.

*   *   *

That night, Jared and Nan packed all the students into the two vans headed for the airport.

Matt waved them out and walked toward the trailer. Part of him was extremely put out—the thought of getting away from the dust and nothingness and seeing some real ruins (and making out with Jenna every day, of course) was definitely appealing. Here, he was just with his dad, the workers . . . *and Taryn.*

Why is she staying? She was definitely more tolerable lately, probably because she looked decent now, and she hadn't actually called him "stupid" for a few days, but she was the last person he wanted to hang out with for three whole days.

Speaking of which, she wasn't anywhere in sight. Matt glanced around as he walked to the trailer, and when he stepped inside, he saw his dad sitting at one of the computers, pulling on his field boots.

"I hear Taryn's hanging out with us too," Matt said almost accusingly as he sank down into the nearest chair. "What's up with that?"

"Well, she's been working closely with Nan, and since Nan's busy chaperoning the next few days—if we find anything between now and when the students get back, Nan has versed Taryn in the protocols of cataloging any artifacts we find."

"Huh? I thought they were just blasting and clearing. They probably won't find anything," Matt countered.

"That's what I told Nan, but she said we'd need a backup . . . just in case, and frankly, she's right. And Taryn's the best for the job. If we do find anything, I would rather have someone to take care of it, so I can be free to explore the site," Ben explained patiently.

Matt scratched his unshaven chin. "Well, okay. Not that I care or anything, it's just sometimes she . . ."

". . . rubs you the wrong way?" Ben supplied.

"Yeah, she does," Matt agreed. "She's just so . . ."

"Blunt?"

"Yeah, blunt. And annoying."

"She may be those things," Ben agreed, "but I think they're defense mechanisms."

"Even I can see that," Matt countered. "And I'm not that bright."

"You're bright enough. It's just—she's been shunned her whole life because of her looks, and being in the shadow of her brothers." Ben put his foot up on the table to lace up his boot. "But she's incredibly resilient, and I think she's in a new world here with what your mother did for her and having that Ross boy attentive to her. It's probably the first time in her life any boy has noticed her at all, apart from teasing her."

"Boo hoo," Matt mocked, leaning back in his chair. "Is she confiding in you, now?"

"I was her bishop once, remember?" Ben replied. "And you two have known each other since you were babies. Try not to be so hard on her, if you can help it. She's a good girl."

"I'm not mean to her," Matt retorted. "I just . . . *avoid her.*"

Ben shook his head. "That's the same thing, in my book." He smiled. "Look, I'm not asking you to take her out on a date, or anything, just maybe . . . become her friend. A *platonic* friend, of course. Just for the next few weeks. There's nothing wrong with that."

"Platonic is right," Matt huffed, rolling his eyes. "If she keeps her insults in check, maybe I'll give it a try."

He certainly had no intention of doing so, but he thought Ben might like to hear it. At this point, his only motivation for staying was Jenna, and she was gone for the next three days. *It would probably feel like three years until she got back . . .*

"Thanks, son, I really appreciate it," Ben finished, thumping both boots on the floor and standing up. "Now, you want to come with me to the site? Chuck wants to show me their game plan. I don't need them blowing up anything important."

16

AD 33

HELAM WAS GROWING IMPATIENT. HE PACED BACK AND
forth behind the hut, waiting for Nuria. The sun had gone
down hours ago. Surely she hadn't gotten scared? Surely she
would come to him. *She loved him.* She'd said so.

He heard the sound of footsteps, and, to his relief, Nuria
stepped into the moonlight. "I'm sorry," she made excuse.
"Chem had a bad dream. It took a while for mother to get
him back to sleep."

Helam said nothing but pulled her into his arms. "I
thought you might not come," he whispered.

She broke apart from him. "Helam, I am frightened," she
began, looking earnestly into his eyes. "I know you are part of
the robbers now. My father has just been called as chief judge.
Will they kill him too?"

"How do you know it was us?" Helam asked, careful to not let his eyes betray what he knew.

"Please, Helam. I may be young, but I'm not stupid," she said softly. "Will he be safe?"

"Yes, Helam, that's a good question," Teom said, stepping out of the shadows, startling them both. "What is your answer?"

Helam pushed Nuria away and grabbed for his knife. Teom drew his as well, and Nuria screamed.

"No! Teom! Helam! What are you doing?!"

"He is one of them," Teom said with gritted teeth. "I won't have my sister sneaking around in the dark, meeting with . . . *robbers.*" He said this last word with disgust.

"He is your friend," Nuria pleaded, standing between them, her arms out to both of them. "You two have love for each other. You can't do this."

Teom looked at his sister, then over at Helam, and sheathed his knife. Helam kept his out.

"Do you speak for them?" Teom asked, drawing Nuria closer to him. "Will they murder our father, as they have been murdering all the chief judges?"

Helam sighed. "Teom, do you realize that our ways of government are all but over? Years ago, when King Jacob came from the land southward, they had done away with chief judges. Hagoram himself told me. We are one of the last cities to hold on to the old ways." He sheathed his knife. "Jacob only wants a peaceful kingdom. Yet there are some who would fight him, and they will *lose.*"

"You mean men of God? Like my father?" Teom snapped. "If Jacob wants our ways to be done away with, it should be so? Just because he wishes it?" He narrowed his eyes at Helam. "He is a corrupt king, Helam. You have known this ever since they took over that city. And now, their city has become too crowded for them, and they are coming here, to *our city*, where we have always lived peaceful lives . . . except for the Lamanites," he added, remembering Helam's father. "Do you really think he will allow us to worship our God and live free if we are under him?"

"Of course you can," Helam said simply. "Jacob doesn't want us to be tied down by rules. We are free to do as we please, as long as we bow down to him. We can believe what we want and live the way we want, free from the strictness of the old ways."

"But Helam," Nuria said softly. "The 'old ways' are God's ways. They are his laws. Jacob scoffs at his laws. Jacob's subjects live in iniquity. We don't want to live like that. We are obedient to all of God's laws."

"Then you will never be free," Helam replied. "If you come with me to Jacobugath, we can be free. You can worship as you wish. No one will harm us."

Teom's eyes glittered at Helam like flint. "She will never go with you," he threatened. "Not while I am alive."

Nuria looked at Teom. "I am old enough to decide on my own, brother," she reminded him coldly.

Helam looked at Teom in triumph. "You hear her? She is old enough to make her own decisions, without you."

"Yes, I am," Nuria said, turning her cold eyes on Helam. "But I won't go against my God. And I won't go with someone who is part of a people that might cause my father's death. He is a righteous man."

Helam's mouth dropped open, and he said nothing.

"Helam, I love you," Nuria said, her voice softer, and she stepped forward to touch his arm. "And I always will. But you aren't the man I want to spend the rest of my life with. Your ways have changed. *You* have changed. You are not the Helam I used to love."

"You tell me this now?" Helam said angrily, pushing her hand away. "After all your proclamations of love and promises? Were they all lies?"

Nuria choked back tears. "No, they weren't. But now I see what you have become, and I can't be a part of that life, Helam. I see the city now. I see the corruption and filth of the people. I can't live like that," she explained. "And it saddens me that you don't see what I see. You embrace their iniquities, and I . . . can't."

Helam stared at Nuria for the longest time before he finally spoke. And when he did, his voice shook with controlled rage.

"Then stay here with your family and your God. One day, they will forsake you, as you have forsaken me. And I won't protect you. I will not even know you!" And he turned and ran away from them as Nuria collapsed into Teom's arms, weeping.

Teom comforted his sister. "You are safe with us," he said, stroking her hair reassuringly. "I will always protect you, and Mother, and Chem, as long as I live."

"I know," Nuria choked. "But I *love* him, Teom! He was my only love!"

Teom broke apart gently from her. "You did a very brave thing, Nuria," he said firmly, looking into her eyes. "You did the right thing. God will bless you for your obedience."

"Oh, are you God's prophet now?" Nuria hissed, pushing his arms away. "Did God tell you I was meeting Helam tonight? Do you speak for him?"

Teom folded his arms. "No. But you know what Father has always taught us. As long as we obey God's commandments, we will be blessed. All the prophets have spoken it, always."

"And most of them have been stoned or slain by Jacob's

followers!" Nuria argued. "What does that tell us? That those who stand up for God are not saved! Just like our father won't be saved! He'll die, just like all the other righteous men God has allowed to be murdered in his name!"

Teom stepped forward and embraced her again, to stop her words, and she wailed, collapsing against him. He held her for a long time, allowing her to cry herself out until she was only hiccupping and sniffling. Then he lifted her chin with his hand. "Father is a brave man. And he is a righteous man. Whatever God wills will happen. We can pray that he will be kept safe."

Nuria nodded mutely, and Teom put his arm around her shoulders, to walk back home.

She was completely calm by the time they reached the gates of the city. "How did you know where I'd gone?" she asked, before they walked inside.

Teom smiled. "I'm a prophet, remember?"

Nuria smirked and laid her head on his shoulder as they walked. "But really . . . how?"

"You made a lot of noise for someone trying to sneak away," he replied honestly. "And I followed you."

"Oh!" she exclaimed breathlessly, embarrassed.

Teom put his arm around her shoulders again, and they turned onto the street, entering the house where their family lay sleeping soundly.

17

BOOM.

Matt jerked awake, adrenaline pumping through his veins. *Was the bed shaking in my dream?* He wasn't sure. Then he remembered. They were dynamiting the fissure this morning. He lay back down on the pillow and looked at his watch. *6:15. Yuck.*

He rubbed his eyes, remembering the events of the night before. His dad had taken him, Manny, and Taryn in to Cholula, where they'd had a nice dinner, just the four of them. And then they'd seen the great pyramid of Tipanipa. Matt had been amazed at its size. He remembered looking at pictures of it when he was little, in the coffee table book his dad kept in the living room, but seeing it in person was a much different experience.

Taryn had acted odd the whole time, jumpy and quiet,

and when they'd come back to camp to go to bed, she'd stopped Matt in front of the barracks and told him point-blank she hadn't known he was staying behind too.

"I thought you were going to Palenque with the rest of them," she'd said stiffly. "Just in case you wondered. Good night."

Matt had watched her disappear inside the girls' barrack, shaking his head, perplexed at her behavior.

Now, as he lay in bed, he wondered what she'd meant. After a while, he gave up and laid his head back down on the hard pillow to try and go back to sleep, but he couldn't. He sat up, stretched, and shuffled off to the showers.

Afterward, he dressed quickly and left the barrack, surprised at how hot the air was as it hit him when he stepped outside. The food tent next to the kitchen was buzzing with clanking and sizzling noises and the sound of the undercooks chattering together. They seemed cheerful and relaxed, since Terrence wouldn't be getting out of bed to cook for only a portion of the camp. He was probably still asleep, unless the blasting had woken him too.

Matt peeked inside the operations trailer to find it empty. Everyone was probably at the fissure. He started walking through the trees to the other side of the camp, when another loud boom startled him. The ground shook beneath his feet, and he stopped, feeling nervous. *Were they trying to cause another earthquake?*

He came out of the clearing to see a large cloud of dust settling over the site, far away. He could see his dad and the workers and Taryn wearing hard hats and crouched behind some rocks. Then another charge went off: *BOOM.* Another huge cloud of dirt and smoke shot into the sky. It looked like something out of a war movie.

"*What the h—*" Matt gasped as he walked toward them.

Taryn had her hands over her ears. She looked surprised when he reached them.

"You're up early," she yelled over the commotion.

"Yeah, well, it's a little hard to sleep with people blowing up stuff right in my ear," he yelled back.

Ben smiled at him. "Good to see you, son. You ready to see what we've been up to?"

Matt nodded, and Ben handed him a hard hat. He put it on, and they walked out from the shelter of the rocks, waving away dust and dirt that still hung thick in the air. As they picked their way through the rubble toward the fissure, the dust cleared and Taryn gasped.

The fissure was gone. Instead there was a wide crater in the earth, about two hundred feet in diameter.

"Nice. Now we have the Grand Canyon instead of a big ol' crack," Matt commented as they looked down into it. There were large boulders and rocks everywhere, and the hastily constructed shelter they'd built over the cenote was clearly visible, since there was a bank around it. The insides of the newly hewn canyon were striped; the layers stacked up on each other through the ages were clearly visible.

Ben whistled. "Look at that strata."

"*Que ghido*," Manny whistled low.

"Wow is right," Taryn said. "Just think what it will be like when we uncover the cenote. It will be the first time in two thousand years the water has seen air and sunlight."

To Matt it seemed strange, like they were disturbing something that wasn't meant to be disturbed.

"What's that?" Taryn asked, pointing down into the hole.

"What's *what*?" Ben and Matt asked in unison.

"There's something shiny down there, I saw it . . . look! There it is again!" Taryn pointed, and they all followed the direction of her finger. Something indeed was catching the sun, and it glinted at them briefly. Taryn leaned forward as if to start walking, and Ben held out an arm to stop her. "Not in a million years, Taryn. It's not safe for anyone to go down there. They've got to clear the rubble first."

"But can we trust the workers, if they find anything?" Taryn worried.

"It's taken care of," Ben replied. "I told the foreman if any of his workers find something 'not' rubble, if they turn it in to us, and it's something special, I'll pay them a thousand pesos."

"A *thousand* pesos?" Matt nearly choked. "Isn't that a lot?"

"It's about a hundred dollars," Ben replied. "But it should keep them honest."

"I want to see what's down there," Taryn pouted.

"So do I, believe me," Ben told her. "But none of your lives are worth anything we could potentially find down there. We'll have to wait."

Matt was actually disappointed about it. But he understood. And his stomach was making loud noises all of a sudden. He turned to his dad. "You think breakfast is ready?"

Ben chuckled. "Always thinking with your stomach. Yes, let's go see. These guys will want us out of here anyway."

Manny had to go back and pull Taryn gently away from the edge of the site. She joined them reluctantly as they walked back to the main part of camp. A heavenly smell of pancakes and bacon wafted out of the meal tent toward them.

"Now, that's what I'm talking about," Matt said happily as they entered the tent and saw what was set out for them: pancakes, waffles, eggs, bacon, sausage, and assorted juices and fruit.

The DIG guards had already helped themselves and were seated at one of the tables, laughing and joking in Spanish.

Matt noticed they wore guns in holsters. It was only natural, since they were guarding a site full of extremely expensive and advanced technological equipment, but seeing the guns made it all the more real.

Matt walked over and heaped pancakes, bacon, and eggs on a plate and sat down at the nearest table. Taryn thumped a plate down across from him, then another, and then another: one with waffles, one with eggs and bacon, and one with fruit.

Matt shrugged and poured syrup over everything on his plate.

Taryn watched him do it and shuddered.

"Is there a problem?" Matt asked as he put a large mouthful of syrup-covered eggs and pancakes into his mouth.

"Well, if you must know, yes," Taryn replied. "I can't do that."

"Do what?" Matt asked.

"I don't like my food to touch," Taryn said, blushing. "Like syrup on eggs. Eggs are supposed to be salt-and-peppery. Not *syrupy*. That's . . . gross."

Matt stopped chewing and looked at her. "But you have eggs and bacon together." He motioned at one of her plates.

"But they're both *salty*. They go together," Taryn explained.

Matt swallowed and shook his head. "You're a strange duck, Gilley," he said, mopping his eggs in the syrup on his plate and forking them into his mouth.

Taryn shuddered again. "Quack, quack," she said, pouring syrup over her waffles.

*   *   *

After breakfast, Matt decided to ditch and take a nap. Nothing exciting was going to happen for a while anyway, since the crew had to clear all the rubble and debris from their blasting.

He stripped off his shirt and got into bed, sighing heavily as everything grew dark around him . . .

*   *   *

Later, he woke up to the lunch bell just after noon. He pulled his shirt back on and went outside to the tent, where there was an assortment of deli sandwiches and bags of chips and drinks. He grabbed three sandwiches and two bags of chips and sat down next to Ben and Manny, who were in deep conversation at a nearby table.

Ben looked up as Matt sat down, and they were both immediately silent. "Hello, son," he greeted as Matt reached over for the pepper. "How's it going?"

His dad sounded silly talking that way, and Matt shook his head. "It's cool, Dad. What's up with you guys?" He noticed Taryn was nowhere in sight. "Where's Gilley?"

He saw Manny smile quickly and take a bite of his sandwich, and immediately Matt realized he may have given the foreman the wrong idea.

"I mean, she's probably out there spying on the workers to make sure they find that shiny thing she saw in the rocks . . . not that I *care* or anything," he added. To his immense frustration, Manny grinned even wider and took another bite.

"Well, that's exactly what she's doing," Ben replied, biting into his own sandwich. "She marched right over there after breakfast to 'watch them,' and she hasn't returned. Maybe when you're done you can take her a sandwich?"

Matt looked at Manny, who grinned back at him. "Um, okay."

*   *   *

About twenty minutes later, Matt, armed with a bag containing a sandwich, apple, and a cold can of soda, traipsed reluctantly through the jungle path in the direction of the dig site. He would have rather been doing *anything* than taking food to Taryn; she would probably get the wrong idea. *Manny already seems to have the wrong idea . . .*

Matt was thinking these thoughts grumpily when something rushed by him, nearly knocking him flat. He only had a moment to register a retreating blur of khaki capris and brown hair pulled back in a ponytail. It was Taryn.

"Taryn! Hey! I have lunch for you!" His voice trailed off as she disappeared around a bend in the path. Why *was she running like that?*

Intrigued, he turned around and followed after her. A few minutes later, when he reentered the camp, he saw his dad and Manny and a few other DIG guards, as well as all the cooks gathered around Taryn, who was facing them with her back to Matt. She was showing them something clearly fascinating, by the looks of awe on their faces.

Ben stepped forward and took the object from Taryn, who seemed reluctant to part with it. He held it up to the rays of the sun, where it glinted at Matt.

"What is it?" he asked as he joined them.

"It's a knife," Ben said quietly.

"Like a really old knife?" Matt asked, leaning forward to see it. It was about ten inches long and crusted with dirt. Patches of gold were visible on the hilt.

That's probably what was shining at us, Matt thought.

"Yes, a *very* old knife," Ben confirmed. "Well done, Taryn. Well done," he mused, turning it gently over in his hands. "We need to get this to the lab and get it cleaned and photographed, and I'll update Sam." He carried the knife almost reverently to the lab, with Taryn in tow, her sweaty face beaming with happiness and triumph.

*   *   *

Matt, after covertly handing the lunch off to Taryn before she made it to the lab, decided to shoot some hoops. He always felt more at ease when he was doing drills with the ball. It always seemed to calm him. And it gave him time to think, since he never really had to think about shooting. It was second nature to him.

He thought about Jenna and how much he enjoyed kissing her. He thought about how fun it was going to be to start school in the fall, and especially how dumb Taryn had been to bribe him with an entire year of tutoring for thirty stupid days out here. And now that he thought about it, why was Taryn so strange about her food not touching . . . ?

And then he thought about the knife. It had looked like it was made of gold. That would mean it was a significant treasure, aside from historical value. How old was it? Was it worth a lot of money?

He paused, gripping the ball in both hands, and decided there was only one way to find out. He ditched the ball in the boys' barrack and walked to the storage lab, where he welcomed the gust of cold air that rushed over him as he stepped inside. Ben and Taryn sat at Nan's long table, with the lamps trained on the knife, which was now clean. Taryn had Nan's camera and was photographing the knife from every angle.

Ben hardly noticed as Matt came to sit beside him. He had the large standing magnifying glass trained on the knife and was peering through it, silent.

"Boo!" Matt uttered, causing Ben to jump.

"Oh, I didn't see you. Sorry, son," he said, bending back to the magnifying glass. "Taryn, did you get this symbol on the hilt?"

"About twenty pictures," Taryn replied, snapping away.

"Wow, that's pretty cool. It looks almost new," Matt commented as he looked at the knife. The hilt was solid gold, which gleamed under the lamplight and the blade, about six inches in length, was a slate color, and seemed to be chipped out of gray stone, not metal, as most knives were. The handle had a small symbol carved into it, and other than that, it was plain.

"It's in remarkable shape," Taryn commented as she put the camera down.

"Protected from the elements in that cavern, you bet it was," Ben replied, pushing the magnifying glass out of the way. "It's incredible, like a Mayan stemmed macro blade, but smaller, with a gold hilt. I've never seen anything like it. And I've got to get scans of this symbol to Gertie. It's a language I'm not familiar with. It isn't Mayan, or Aztec. It could be Epi-Olmec."

Taryn nodded somberly, and Matt looked at both of them. "So, is this the knife that cut out the heart of the sacrificial victims?" he joked.

"No, this is a basic weapon, not ceremonial. The ceremonial blades were mostly obsidian. This one is chert," Ben explained as he put his glasses back on his nose and bent to look once more at the symbol. "Only, you won't find any chert around here. If we can find out what this symbol means, it will help us to know where it came from."

Matt peered down at the tiny glyph, carved into the gold of the hilt.

"It looks like a snail shell," he guessed, blinking his eyes in the light. "I can't tell."

Ben peered at the symbol and grinned. "It sort of looks like . . . ah, don't worry, Gertie will know." He looked at Taryn. "You ready to catalog it?"

Taryn nodded, scratching at her dusty nose. In fact, she was covered from head to toe in dust yet again. Matt saw the lunch sack over on the other table, untouched.

He looked back at the knife. Somehow, he wasn't surprised. Taryn was one of those hardnoses who put archaeology even before food. She was basically a mini Ben.

Without the balding head, of course, Matt thought, smirking to himself.

18

AD 33

TEOM STUMBLED ON A LOOSE ROCK AND RIGHTED HIMSELF. No one had seen his carelessness since it was dark, the night lit only by torches and fires that burned in the city. He followed behind the bare feet of his guide, who maneuvered deftly through the maze of drunken people and makeshift vegetable and pottery stands. Loud curses and laughter filled the night air, along with the stink of foul breath and unwashed bodies. Brightly painted women stepped out of shadows and beckoned to Teom, their jeweled bracelets tinkling, but he brushed them away as he followed the young boy who had arrived at his doorstep in the middle of the night with a message:

Follow me if you value your life and those of your family.

Teom had followed without question. He had a hunch as to where he was going, which was confirmed as the boy disappeared into one of the larger stone buildings of the city, the chief judge's house. Since the last chief judge's murder, robbers had overrun it, and Ammaron had opted to sleep at his own house, rather than move his family into the city, as was custom.

A lot of customs had been broken lately.

Teom entered the great stone house, lit by torches, and smelled the reek of wine and incense . . . and other unpleasant smells. He followed the boy into a cavernous room, where dozens of men and women lay crammed end-to-end, slumbering on the floor in various states of undress. Teom averted his eyes and kept behind the boy, who stepped around the sleeping mass of bodies and disappeared through a doorway into another room.

As Teom entered the doorway after him, Seantum stepped out and barred the entrance with folded arms and a menacing grin. He held his hand out. "Your weapon," he demanded cheerfully.

Teom removed his knife and handed it to Seantum, who looked at him appraisingly and backed away to the side.

Teom swallowed the bile that entered his throat and saw that the room was bare except for the chief judge's chair, where a tall man dressed in a rich robe sat waiting for him.

It was Hagoram.

So *this* was the bloodthirsty leader of the robbers. The one he'd heard all the stories about. He was second only to King Jacob, who years before had taken over the city to the north.

Hagoram's long hair was twisted up and adorned with jewels, and he wore many costly ornaments in his ears and on his wrists. His skin shone bronze in the firelight, and his fierce demeanor alone would have terrified anyone in his presence. But Teom was the son of the chief judge, and more than this common robber's equal.

But the person who suddenly stepped out of the shadows and stood next to Hagoram surprised Teom.

Helam.

Helam's dark eyes glittered at Teom in the firelight. No indication of the friendship they had shared as boys was evident on his face.

Teom stood straight and tall, regarding them both.

Hagoram dismissed the messenger boy with a flick of his hand. The boy bowed low and retreated to the side of the room, where he stood, framed by the brightly colored figures and glyphs painted on the wall.

"Do you know who I am, son of Ammaron?" Hagoram's voice was low and gravelly, and he wore an amused smile on his face.

"You are Hagoram, the leader of the robbers who have overtaken this city, and one who would murder my father," Teom answered boldly.

The amused smile disappeared. "Is that what you think of me? That I am a murderer?"

Teom clenched his teeth. "Yes."

Hagoram studied him for a moment and smiled again. "You are brave, I'll give you that. But let's see if you are smart. Any fool can be brave." He stood and walked over to the far wall and studied the pictures on it.

"You realize, Teom, we are in the middle of a war—a war for power. And in wars, there are casualties." He turned and faced Teom. "You are standing before one of the most powerful men in this land. I rule the city now, and everything I say comes to pass."

Teom bit his tongue against the bitter words he wanted to spew at Hagoram. He knew he was in a dangerous position—the blood coursing through his veins and the pounding of his heart warned him of it. He remained silent.

"King Jacob has long wanted this city added to his kingdom. But the people here were so . . . *resistant* at first. He called me to come here, to persuade them, to show the people of this city that Jacob is truly great. And look what has happened."

Exactly, Teom thought, masking his anger.

"But there need be no more blood spilt," Hagoram continued, gesturing toward Teom. "It depends on you, of course."

"Me? How?" Teom managed to be civil.

"Your father is the new chief judge." Teom watched as Hagoram walked over to Helam and patted him on the shoulder with pride, as a father would to a son. "You know what has happened to chief judges in the past." Teom saw Helam's defiant, proud stare, and his eyes widened as Helam's hand in everything became clear.

Helam had murdered Gilgal, the chief judge.

Not Helam. Not my old friend! Teom's shoulders sagged at the weight of this new knowledge as Hagoram continued.

"It need not be your father's fate to die. You can . . . *help* him."

"And how would I help him?" Teom spat. The words were angry, and out before he could control them.

Hagoram settled into the chief judge's chair with a heavy sigh. "I have been watching you for some time, Teom. You are strong. You are a leader, and I need leaders around me, not whining donkeys." Teom noticed that Helam's smug smile vanished at these words, and he looked at the floor as Hagoram continued. "You could be a great man to us, if you wished it."

Teom knew what he would say next but asked anyway. "What is it you want?"

Hagoram leaned forward conversationally, placing his fingertips on his knees. "Join us, and I will let your father live."

Teom's pulse raced. "Join your band of murderers? And

you would have my father be your puppet? He would never do it. *I* would never do it." He glared at Hagoram, whose mouth became a grim line.

"Don't be so hasty, son of Ammaron. Your father's life hangs in the balance. The only way he will be protected is by your choice. If you choose not to join us, . . . he will die."

"I would never join you," Teom said firmly and angrily.

Hagoram looked inquisitively at Helam, who glowered at Teom in return. "You say that now," Hagoram said conversationally, "but I am not unreasonable. I will give you seven days. Then I will expect your decision. I will only offer once. Do not disappoint me, Teom." He gestured all around the room. "The lands around this city are filled with the rotting carcasses of men who have . . . *disappointed* me. I would not wish that fate for you."

Teom thought it wise to remain silent and nodded his head mutely.

"You may leave us," Hagoram said, waving Teom away and settling back into his chair. "I will see you again in seven days."

Teom turned, and ignoring Seantum's leering grin as he was handed back his knife, marched through the doorway and out of the stone chief judge's house with his head held high until he was out of the main part of the city.

When he was finally on the street in front of his own house, Teom collapsed on the ground by a large boulder, his strength spent. He heaved onto his knees in the dirt, and for the first time since he was a little boy, he sobbed, feeling utterly alone.

*   *   *

Helam fell to the ground, blood spurting from his bottom lip.

"You told me he would join us," Hagoram hissed, turning away and straightening the bracelets on his arm. "It seems you don't know him as well as you claim."

"I never said he would come easily," Helam muttered, rising and wiping the blood from his chin. "He is stubborn. He believes his God is worth dying for, as his father does."

"Yes," Hagoram agreed. "And men like that are very tedious to work with, unless motivated properly. But I have given him proper motivation. If he joins us, we will have a powerful weapon in his father. If he does not join us, we will slaughter his entire family, one by one."

Helam started to protest, but Hagoram held up a hand. "You will find another woman, Helam. The rules have changed. Now go and convince him to join us. If you fail, I will make sure YOU are the one to slit his sister's throat. Go."

Helam departed swiftly, anger pounding in his head at Hagoram's threats. Hagoram had promised Nuria would be spared and given to Helam for his wife.

Clearly all Hagoram's promises meant nothing. And how could they? The promises of a murderer and thief?

Suddenly the foolishness of all his actions, including his induction into the robbers' gang, came down on Helam like a vise, from which there was no escape.

"What have I done?" he breathed to the heavens as he walked outside into the hot, stifling night air.

19

"GERTIE . . . ARE YOU SURE?" BEN ADJUSTED THE HEADSET
better on his ears and typed on the computer keyboard
as Gertie, a plump bouffant-haired woman in her mid-fifties,
nodded on the monitor.

"Yes, I'm sure," her tinny voice replied over the computer speakers. "I reversed the values, and it stood out better.
Definitely Epi-Olmec. It appears to be the symbol for 'jaguar.'"

There was a long pause.

"You there, Ben?"

"Thanks, Gert, I owe you one," Ben finally managed.

"Okay, let me know if you need anything else. 'Bye, Ben."

Ben terminated the connection and sat silent in his seat.

*It couldn't be. Have we really found a knife belonging to one
of them? If it really is, that would mean . . .*

He leaped out of his seat and banged the trailer door open,

jumping out and leaving a flurry of papers sailing quietly to the floor behind him in his wake.

*   *   *

"So what happens if they don't make ten yards by the fourth down?" Taryn asked, blowing a stray hair out of her eyes. She had her chin resting on her hands and a look of intense concentration on her face. She and Matt were seated across from each other at one of the tables outside the food tent, hunching over a piece of paper between them, on which Matt had sketched a crude football field.

"Well, they have a couple of options," Matt explained, turning the sheet of paper around. "They could . . ."

"Taryn! Matt! Come quickly!" Ben shouted as he shot out of the trailer. Matt and Taryn looked at each other and jumped up. They followed as Ben disappeared into the brush of the jungle trail, headed for the dig site.

They had to run to keep up with him, and when they arrived at the silent pit, they were winded. The workers had gone home an hour earlier, and about three-fourths of the rubble was already cleared away. The sun was starting to sink behind the mountains, and the air was already feeling cooler.

Matt made a low whistling sound. "They sure work fast."

"They were paid well to do it," Taryn replied. "What's going on?"

Ben was catching his breath, and he pointed into the pit. "Where did you find it?" he asked between gasps of air.

"The knife?" Taryn guessed. "I found it down there." She pointed to the ground about ten yards from the cenote.

"Let's go down," Ben said, still wheezing. "You lead the way." He gestured Taryn along, and she started climbing down the makeshift road of rubble the trucks had formed coming back and forth out of the pit, with Ben and Matt following close behind.

"Right here," Taryn said, pointing to a small *X* on the ground, made with smaller white rocks. "*X* marks the spot."

"Clever," Matt said sarcastically.

"Actually, it *is* clever," Ben commented, studying the ground around Taryn's rock *X*. "Unfortunately for us, archaeology can be a rather destructive discipline, and the fact that Taryn took the time to properly mark where she made her find makes her good at what she does."

Taryn beamed with pleasure at the compliment. "What are you hoping to find?" she asked.

"Well, Gertie got back with me about the symbol on the knife," Ben replied, bending down and sifting through dust with his fingers. "She thinks it means 'jaguar.'"

Taryn gasped. "Are you kidding me?" She put both hands up to her mouth.

"What? Is that bad?" Matt asked, perplexed.

"No, it's very, very *good*," Ben said matter-of-factly. "I have a theory I've been working on . . ."

"Which has just been proven *true*," Taryn interjected excitedly.

Ben smiled. "Yes, I suppose it has."

Matt sighed impatiently. They were both driving him crazy. "And the theory *is* . . . ?"

Ben didn't answer right way but bent down and looked under a large rock.

Taryn lowered her hands and watched Ben as he looked underneath. "Your dad has a theory about the Gadianton robbers," she said simply.

"Okay, I remember them from Sunday School," Matt nodded. "They were the bad guys who were like, the Mafia back then, right?"

"More like al-Qaeda," Taryn corrected. "They were a bunch of terrorists, basically, who murdered and plundered their way into cities covertly and caused all sorts of problems."

"So, what does this have to do with the knife?" Matt asked.

Ben actually stopped what he was doing and looked at his son. "You really want to know?" he asked, seeming surprised.

Matt dusted off a large boulder and sat down. "Sure. Why not?"

Ben, with a pleased look on his face, sat on his heels in the dirt and looked at Taryn, who was perched on the boulder next to Matt, her skinny legs jutting out.

"In the Book of Mormon—Third Nephi to be exact," Ben began, "it tells of the evil robber Jacob, who terrorized the Nephite cities in the land southward. This was about AD 30."

"Okay, so he lived a really long time ago," Matt repeated, nodding his head. "You think this is his knife?"

Ben put both hands out, smiling. "Whoa there, let me get to it." Matt grinned sheepishly.

"Jacob wanted to be king," Ben continued, "so his followers, through secret combinations used by the Gadianton robbers centuries before, overthrew the existing Nephite government by murdering the chief judges. The Nephites broke up into tribes after that and governed themselves. Jacob got impatient and decided to find a land where he could build his own kingdom, and took all the robbers and Nephite dissenters who would follow him, and they migrated to the land northward."

"Where's the land northward?" Matt asked.

"You're sitting on it," Taryn said quietly. "Basically, it's Mexico. At least, that's what a lot of people think."

"Oh," Matt said simply.

"This is what *I* believe, anyway," Ben said quickly. "And

when Jacob arrived here, he took over existing cities by systematically destroying their governments, as he had in the land southward. He named the cities after himself and began to rule them as he saw fit, which was pretty . . . well . . . *inappropriate*."

"He was basically an evil king, and all his subjects were living a hedonistic life of iniquity," Taryn added.

"Okay, I get it," Matt nodded. "They were really bad people."

"Yes," Ben agreed. "They were. And in AD 33, immediately following Christ's crucifixion, the cities of Jacobugath and Jacob were burned and sunk, respectively."

"How do you know they were?" Matt asked.

"Because in Third Nephi, chapter nine, Christ himself speaks to the people after the three days of darkness, and names the cities that were destroyed," Ben answered. "Jacob's cities were destroyed because they were an abomination to him."

Matt was silent for a moment. "Can you show me later where it says that? Unless you have a Book of Mormon in your back pocket."

Ben chuckled. "No, I don't. I'd be happy to show you later, though. But about the knife—the *symbol* on it is what's most important. My theory is the robbers had a symbol for themselves, a symbol of power that the people would recognize and fear."

"The jaguar," Matt said quietly.

"Don't you see?" Taryn interrupted next to him. "If this knife belonged to one of the robbers, or even to their followers, it's proof that they once roamed this land."

Matt shrugged. "Do you know for sure?"

Ben sniffed. "Not really. Its mostly guesswork. After all, it's sort of difficult to look through history and attempt to find documentation on a secret society, when, after all, their very nature was to be secret."

"Yeah, that would make sense," Matt agreed, nodding.

"And what's even worse, is the lack of preconquest material," Ben added. "After the Spaniards arrived, they destroyed most of the records and documents the Mesoamerican people had in their archives."

"They wrongly dismissed their records as satanic and burned them," Taryn sniffed, making a face.

"That stinks." Matt picked up a stick and began stabbing it in the dirt. "What happens now?"

Ben stood up, brushing the dust from his cargo shorts. "I'm going to set up a grid in this area, and Team One will work on it when they get back tomorrow. Team Two will start a grid over there," he said, motioning to the part of the cavern where the water jug had been found, "and maybe we'll find something to write home about."

Matt stood up and dusted his shorts off as well. He looked at Taryn, who hadn't moved. She had pulled her knees up under her chin and looked thoughtful.

"What about the core samples?" she said finally.

"Already taken care of," Ben replied, looking at the setting sun. "The drillers arrive in two days."

Matt wasn't sure of what they were talking about, but his head felt so full of thoughts that he didn't dare ask for any more explanations.

Taryn hoisted herself up off the rock and stumbled a little, righting herself. They walked up out of the pit and dusted themselves off.

"Does it ever rain here?" Matt asked, making large clouds of dust as he beat his shorts.

"Yeah, it does—we've just had an amazingly long streak of sunny days," Ben answered.

They walked back to the camp in silence, each of them lost in their own thoughts.

"You know what?" Ben said as they came out of the trail. "Everyone gets back late tonight, so why don't we take the jeep into Cholula for dinner?"

"Sounds good to me," Matt piped up immediately.

To their surprise, Taryn shook her head. "I'm feeling kind of tired," she admitted. "I think I'll skip dinner tonight."

"When's the last time you had a good night's sleep?" Ben asked.

Taryn looked sheepish. "A while."

"Should we bring you back something?"

"No, thanks," Taryn replied, pausing at the doorway of the girls' barrack. "I think I'll just grab a piece of fruit and go to bed."

"Your loss," Matt mumbled as they continued walking and she stepped inside.

All he knew was that he was *starving*.

*   *   *

After they returned from dinner, Ben told Matt he had a call on Skype. Matt, thinking it was his mom, sat down in front of the computer monitor, but to his surprise, it was Dave and Adam, his friends from home.

"Dude!" Dave exclaimed when Matt greeted them. "Nice of you to leave without telling us!"

"Man, I'm sorry, guys," Matt said, rubbing his eyes. He had eaten too much at dinner and was sleepy. "It was a sudden thing. I hardly had time to pack." Matt heard the click of the trailer door shutting and realized he was alone. His dad had left the trailer to give him some privacy.

"Your mom was nice and let us in," Adam chimed in. "She said we could talk to you this way. It's cool!"

"So, what exactly are you doing down there?" Dave asked, smirking. "Lying on the beach with all the hot chicks?"

"Actually, no beach, just a dig site," Matt said, feeling embarrassed.

"No chicks?" Adam asked, bewildered. "Man, what are you *doing*?"

"Being bored," Matt said, half laughing. "But I'm hanging with my dad."

Dave and Adam leaned in close to the monitor. "Okay, here's the deal," Dave said covertly. "My parents are leaving for the Bahamas for three weeks, and they told me I could have the lake cabin while they're gone."

"Only because they're worried he'll trash the house partying," Adam interjected, grinning.

Dave nudged him. "And I've invited some of the guys from the team and most of the cheerleaders."

"He invited Crystal Lessner," Adam said cheerfully. "And she thinks you're gonna be there."

"*She does?*" Matt asked, flabbergasted.

"Yes, and she is *sooooo fine* . . ." Adam taunted. "C'mon, you *have* to come home and hang out with us! A whole week at the lake!"

Matt felt an uncomfortable tug in his gut. He could see himself spending seven days waterskiing and lying around a beach, not to mention doing it all in the company of Crystal Lessner. "Aw, you guys are killing me!" Matt protested. "Why didn't you mention this before I left?"

"My parents decided to go spur of the moment," Dave replied. "Sort of like *you*. But they gave me The Card. We'll have unlimited 'fun' drinks."

"Drinks, women, and song, my friend!" Adam cheered, and Dave shushed him. He looked behind them, and leaned forward again. "It's simple," he began, lowering his voice. "You tell your dad you're feeling sick and need to come home. You get on the private jet, and in four days you'll be making out with Crystal Lessner and not worrying about rules."

"Everything okay in here, boys?" Matt heard his mom's voice, and Dave and Adam scooted away to let her into the frame. "Hi, honey, you enjoying yourself?"

"Loads, mom," Matt retorted, his voice flat. He noticed Dave and Adam smirking behind Karen's back.

"Well, tell your dad I forgot to remind him about Nancy's birthday, and Beth says hi."

"I will, Mom, thanks," Matt said, fairly squirming.

"We were just about finished anyway," Dave said, turning his mega-watt charm onto Matt's mom. "We'll talk to you later, dude?"

Matt nodded. "Later."

"And our proposition?" Adam said cryptically.

"I'll definitely be giving it some thought," Matt said, nodding.

When they were gone, Matt sat back in the chair, and it creaked with his weight. His wrist was itching from a new mosquito bite under his watch, which he took off and set beside the computer, scratching at the bite thoughtfully. *Crystal Lessner.* She was hot. And she liked him. A whole week at a lake cabin with her, and he would be loving life, for sure.

But what about Jenna? She was fine too. And she was *here.* But she was a goody-goody. All they ever did was kiss.

Which is all you should *be doing,* a voice told him sternly inside his head.

Matt scowled. He was torn. It wasn't that bad here. But a week of debauchery with his best friends . . . it was all tempting. He couldn't think about it right now. Right now, he needed to go find some antacid.

*   *   *

Late that night, everyone arrived from the airport in the white vans. Ross and Andy were the first ones in the barrack. They flipped on the light and startled Matt awake.

"Sorry, man, I honestly forgot," Ross apologized as the rest of the boys trooped in loudly behind him.

"It's okay," Matt said, sitting up and stretching. "What time is it?"

"Just after eleven," Ross replied. "Didja miss me?" He tossed his duffel on the bed and sat down, unzipping it. "Man, I'm going to sleep like the dead tonight. Those girls yakked nonstop on the plane back; it was torture. I couldn't catch a wink!"

"So, how did it go?" Matt inquired as Ross removed his shirt and threw it under the bed.

"It was amazing. We stayed in a hotel in town and studied ruins all day. Pretty much like being on vacation."

"And Mitchell got some kissy action," Andy teased.

Matt looked at Mitchell, who was busily unpacking his perfectly rolled shirts. "*Mitchell?*" Matt inquired with one eyebrow raised. "Is this true?"

Mitchell didn't stop unpacking but blushed to the roots of his hair.

"Well, I can't help it if Pakal's Temple by moonlight is . . . *inspiring*," he said smugly.

"NO WAY!" Matt yelled and began chanting. "*Mitchell got some! Mitchell got some!*"

"Please don't say it that way, it sounds so . . . *derogatory.*

It was rather pleasant," Mitchell sniffed, which made the boys laugh even harder.

"Speaking of lady loves, how is my Miss Taryn?" Ross inquired quietly after the laughter and teasing had died down.

"Oh, fine, I guess. She found a gold knife at the dig site," Matt said casually.

"A *what?*" Ross and Andy proclaimed in unison.

"Yeah, it's pretty amazing. You'll hear all about it tomorrow."

Ross shook his head. "That girl is a magnet for discoveries. She's like a lucky charm."

"She's *obsessed*, that's what she is," Matt countered tiredly. He was tired of talking about Taryn. "How is Jenna? Was she sulking for me the whole time?"

He saw Andy and Ross exchange the smallest of glances. "Well, she's . . . *tan*," Ross divulged, and Matt dove for him.

After Matt gave Ross a sound thrashing, they flipped off the lights and got into bed, whispering in their bunks. Matt told Ross and Andy about the symbol of the jaguar in the hilt of the knife, and his dad's theory about Jacob and the robbers. They listened in stunned silence.

"I wonder if we'll find any remains or anything," Ross whispered. "Can you imagine?"

Matt shook his head. "No, I can't."

"Well, how about you get some sleep, and we won't have to imagine until morning?" Jack's annoyed voice spoke from the darkness.

"SHUT UP, DANTE, WE CAN'T SLEEP!" Andy yelled loudly.

Jack scowled and turned over in his bunk.

Matt grinned in the moonlight streaming through the barrack window. It was good to have them all back. And he would see Jenna tomorrow.

And maybe I'll do more than "see" her, he thought happily. He decided he didn't want to think about what Dave and Adam had proposed, earlier.

He couldn't think about that right now.

20

THE NEXT MORNING, MATT DISCOVERED HE DIDN'T MIND waking up at six so much. He joked with Ross and Andy while they all showered and dressed, and they walked to the food tent in high spirits.

The tent was crowded with boys and girls laughing and talking. Mitchell was seated with Claudia, and Andy sat by them. Ross and Matt stood with their food, looking for Taryn and Jenna. They didn't see them anywhere. Ross shrugged at Matt, and they joined Andy and sat down.

Matt stood up before he started eating. "I'll be right back," he said and left the tent. He'd left his watch in his dad's trailer the night before, but he was using it as an excuse to catch Jenna alone.

He didn't see her anywhere as he walked to the trailer and opened the door. The trailer was empty, so he got his watch, closed the door securely, and made his way back to the food tent.

Then he heard girls' voices speaking quietly and realized it was Taryn and Jenna walking ahead of him toward the food tent. They had stopped, and Jenna said something to Taryn, who looked at her as if she'd rather be getting a root canal.

Matt sneaked up on them unseen, hiding behind a tree to hear what they were saying.

". . . the best way, anyway," Jenna was telling Taryn. "And thanks for the advice, but I can handle myself. Now, I'd like to give you some advice just for you."

Taryn folded her arms. "What's that?"

Jenna smiled sweetly at Taryn. "If I were you, honey, I'd lay off the SPF 70. That *is* the strength you're using, right? Well, you'll never catch any guys if you look like a fluorescent lightbulb."

Taryn looked down at her legs, and Matt chuckled silently behind the tree. *Jenna's right. Taryn's legs are pretty white . . .*

"I don't want to get melanoma," Taryn said back, just as sweetly. "Especially since I'm going to spend most of my life in the sun. I need to protect the skin I have."

Jenna sniffed. "Well, that's fine, but when you're young and trying to catch a man, you shouldn't be worrying about stuff like that."

Taryn stared at Jenna like she was from another planet, and Jenna rolled her eyes in frustration.

"Look, just take it down to SPF 30 or something, okay? If you really want boys to look at you, you have to have *some* color!"

"But I don't want boys to look at me," Taryn countered honestly. "Not for another five years anyway."

This time it was Jenna's turn to look incredulous. "You really are *something*, aren't you?" she said, clearly annoyed. "I feel like . . . oh, never mind. I just can't talk to you." And she walked off, leaving Taryn behind. Matt looked at Taryn, who smiled a small amused grin.

Matt wasn't exactly sure who had triumphed in that conversation, but he was intrigued. He waited until Taryn had followed Jenna into the tent before he stepped out from his hiding place.

Girls are definitely weird.

*   *   *

The next week was busy. Teams One and Two were put to the task of grafting and documenting their respective sites, and the dig instruction had officially begun. Every few hours or so there would be a shout as something was found: a broken shard of pottery, a piece of colored stone, a flint that looked like something significant.

Matt spent most of his time at the site as well, helping his dad or watching the others excavate their own little spaces. It was monotonous work, but with the likes of Ross and Andy around, making jokes and telling stories, it all seemed fun. And Ben seemed pretty happy to be working side-by-side with Matt observing, doing the work he loved to do.

For the first time in a long time, Matt actually felt content, which was an unusual but welcome feeling. In fact, as time went by, he stopped thinking about Dave and Adam's offer. He figured they were big boys; they could handle things without him.

Jenna was acting a little strangely, though, he noticed. Before Palenque, she couldn't seem to get enough of him. Now she was always "too busy" or "too tired" to meet him secretly. It couldn't possibly be anything to do with *him*, so he just shrugged his shoulders and kept trying to get her alone. He did manage one night at the rock pile, but Jenna seemed different, even her kisses weren't as enthusiastic. She seemed to like him still—the way she would sidle up to him in the food line and make eyes at him, or hold his hand at the end of the day and head tiredly back to camp for dinner with him gave him hope—but something was definitely different.

All the students became deeply tanned after a week of being out in the sun twelve hours a day, *including Taryn*, Matt noted. She must have taken Jenna's advice and stopped wearing so much sunscreen. Even *Claudia* looked good. When the girls walked around, it was as if bronzed goddesses had invaded the camp.

Matt thought it was odd seeing a tan on Taryn. She actually looked . . . *good*. Ross, of course, was completely smitten. He was always at her side, and they were always whispering together, or walking to the food tent together. Eventually they became inseparable. Matt couldn't help but notice a change in Taryn. She seemed much more confident and happy with Ross, and even . . . *nicer*.

When Sunday came, and everyone got ready to go to church in the town, Matt faked a migraine so there wouldn't be any awkward questions. He watched through the barrack window as Ross met Taryn at the white van. Taryn had her hair down, sleek and straight, and she beamed at Ross as he took her hand and they got into the van.

Matt flopped down onto his bed, feeling strange. He dumped an ice pack that was on his bed onto the floor. Jenna had come by earlier with the ice pack and some kisses, looking pretty in a short skirt and floral top. For some reason, it bothered Matt her skirt was a little *too* short, as usual, but he didn't say anything. That was her business.

He turned onto his stomach and tried to sleep, but he

couldn't. After he was sure the vans had left, he went outside and shot hoops and ran drills. After a while, even that was boring.

He found himself thinking about the dig site. Would anyone care if he poked around? *As long as I don't touch anything . . .*

After cooling down, he changed into a fresh shirt and shorts and walked to the dig site. It was now a huge square pit carved out of the earth like a rock quarry. At the bottom was the cenote, roped off, the water glistening in the sunlight, no longer dark. It was fairly clear, with mossy rocks visible a ways down. Both dig sites were covered with tarps to protect them, and Matt walked down into the pit, feeling strange and alone. Every step he took echoed in the small canyon. He'd never noticed how enormous it was before because he was always with a bunch of people, and there were always clanking noises and voices.

Not now. The pit lay completely silent in the morning sun. Matt looked around, feeling like an intruder. He looked over at the cenote, and at the path that had been worn in the stone by many feet thousands of years before. He followed it around the Team Two dig site, and stopped at the wall of rubble that hadn't been cleared yet. The path seemed to end a few feet before, but he walked over to the large rocks and surveyed them for a minute.

Then he got a strange feeling, like he should look in those rocks. He brushed the feeling away, but the feeling came back stronger. He stood at the rocks, hands in his pockets, and decided it wouldn't hurt to just look.

He lifted the smallest stone and discarded it to the side; he saw something. It was the tip of a large rock.

The corner was a little *too* rounded to be a natural rock . . .

He picked up another rock from off it, and another. Soon

he found himself out of breath as he hefted rocks out of the way. Some were big and heavy, and some he really had to lift with his legs to heave them to the side. He worked quickly and silently and finally started to dig around it with his hands to lift it out, but he stopped, backing away.

It was too big. In fact, it was *huge*.

He jumped forward and dug around it more frantically. *I need a shovel*, he thought, but all the tools were locked up in the storage sheds, and the keys were currently with Ben, at the church in Cholula. *But there might be keys in the trailer . . .*

He didn't want to waste time going back. He looked around for a rock that was long enough to dig with, and found one that would work. He uprooted the earth around the rounded point, and realized with a jolt of jubilation it was not just any rock, but the large tip of some sort of carved stone, buried in the clay. He dug frantically, clearing away as much dirt and clay as he could, until he had uncovered the top, which had four rounded sides. Whatever it was, it was *big*.

He backed away again, sitting down hard in the dirt, his heart pounding.

I found something, he thought in shock.

Suddenly he understood. *This* was what his dad felt like when he explored. This feeling must be what kept him going and kept him searching for the past. It was an incredible feeling: a mixture of elation and adrenaline. Matt liked it. It was a *great* feeling. Sort of like his junior year, when he'd sunk a perfect three-point shot with one second on the clock to win a game.

But this was different. In some ways, it was even better.

He would for sure have something to tell his dad when they all got back from church!

21

AD 33

"TEOM, WHAT'S WRONG?" NURIA'S VOICE BROUGHT TEOM out of his thoughts. They were at market, and Nuria had been nudging him for the last fifteen minutes, showing him a squash or an ear of corn, and he had no interest in such things. He was only with her to protect her, and he wished she would hurry so they could get out of the main part of the city and back to the safety of their home, near the city's entrance.

Nuria shrugged and finished her selection. As she spoke to the elderly woman tending the vegetable stand, Teom looked up and caught sight of a familiar face in the crowd. It was Helam, striding across the square toward one of the pottery merchants' stands. Teom narrowed his eyes as he watched Helam have heated words with the owner of the stand, a short, stout man with a balding head. The man held up his hands helplessly and shook his head, and Helam, angry, dumped the man's entire selection of jars and jugs onto the ground, shattering them.

Nuria looked up in surprise. "What has happened?" she asked.

Teom went to her swiftly and hurried her away from the commotion before she could see the cause of it. "It's nothing—just some mischief-makers in the market," he made excuse.

They walked home, Teom still saying nothing. Finally Nuria stopped in the middle of the road and faced Teom, a stern look on her face. "What is it, Teom? Why are you sulking? I told you I wouldn't meet Helam again. I promised . . ."

Teom nodded at her and put his hand on her arm to keep her walking. "I know, Nuria, I know. It's something else. Something I have weighing on my mind."

"Have you talked to Father about it?" Nuria suggested as they walked. "You always tell Father your problems. He is wise."

"I . . . can't tell him," Teom confessed, looking around. He said no more. He'd already said too much. Nuria's forehead wrinkled as she frowned.

"There isn't anything you can't tell Father, Teom," she said gently. "You know that by now. Especially if it has to do with the robbers."

He looked at her quickly but realized she had only made a lucky guess. He arranged his face into a stern look. "Don't worry, Nuria, I will work it out on my own."

"Sure," she said knowingly. "Because you have *all* the answers, after all." She darted inside the door to their home, and Teom scowled.

Nuria was right. He needed to talk to his father. Ammaron was the spiritual leader of the community now, even if in name only, but he was still Teom's father.

And Teom needed advice.

*　　*　　*

A few hours later, Ammaron closed his eyes and sighed. "This is a quandary indeed," he murmured. "I am glad you told me, my son."

Teom's shoulders relaxed, as if a great weight had been lifted off them. He and his father were in the back room of the house, away from listening ears.

"Father, I cannot join them. I would never betray you, or God."

"I am proud that you wouldn't," Ammaron replied. He didn't say any more, but Teom knew what would happen next.

"But if I refuse, Hagoram will have you murdered. And they will shout it from the rooftops, and everyone will know that another chief judge has been slain. And the people will succumb to Hagoram," Teom concluded. "Jacob will ride triumphantly into the city and claim it as his own." He spat. "The City of Jacob."

"Hagoram has already won," Ammaron concluded. "Even with me as chief judge, Jacob has proclaimed the city his. As you have concluded, it bears his name. It is no longer safe to go into the city, so I stay here. The other priests have fled. Or at least I hope they have fled. I am the only one who remains. I cannot fight an entire army of robbers."

"Does Hagoram know this?" Teom asked, surprised.

Ammaron nodded solemnly.

"There is no way we can defeat them," Teom muttered gravely.

"No," Ammaron agreed. "I must retire and pray about this,

as should you. Let us find out what God would have us do."

Teom nodded somberly and left. He needed to find a place to pray.

*   *   *

"Teom!"

Teom started up from his knees and drew his knife. He had gone to the small grove by the place of water surrounded by large boulders, where he and Helam had played as boys. He thought he was alone.

To his surprise, Jahza stepped out from behind one of the tall rocks. She had a frantic look on her heavily painted face, and she came forward, clasping Teom's hands tightly. "I have escaped Seantum, but he will be looking for me. I have little time," she told him quickly.

"What is it, Jahza?" Teom asked, releasing her. She stepped back and bowed her head shamefully.

"While I was . . . with Hagoram, I heard him tell his men that if you are not to join them, they will kill your entire family," she whispered.

Teom's eyes widened in shock. "My mother? Nuria? Chemish?"

"All of them. No one will be spared," she answered quietly. "But that is not all."

"What more could there be?" Teom asked, dismayed.

"Hagoram said," she continued reluctantly, "that when you join them, Jacob will come to this city and Hagoram will offer your father up as a blood sacrifice to Jacob to let the people see that the last chief judge is dead and that Jacob is their true king."

Teom was crestfallen. But he believed her words.

"So, whether or not I join them, my father dies."

"You must flee the city, Teom," Jahza said suddenly. "It is the only way to save yourself and your family. Flee before they can find you. If you stay, your father will die."

Teom looked at the girl he had known his whole life. She was barely a woman, and she looked small and afraid in her costly apparel and layers of jewels. He was touched she had taken such a risk for him.

"I am praying to God to know what I must do," Teom said, touching her arm. "I am grateful you have come to tell me this."

Tears streamed down Jahza's face. "I could not see you or your family harmed, Teom. I had to tell you." She bowed her head again. "Pray to your God for me too if you would."

Teom placed a strong hand under her chin and lifted it tenderly. "He is *your* God too, Jahza. Never forget that. He is a forgiving God who loves his children."

Jahza nodded silently, tears dropping from her eyelashes onto her cheeks. "I must hurry and go back. Fare thee well, Teom."

And she was gone before Teom had time to speak.

Teom stood still in the grove, unmoving, a massive turmoil of thoughts racing through his head.

He looked around to make sure he was alone and got back on his knees.

*   *   *

It was dusk before Teom arrived at the house. The evening meal was ready, and Alba and Nuria were bustling about as Chemish got in everyone's way, as usual.

Teom walked directly into the back room of the house,

where he could be alone with his father.

Ammaron had his hand on the shoulder of Jacom, one of the cement workers who lived outside the city. They both looked up when Teom entered.

"I will see thee on the morrow, Jacom, and all will be well," Ammaron said, and the tall man bowed to Ammaron and smiled at Teom as he departed.

Teom wasted no time. "Father, I prayed to God about what must be done, and I have received an answer," he said, stepping forward.

"As have I," Ammaron replied, lowering his voice. "We are agreed that we cannot fight the robbers?"

"Yes," Teom replied.

"Then you know we must join them?" Ammaron asked.

The silence was heavy between them.

"Yes, I do, Father," Teom finally replied.

"Then, may God forgive us, but we must join them," Ammaron said softly.

"We must join them or perish," Teom agreed.

22

MATT WASN'T SURE HOW HE WAS GOING TO EXPLAIN HIS finding a big old artifact at the dig site when he was supposed to have a migraine, but he didn't know what else to do. Eventually he decided to tell everyone he'd miraculously felt better after a while. But there was also a strict rule about working on a Sunday, so he wasn't exactly sure how he was going to get around that one.

It had been two hours since his discovery, and he had succeeded in unearthing about two feet of the stone. It was *big*, whatever it was. The top was about fourteen inches by twenty inches, and it was buried lying down in the clay at about a fifteen-degree angle. There were carvings in the stone, but they were so crusted with dirt that he couldn't make anything out.

At one point he had run back to the camp, grabbed a shovel out of the storage shed, taken one of the walkie-talkies, and put a note by the other one in the trailer, where his dad was bound to see it:

Dad,

Call me on channel 9 when you see this. I have something important to tell you.

Matt

Then he'd run back and commenced digging. But now he sat down in the dirt and rested because he was tired. This thing had to be a significant find. Maybe as significant as the knife. Maybe all those know-it-all students with their big vocabularies would respect him now, after this. They *had* to.

Crackling static on the walkie-talkie jolted him out of his daydreams, and he heard his dad's voice come across the band: "Matt? Is everything okay? Over."

He scrambled and grabbed the walkie-talkie. "Dad, I'm at the dig site. You need to come here, quick."

"Why are you there?" came his dad's alarmed voice. "Is something wrong?"

Matt smiled. "Actually, no, I have something you need to see."

"I'm on my way. Over," Ben replied, and the line began to crackle. Matt shut the walkie-talkie off and stood up, brushing his shorts off and surveying his handiwork.

"Dad's gonna pee his pants," he thought out loud.

*   *   *

A few minutes later, Matt climbed out of the pit and saw his dad emerge from the jungle trail, still wearing his shirt and tie from church. He was two hundred yards away, but Matt could tell he was running.

Matt walked forward to meet his dad, a large grin on his face.

It seemed to take forever for Ben to reach him, but he did, gasping, still holding the walkie-talkie.

"What . . . what is it, son?" he asked breathlessly.

"Come here," Matt said, grinning and motioning for his father to follow him.

"So I was walking around here, just thinking, while you guys were gone," Matt began as they neared the pit, "and I got this feeling that I should look under some rocks."

Ben looked alarmed. "*Some rocks*? What do you mean? Son, you didn't touch anything, did you?" His voice went up in pitch. "You could compromise the site . . . Every rock, every seemingly insignificant piece of dirt is important! To untrained eyes . . ."

"Relax, Dad," Matt interrupted. "It's a place you guys haven't gridded. Just come and see." Ben nodded and followed Matt to the mouth of the pit.

"What the . . ." Ben began, his mouth dropping open. "Is that . . . ?"

"Yes, I believe it is," Matt finished triumphantly for him. Then he added sheepishly: "Well, do you know what it is? Because I don't. I just think it's *something*."

Ben didn't reply. He stumbled down the rock path into the pit and walked toward the partially exposed stone as if he were in a dream.

"No, it can't be," he whispered. "*It can't be.*"

"So, Dad, did I do good?" Matt asked, standing beside his father.

"Mattie," his dad whispered, calling him by a name he hadn't called him in years. "You definitely hit the jackpot this time."

"Cool," Matt mused. "What exactly is it?"

"It's a stela," Ben replied, crouching down to study it.

"What's that?" Matt asked, watching his dad caress the stone.

"They used them in ancient Mesoamerica as territorial markers or to commemorate events," Ben said, standing up and producing a handkerchief. "Usually they had them posted around cities." He wiped his sweaty brow.

"There aren't any cities around here," Matt said, looking at the striated walls of the pit.

"Then it makes no sense for this to be here," Ben replied, surveying the walls as well. "No sense at all . . . unless . . ." He trailed off, lost in his own thoughts.

"What are you going to do?" Matt asked after a moment.

Ben turned around and looked at him. "Call in the cavalry, of course. But not until Monday."

"Are you serious?" Matt asked, flabbergasted. "This is a big deal, and you're just going to let it sit until *tomorrow*?"

Ben smiled and put his hands on Matt's shoulders. "Son, I want more than anything to start excavating this. It's a marvelous thing you've found. But I also want to honor the Sabbath. Not to mention how it would look to the other students if I suddenly decided not to follow my own rules."

Matt sighed, feeling foolish. "You're right, I guess," he said reluctantly.

"Now," Ben clasped his hands eagerly together. "Help me get a tarp out of the storage shed so we can cover this beautiful thing up, in case it rains!"

*   *   *

When Ben and Matt entered the camp as inconspicuously as they could, it was quiet except for sounds and smells coming from the cooking tent as Terrence and his assistants prepared lunch.

"I think everyone is asleep," Ben commented as they looked around at the deserted camp. "I heard some of the boys mentioning a nap when we got back."

"Sounds good to me," Matt grinned.

"As if I could sleep if I wanted to," Ben said in a hushed tone. "I'll be thinking about that stela until tomorrow morning!"

"You're welcome," Matt said cheerfully and entered the boys' barracks.

His dad was right. All the guys were sprawled on their beds, most of them snoring away. Only Ross's bed was empty.

Matt looked up to see Ross emerging from the bathroom. He had changed out of his church clothes into a T-shirt and shorts. He lifted a hand and greeted Matt silently.

Then, to Matt's surprise, he motioned for Matt to go outside with him. Matt was hot and dusty from being outside, but he shrugged his shoulders and followed after him.

"Your headache gone?" Ross asked as they walked out of the camp in the direction of the dig site.

"Yeah, it finally went away," Matt lied. He was hoping they weren't walking to the excavation pit, or Ross would see what he had been up to.

"I used to get migraines when I was little," Ross said conversationally. Matt was relieved when he turned to the right instead of going straight. Apparently they were headed for the boulders of the original dig site—the same place he and Jenna had first kissed by moonlight.

"I remember they were all-day headaches. And I'd throw up. It was awful," Ross mused as they continued walking. "You're lucky yours came and went so quickly."

"I have some good medicine," Matt said, unsure if he

liked the direction the conversation was taking. *Is Ross accusing me of something?*

They finally reached the boulders, and Ross jumped nimbly onto the highest one. Matt joined him as he sat down, looking out over the landscape. They could see the spires of Cholula far in the distance, as well as the Great Pyramid.

"So, what's up?" Matt asked. "I'm getting an 'I want to talk' vibe from you."

"Taryn told me about you," Ross said simply, turning to look at him. "She told me you haven't been active in the Church for years."

Taryn. "She did, huh?" Matt asked calmly. Inside, his guts were churning with anger at the betrayal. *Why would she do something like that?*

"I guess I just wanted to find out why," Ross continued, looking up at the puffy clouds overhead. "I figure you must have a heck of a reason."

"She didn't tell you?" Matt asked bitterly.

"No, she said if I wanted to know, I should ask you. So here I am," Ross answered honestly.

"It's a long story." Matt flicked a large bug off his forearm.

"I've got time," Ross looked at him. "That is, if you want to tell me."

Matt discovered, to his surprise, he *did* want to tell this boy he'd only known for a few weeks. And so he told him. As the clouds rolled by them in the blue sky, Matt told Ross about his dad, his job, and his neglect of family for archaeology over the years. Matt talked about the time he ended up in the hospital, and how his dad didn't even come home to be with him. How he wasn't interested in his games or anything Matt liked.

After Matt had talked it all out, he felt much better. In some strange way, he felt like he had just extracted a large splinter. Only this particular splinter had been festering for a long time.

"*Wow*," Ross breathed after a thoughtful moment. "I think I understand now."

Matt picked up a stray stick and stabbed it in the dirt. "I don't know. It's been crazy. I guess the more you don't go to church, the harder it is to go, if that makes any sense."

"So you gave up," Ross said simply.

Matt shrugged. "Yeah. Something like that."

"It must bug you a ton when Andy and I go on and on about our missions," Ross continued, folding his arms. "You've never acted like you weren't going. In fact, I never got that vibe from you."

"What, the heathen vibe?" Matt joked, but he saw Ross was serious. "Yeah, well, I didn't think you guys needed to know about all my problems."

"Now I just feel stupid," Ross said. He looked at the sky. "You know what? I take that back. I don't feel stupid. Because I know we're following the truth. Lucky for us, we don't have to dig. All we have to do is *read* to know the truth of things."

"You're talking about the Book of Mormon, aren't you?" Matt volunteered. "It doesn't make sense to me. I mean, it seems all the masses are just 'going by faith' most of the time. I like to see proof of something before I waste my entire life following the principles of it."

"Fair enough," Ross agreed, nodding his head. "But have you read it?"

"Read what?" Matt said quickly, knowing exactly what he meant.

"The Book of Mormon. Have you read it? And I mean *really* read it?"

Matt suddenly felt stupid. "No. I haven't," he admitted.

To his surprise, Ross tilted his head back and laughed.

Matt flushed dark red with embarrassment.

"Well, there's your whole problem, man," Ross said after he'd recovered. "How can you dismiss something when you haven't even given it a chance?"

"So you've read it?" Matt asked, feeling even dumber.

"Yeah, a few times." Ross grinned. "I don't want to sound arrogant or anything, but if you've really *read* the book, you wouldn't need 'proof' or a sign. You would just *know*."

"Now I suppose you're going to give me a copy and ask me to read it and ponder it in my heart," Matt said sarcastically.

"Actually, no. Not unless you want me to," Ross replied, grinning. "But I will ask you to consider something. Well, a few things."

"What's that?" Matt asked.

"Well, first—don't be mad at Taryn," Ross requested. "She only told me because she cares."

Matt nodded stiffly. "Okay. Got it."

"Second, stop being such a dang Israelite," Ross said with a frustrated tone. Matt raised his eyebrows. "They gave Moses such a hard time, because they were always requiring 'signs' from him," Ross explained. "As if the parting of the Red Sea wasn't enough. Or manna. Or water from the rock. They always needed more signs."

"What do you mean?" Matt asked, genuinely confused.

"Well, think about it. All the miracles around them, and they still didn't believe and acted like a bunch of nuts most of the time," Ross clarified. "Here we are, in Book of Mormon lands, and you see evidence of the people of the Book of Mormon all around you, and frankly, that should have *some* effect on you. You want some proof? The evidence is all around us."

"I don't see any," Matt countered.

"Well, not right where we're *sitting*," Ross amended. "But

they're discovering more and more every day. Did you hear about the gold plates they found in Bulgaria?"

"No," Matt replied, interested. "What gold plates?"

"They were digging in some tomb in southern Bulgaria and found them. They're on display in the National History Museum in Sofia. They're from Lehi's time, about 600 BC."

"I didn't know that," Matt mused.

"Lots of critics have scoffed over the ages at the concept of bound metal records, not just because Joseph Smith said he found some, but because they hadn't *seen any*. Now it's proven they exist," Ross continued. "It boils down to the fact that we finally have the *technology* to find these things and find evidence of the Book of Mormon if we want to. Kind of like that jaguar knife Taryn just found. Stuff like that."

Matt was silent. Ross was right.

Ross took advantage of the silence. "And the last request I have is that, yeah, you *do* read the Book of Mormon."

"I knew it," Matt said, grinning. Then he became serious. "I don't know."

"How about I triple-dog-dare you then?" Ross asked, grinning back. "Think about it—the entire setting of the book is on this continent. Parts of it took place where we're standing. It's pretty incredible if you think about it."

"Here?" Matt repeated. "Are you sure?"

"Pretty much," Ross replied. "You know the story of the Tower of Babel? How God confused the languages of the people?"

Matt nodded. "Of course."

"Well, it's believed that the Brother of Jared and his people landed right off the coast of Mexico. You've heard of the Olmecs?"

"I have recently, yes," Matt replied.

"Well, they could be the Jaredites of the Book of Mormon.

In fact, it's a real possibility." Ross went on. "And Lehi, when he migrated from Jerusalem, they may have landed not far from here, on the coast in Chiapas."

"I wanted to ask my dad that," Matt swatted at another mosquito. "You know, where he thought stuff from the Book of Mormon happened."

"Well, I've been studying it since ninth grade—driving my parents crazy, actually," Ross joked. "You know that big map in the trailer? I could show you lots of stuff on it, if you're interested."

"Thanks," Matt said. "So you really triple-dog-dare me to read the Book of Mormon?"

"Yep. It's actually a fairly good idea, since we're probably smack-dab in the middle of where it's set," Ross responded. "And I won't tell anyone, I swear," he added quietly.

Matt thought for a moment. *It couldn't hurt.* Besides, he would definitely be seeing the book in a different light this time around. As a child, he had always thought the Book of Mormon was some boring tome that yielded a few good quotes now and then. At least, that's how *he'd* felt.

"Okay, you're on," Matt said, scratching at his long hair. "Can we get out of this sun now? I'm boiling out here."

"I figured I could persuade you if I got you into the hot seat," Ross kidded as they jumped down and started walking back. "Actually, a nap sounds really good." He grinned at Matt, who returned the smile.

A nap *did* sound good.

23

MAN, YOU SUCK! I CAN'T BELIEVE YOU DIDN'T TELL ME! WE were *right next to it* yesterday!"

It was early morning. Matt sleepily opened one eye and looked at Ross, who was standing at the side of his bed, arms folded indignantly. Andy was next to him, also with folded arms.

"Tweedledee and Tweedledum?" Matt observed. "Sorry, guys, I was sworn to secrecy." He turned over, only to have the blanket snatched off him. "Hey!"

"Oh, no you don't," Ross chided. "You're getting up right now and telling us how you found it."

"What time is it? How did you guys find out already?" Matt slurred.

"Well, your dad told Manny, who told Jared, who told us," Andy explained. "We thought you were our friend. What are we, riffraff?"

Matt sat up and saw they were both grinning at him. "I told you, I promised my dad I wouldn't say anything. Besides, I found it on Sunday. Couldn't touch it."

Then he was smothered in pillows as Ross and Andy attacked him.

*   *   *

Later, at breakfast, Mitchell was talking excitedly about the stela to Jack when they all sat down.

"They've been excavating it since four this morning. They've uncovered most of it. It's big."

"How big?" Ross asked after he took a large gulp of orange juice.

"Big," Taryn commented, sitting down at their table with a tray, with Claudia and Candace in tow. "About ten feet long and two feet wide." She smiled radiantly at Ross as she said it.

Matt noticed Jenna wasn't at their table. In fact, he didn't see her anywhere.

"Where's Jenna?" he asked casually.

Taryn looked at him. "Overslept."

"What does it have on it? Any glyphs?" Mitchell asked, leaning in.

"That's what's strange. It appears to have a depiction of an important man on it," Taryn answered, taking a bite of scrambled eggs. "And there are some glyphs, but they're incomplete."

"Incomplete? How?" Mitchell inquired.

"Well, the glyphs just . . . *end* suddenly, like they didn't have time to finish them or something," Taryn replied. "But they'll know more after they clean it. Then they can reinsert it."

"*Reinsert it?*" Matt asked curiously. "What does that mean?"

"Just that. It's too heavy to transport for now, so they want to basically stand it up in its original position in the ground," Taryn explained.

"It must weigh a ton," Ross mused. "I wonder what force could be powerful enough to knock it over like that?"

"Ross's morning breath?" Andy offered. "Ouch!" He rubbed his head after a flying plastic spoon, courtesy of Ross, hit him squarely in the temple.

"You deserved that," Ross sniped. "But really, that thing must weigh a ton, at least. I bet it was no easy task knocking it sideways."

They all were silent, shaking their heads with wonder.

*   *   *

Later, as they all trooped over to the excavation pit, they were amazed at the sight before their eyes. The stela had been completely uncovered, and Nan, Jared, Manny, and Ben were cleaning it with bowls of water and brushes.

The rest of the students were gathered around, watching silently and talking quietly among themselves. Some of them sketched the large stone in small handheld notebooks.

"It's beautiful, isn't it?" Taryn whispered, and Matt looked at her just as she took Ross's hand. Matt looked away quickly.

"How old is it, Dad?" he asked, and Ben looked up.

"Same age as the water jar, we think," he said, rising and dusting off his shorts. "Come, gather round, everyone."

Everyone crowded around the stela as Nan, Jared, and Manny backed away so they could get a better look. A collective gasp rippled through the students as they saw the detail carved into the stone: a man wearing an elaborate headdress, and it looked like he had a knife in one hand and several smaller people clenched in the other hand.

"What's your evaluation?" Ross asked Ben.

"Well, it's derived from the Olmecs, but it's clearly different in composition," Ben replied. "See here? This man is very important. He is wearing either royal attire or ceremonial garb." He pointed at the carving. "And it looks like the people he holds in his hand are all his enemies, as are all these people he's crushing underneath his feet." They all looked and saw more people, twisted and contorted in the scroll carving underneath his feet.

"Clearly he thinks a lot of himself," Ben observed. A few of the students chuckled at this. "I'm guessing he was a king of some sort, and this was carved to commemorate his success in battle or his conquering of a people."

"Ben, look at this," Nan said, pointing to the knife the man held in his extended hand. Ben peered in closer and gasped.

"Well, I'll be . . ." he said quickly.

Matt became aware that Taryn had materialized at his side, and she poked him in the ribs. "It looks like the knife we found," she whispered.

Matt looked down at her and back at the stone. He squinted. It *did* look like the jaguar knife—the shape was similar. "Is that the knife we—I mean Taryn—found?" he asked out loud. "It sure looks like it."

Ben backed away, removing his hat and wiping his brow. As he replaced it, everyone was silent, waiting for him to speak.

"You know, it very well could be," he said at last. "I'll have to look into it."

Suddenly one of the boys started cheering and clapping, and soon everybody was doing the same. They had found something significant. *Matt* had found something significant. Matt felt Ross and Andy clap him on the back, and Taryn took his hand and squeezed it briefly before Ross embraced her and lifted her off the ground.

Everyone was cheering, and when it all died down, Jared and Nan shouted directions to their two teams. Everyone scattered to get their tools, and it became quiet again.

Matt stayed with Ben after all the students had reluctantly gotten back to work, and he stared at the stone monolith. "What are you thinking, Dad?" he asked. "Do you know who this guy is?"

"It's just a theory I have, Matt," Ben replied, bending back to the stone. "I promise I'll tell you all about it after we get this thing cleaned up and remounted."

Matt looked up and saw Jenna striding toward them, her tool kit under her arm and a large smile on her face. "Later, Dad," he said, and walked toward her, grinning widely.

24

AD 33

"YOU HAVE MADE A WISE CHOICE, YOUNG TEOM," HAGORAM spoke as the firelight flickered and reflected in his dark eyes. "We will have revelry tonight, and you will stay here, with us. I will send word to King Jacob, and he will come to celebrate your appointment with us."

"The king himself?" Teom asked, pretending to be startled. "He would come here? To this city?"

"Yes, he would," Hagoram replied, smiling. "It will be a very . . . *memorable* occasion for you."

Teom gritted his teeth and was silent. He hated Hagoram. He hated the robbers and their secret combinations and murderous ways. He hated everything about them. But mostly he hated himself, because he had no choice but to join them. And join them he would. To save his family.

Hagoram rose from his seat and came forward to place his hand on Teom's arm. "Come, let us join in the celebration." He led Teom out of the chief judge's chamber and into the cavernous inner hall, where there was music and merrymaking.

Hagoram motioned to the tumult of bodies on the floor of the room. "They celebrate you, Teom," Hagoram said proudly. "Join them tonight. Are there any ladies here you desire?" He motioned to the group of richly dressed, brightly painted women who sat on the steps, watching the celebration.

Teom saw Jahza sitting with some younger girls, and she stopped talking and looked at him.

Hagoram chuckled. "I see you like my favorite."

Teom turned to him. "No, I would never presume," he began, and Hagoram laughed, amused.

"Please, you are one of us now. My favorite is your favorite." He motioned for Jahza to come to them, and when she reached them, she bowed low and looked at her feet.

"My master Hagoram," she uttered over the din.

"This is Teom, who will soon be our newest member," Hagoram told her, slapping Teom on the back. "I expect you will give him a nice welcome?"

Jahza looked at Hagoram and bowed her head once more. "As my master commands," she said complacently.

And before Teom knew what has happening, he was whisked away from Hagoram as robber after robber slapped him on the back and congratulated him heartily. Jahza led him into one of the darker chambers of the house, a small room where there were soft mats and pillows on the floor and wine and cups set out.

Things were getting out of hand. Teom knew what was expected of him, but he wasn't going to insult Jahza—or himself.

Jahza offered him wine, but he declined. He sat on the

mat and patted the place next to him, and she sat down, look-ing at him intently. "I will not lie with you, Jahza," he said quietly. "I may be joining them, but I am not one of them yet."

Jahza seemed relieved. "I am grateful to you, Teom," she said. "May I sleep? I am up all night with Hagoram and his men while they drink. They like us to be awake with them, and sometimes it is difficult."

"Rest, Jahza," Teom said, smiling at her. "I will see you soon." He put a hand up to her cheek and left quickly. Jahza removed her headdress and lay down on the bed, closing her eyes and sighing heavily.

*   *   *

Teom's heart was heavy as he made his way out of the city. He had slipped unnoticed out of the robbers' den and headed home. As he walked, he felt someone fall in step beside him.

It was Helam. Teom stopped and stared at his former friend. "What do you want, Helam?" he asked angrily.

"I need to speak with you," Helam said, looking around for anyone who might be watching. "We need to speak . . . alone."

Teom regarded him sternly, arms folded. "What could you possibly have to say to me? You try to take my sister from her family, and then you tell Hagoram that I will join the robbers."

"But you *have* joined them," Helam countered. "I was right."

"You have been wrong about many things," Teom hissed back. "You don't know anything."

"I know more than you think," Helam replied, lowering his voice. "Please, we must talk somewhere else."

Teom looked at him for a moment. "My house," he said

quickly. "But only for a short while. I don't want you any-where near Nuria."

Helam's face blanched visibly at Nuria's name, but he nodded. "I understand."

They walked quickly and silently back to the stone house just inside the city. Before they entered, Teom reached over and took the gold knife Helam wore at his side. "My father is the chief judge," Teom explained as he tucked it into his own side. Helam looked surprised, but nodded.

Nuria screamed and dropped the jar she was carrying when she saw Helam enter the house behind Teom. Alba appeared with a lamp, and shushed her, for Chemish was asleep on the floor. Then she too gasped when she saw whom Teom had brought into the house.

"He is only here for a short while, Mother," Teom reas-sured her and led Helam swiftly into the back room, where Ammaron was alone on a mat, praying.

They waited until Ammaron finished. He rose slowly to his knees.

"Helam, it is an unexpected surprise," he greeted. Helam looked ashamed and hung his head.

"He approached me in the city and said he must speak with me, Father," Teom explained. "He is unarmed."

"Then I suppose I shall not fear for my life." Ammaron replied, with a shadow of a bitter smile across his face.

The joke was lost on Helam, who looked at them both with boldness. "I am not proud of the things I have done," he ejected. "I have come here to make amends. I wish you would not mock me."

"Helam, Helam, we are not mocking you," Ammaron sighed. "It is difficult. I see only my son's childhood friend in the man standing before me. For all I know you are here to slay me by Hagoram's command."

"Hagoram has commanded no such thing," Helam said quietly. "He bides his time. He is a clever, cunning man. He knows how to make people do his bidding. Then, when he has what he wants, he twists his words so his promises mean nothing."

"What, did he promise you my sister if you killed my father?" Teom spat. Ammaron's eyebrows rose at this.

Helam looked down at the ground. "Yes. But not for killing your father. He said if I joined them, I would have all that I wanted." He looked up at Ammaron. "I love your daughter. I wanted to take her with me."

"She is young, Helam," Ammaron sighed heavily. "Too young to be caught up in all this."

"We are all caught up in it now," Teom said angrily. He began to say something else but thought better of it and was silent.

There was a commotion in the front room, and both Nuria and Alba let out a scream. The men dashed into the room to see Hagoram and Seantum and a few other robbers entering the house. Chemish stood wrapped in his mother's arms, terrified.

"Good evening, Ammaron," Hagoram greeted cordially. "I have come to inquire why your son left us so early this night."

"My son would have nothing to do with you!" Alba hissed, and Hagoram turned to her.

"On the contrary, woman. Your son is joining us. You shall be a proud mother this night."

Alba wailed at this horrible news and hugged Chemish closer as tears streamed down her face.

Teom wanted to step forward and comfort his mother, but he did not move. He merely looked at her. He turned to Hagoram, who was watching his every move with interest.

"I spoke with Jahza, Teom. She told me you had come back home because you'd forgotten something. I trust you have found it and are prepared to come back with us?"

"What is this treachery, Teom?" Ammaron demanded loudly, acting upset. "Is it true? Have you joined this man and his band of murderers?"

Teom stood firm. "Yes, Father. I have," he said proudly, with his head up.

Ammaron cried out in feigned agony and collapsed to the earth, and Nuria flew to his side to support him. She looked up at Helam and her brother, disbelief and betrayal in her eyes. "You did this," she hissed at Helam, who flinched at her words. "You brought the robbers to our door and convinced my brother to join them. I hate you!"

Hagoram laughed cruelly. "Such spirit! I can see why you like her," he said to Helam, whose shoulders had slumped miserably.

Teom nudged Helam after Hagoram turned away, and he straightened up, an angry fire in his eyes. "Do not speak to me, girl," Helam told Nuria. "I am finished with you."

Nuria's eyes widened in shock and filled with tears as she bent and buried her head in the arm of her father's robe.

"Please, Teom," Alba pleaded, holding tightly to a frightened Chemish, who had tears streaming down his face. "Please do not go with them. They are evil men. They would have you become evil like them."

"I begin to tire of this," Hagoram announced, and Seantum drew himself up, bestowing a menacing look on them all. "Teom and Helam will come with me," Hagoram said, folding his arms. He looked at Ammaron, who was still kneeling on the floor, with Nuria's arms around him. "Ammaron, you must thank your son, for because of his choice, you are yet alive," he warned. "Do not do anything foolish. We will speak again."

He motioned for Teom and Helam to follow him, and they all departed as Alba shrieked and sobbed inside the house for her eldest son.

As they walked away into the darkness, Teom walked with his back straight at the side of Hagoram, Teom's mother's cries growing quieter and quieter until they couldn't be heard at all.

*   *   *

"You disappoint me, Teom," Hagoram said as they entered the chief judge's house. "My favorite claimed you would not lie with her."

"I saw Helam slip out," Teom answered quickly. "I knew he was going to see my sister. I wanted to stop him."

"Why?" Hagoram inquired. "He is your brother now. You should be happy that he shows attention to her."

"As my father said, she is young," Teom replied. "It is a long story."

"One I'm sure you may tell to Jahza," Hagoram said, smiling. He motioned to the room where Jahza had taken Teom. "She awaits you." Then one of the women slipped her arms around Hagoram and led him away.

Teom stood, looking at Helam. He handed back Helam's knife. "We are not finished," he said in a low tone before walking away toward the back room.

Teom entered through the curtains and fastened them behind him. Jahza sat on the mat, looking nervous. She started to speak but stopped when a shadow passed before the curtain. They were being watched now. Teom would not be able to leave again.

Teom looked at her for a moment, and undid the sheath around his middle. Then he removed his sandals, and motioned for Jahza to lie down on the bed. She seemed surprised but obeyed him.

She was very pretty, and Teom *was* tempted. Especially since she was there for only one purpose. Teom prayed silently to God for strength and lay down next to her, keeping a few inches between them.

"I told you I would not dishonor you in this way, Jahza," he whispered into her ear. "Sleep. I will sleep too." He put his arm around her side and scooted her close to him, smelling the scent of her hair.

Jahza, relieved, clasped Teom's hand in her own and drifted off to sleep quickly.

Teom lay at her side, his eyes open for a long time. He couldn't sleep, with all the thoughts running through his head. The soft, sweet-smelling girl beside him wasn't helping things much either.

Finally, hours later, after the revelry in the other room had died down and faint snores were coming from within, Teom closed his eyes and drifted into a troubled sleep.

25

I T WAS TWO IN THE MORNING. EVERYONE WAS ASLEEP except Matt. He lay on his stomach on the bunk, a leather-bound set of scriptures open in front of him. He had propped a flashlight on the covers so he could read. He had been reading every night for the past few nights since Ross had handed him the scriptures.

"My parents gave me these for graduation, so be careful with them," Ross had warned, grinning as Matt took them from him.

Matt was already in Second Nephi, at the part where Lehi spoke to his children right before he died. Matt mouthed the words silently as he read:

"Wherefore, men are free according to the flesh; and all things are given them which are expedient unto man. And they are free to choose liberty and eternal life, through the great Mediator of all men, or choose captivity and death, according to the captivity and power of the devil; for he seeketh that all men might be miserable like unto himself."

Matt put the marker in the scriptures and closed them. He remembered this scripture vaguely from seminary, which he had attended until his sophomore year in high school. But this time it was different. Here, sitting on the same land Lehi's descendants had occupied and picturing Lehi on his deathbed with his children surrounding him, the words seemed more powerful.

Matt suddenly realized that he hadn't been happy the past few years. In fact, he'd been the opposite. Filled with anger toward his dad and with bitterness at his dad's lack of enthusiasm about basketball, Matt had ostracized himself from his family and the Church. He had chosen to be miserable.

Lehi's words made him squirm: "*He seeketh that all men might be miserable like unto himself.*" It made sense. Matt wasn't happy. Since he'd stopped going to church, he was always in conflict with himself. He had changed, and not for the better.

Ross and Andy seem so . . . content all the time, he thought. *Happy, even.*

Matt realized he was happier when he was around Ross and Andy and the other students, much more so than when he was back home with Dave and Adam.

And now that he'd been spending time with his dad and seeing how he worked and the atmosphere he worked in, Matt sort of understood. *Sort of.*

Matt suddenly felt an urge. It was foreign to him—an urge he hadn't felt in a long time, a few years at least. It took him completely by surprise. He felt awkward. He glanced around the room. All the guys were dead asleep. He looked down at the scriptures in front of him and made a decision.

Slipping the scriptures underneath his bed, Matt got down on his knees to pray.

*   *   *

The next morning it was dark outside, and a steady rain was falling. No work could be done on the site in a downpour, so the students spent their time in the barracks.

Matt had gone immediately back to sleep as soon as the announcement was made—he'd been up most of the night and was exhausted.

Ross went back to sleep as well, but at ten, Andy burst into the barrack, dripping wet with visibly shorter hair.

"Hey, free haircuts over at the girls' barrack," he announced. He ran his hand over his newly shorn head. "Beats going into town and getting overcharged."

Matt and Ross looked up from their bunks at each other. Matt definitely needed a trim. His hair had grown over his ears, and it was uncomfortably scratchy lately.

Ross ran a hand through his own scruffy hair. "Sounds good to me. You game?"

Matt nodded, and they got out of bed, pulling on clothes.

When they entered the girls' barrack, dripping wet even from the short jog over in the rain, there was a line. The girls had set up two chairs in the main sleeping area, and Matt saw that Taryn and Claudia manned the chairs and were busy clipping Jack and Carl, a guy from Team Two.

"Hey, guys," Jenna materialized out of nowhere and slipped her arm through Matt's. "You want a haircut?"

"You guys know what you're doing?" Ross asked. He directed the question at Taryn, who blushed and smiled back at him.

"Ouch, you nicked me," Jack complained.

"Sorry!" Taryn said quickly, blushing an even deeper red. "I get distracted by handsome guys."

This time it was Jack's turn to blush, as he misunderstood the obvious target of her compliment. Taryn gave a small sideways look at Ross, who winked at her.

Matt sat down on one of the beds, with Jenna firmly bulwarked at his side, and looked around the room. Except for the mess of hair on the floor, the room was immaculate. Every bed was made to crisp perfection, with luggage stowed neatly underneath.

"Wow, you guys are pretty clean," Matt mused as he looked at Jenna, who was wearing her hair in a loose ponytail. Tendrils of hair drifted around her face, and he found he wanted to touch them, so he reached up and brushed one behind her ear as she grinned at him with her perfect smile.

"Next!" Taryn announced loudly as she whipped the towel off of Jack's shoulders.

Jack, acting like a stunned puppy, stumbled from his seat, and another one of the guys took his place, a blond named Dan.

"Just buzz it off," he told Taryn, who was brandishing a pair of electric clippers. "It's so dang hot here, I'd rather be bald."

Jenna made a snorting noise of disapproval, and Matt looked at her.

"You want it at a two or a three?" Taryn asked.

"One," Dan replied. "I want a military cut."

"My specialty," Taryn commented with a grin and started buzzing his head.

Matt and Ross winced at each other as Dan's hair fell to the floor.

"Like shearing sheep," Ross whispered out of the corner of his mouth.

Claudia whipped the towel off of Carl's shoulders and said "Next!" as Mitchell eagerly stepped into the chair.

"Just a little trim, my dear," he said, gazing up at her. Claudia smiled back down at him adoringly and ran her hand through his curly locks.

Jenna stuck a finger in her mouth and mimed throwing up. Matt chuckled.

Matt watched as Taryn finished with Dan and announced, "Next!"

It was between him and Ross.

"Go ahead." He gestured for Ross to go, and Ross grinned and replaced Dan. Taryn draped the towel around his shoulders, picked up a plastic spray bottle, and dampened his hair, working her fingers through it. Ross sighed as if he were in heaven.

Matt turned to Jenna. "Where did you guys get the spray bottle? Just happened to have it with you?"

"Taryn stole it from the lab—from Nan's cleaning tools," Jenna confided. "She's clever, that one."

"Yes she is," Matt said appraisingly. His tone must have been a little *too* appraising, because Jenna stiffened next to him and withdrew her arm.

"I could never cut someone's hair," Jenna said, leaning forward and putting her elbows on her tanned knees. "I'd make a mistake, and it would be all lopsided."

"I'm sure they'd forgive *you*," Matt reassured, stroking her back. She leaned back and smiled at him, happy again.

"Next!" He was startled by Taryn's loud announcement. *She's done with Ross already?* Matt looked at Ross as he stood up, his hair much shorter and spiked at the front.

Claudia was clearly going to take her time with Mitchell, so Matt shrugged and left Jenna's side.

As he sat down, the lunch bell rang outside. Everyone

stampeded out of the barracks, leaving only the two haircutters and their victims. And Jenna. She was sitting on the bed, smiling at Matt lazily.

Candace poked her head through the doorway. "Jenna, you coming?"

An annoyed look crossed over Jenna's face, but then it disappeared as quickly as it came. "Sure," she answered, her tone unenthusiastic. "I'll save a seat for you, sweetie," she told Matt as she grabbed the lone umbrella propped by the door and slid outside.

"*Hey!*" Matt sputtered as a sudden spray of cold water hit him full in the face.

"Oh, *I'm sorry*," Taryn said sweetly, feigning innocence. "Did I get you?" She sprayed a few more times, running her fingers through Matt's hair. "I figured you needed a . . . cooling off."

Mitchell and Claudia both chuckled next to them, and Matt felt himself blush.

"Yeah," he agreed. "I appreciate it." Taryn snorted in disgust behind him and ran her fingers through his hair, massaging his scalp as she'd done to Ross. *Dang, that feels nice*, he thought.

"So you want me to whack it all off like that Dan guy, or do you just want it braided so it will be easier to take care of?" Taryn sniped.

"Hey, it's not *that* long," Matt protested. "Just give me a haircut. A trim, like Mitch over there."

"*Mitchell*," Mitchell corrected as Claudia kissed the top of his head and whisked the towel away.

"Sorry," Matt apologized as Mitchell stood up and waited for Claudia to put her scissors away.

"We'll see you guys at lunch," Claudia announced, taking Mitchell's arm. "Try not to kill each other, okay?" And with a sly smile, she allowed Mitchell to lead her outside.

The door clicked shut and echoed in the room. Matt and Taryn were alone. Matt felt like he needed to say something to break the silence. But then again, this was *Taryn*. He shouldn't feel awkward at all.

Taryn spoke first. "So, a little bird told me you're reading the Book of Mormon."

Matt looked up at her in disbelief. "Is anything a secret around here?" he demanded. He folded his arms, scowling.

"Hey! Don't be mad—I think it's really neat you're reading it," Taryn said hurriedly. "You shouldn't be so defensive about it."

"I feel stupid," Matt blurted. "Like I'm Ross's pet project."

"That's just pride," Taryn said bluntly, combing his hair forward. "But you've always been prideful. Hold still."

Matt was fidgeting. He was angry Taryn knew about his reading. But of course she'd know; she was Ross's girlfriend.

"It's really fitting you're reading it, anyway," Taryn continued as she quickly parted and snipped at his hair. "I've been reading too. It's the perfect setting out here . . ."

"I know, I know, *in Book of Mormon lands*," Matt finished for her. "Ross and I already talked about it. But of course you knew that."

Taryn was silent for a moment, snipping his hair. "Ross doesn't tell me everything, Matt," she said. "My point is, I'm glad you're reading. It's a *good thing*."

Matt felt stupid. Taryn came around to the front and bent down with her hands in his hair, her face only inches away from his. *A little too close.* He pushed the thought out of his brain. "What are you doing?" he asked, perplexed.

Taryn's mouth turned into a smirk. "I goofed."

"WHAT?" Matt ejected. "What do you mean, '*goofed*'?"

Taryn stayed where she was and looked at him. "Well,

I meant to make the sides equal, but one is shorter than the other."

Matt grabbed the mirror on the bed and looked at his hair. "It's completely lopsided! I thought you could cut hair!"

Taryn blushed and took the mirror from him. "I only really know how to do one cut. The cut I always give my brothers and my dad."

Matt sighed heavily. "Then give me the cut. Ross and I will just have to be twins."

Taryn let out a laugh. "Ross could never . . ." she started to say, but she stopped and cleared her throat. "Well, I could always buzz you, like Dan."

"No, thanks," Matt retorted. "Just give me 'The Ross.' I'm hungry."

He winced as Taryn powered up the hair clippers. He held still as she quickly buzzed the back and sides of his head and trimmed his sideburns. Then she took the scissors out and began to snip, and he watched as chunks of hair fell down in front of his eyes, into his lap.

"Done," she finally said after a few agonizing minutes. His head definitely felt lighter. She held up the mirror, and he checked his hair, trying not to look too disappointed. But it was out before he could stop it.

"Aw, Taryn, I look like a *little kid*!"

"I think you look nice," Taryn replied briskly, taking the mirror away and brushing his neck before taking the towel off. "You look like you used to look."

"When was that? When I was *ten*?" Matt shot back.

"No, our junior year," Taryn mumbled. "You wore your hair really short."

Matt reached up and scratched the back of his neck. "Yeah, you're right. I guess I did. That's quite a memory you have."

"I have a semi-eidetic memory," Taryn said. "I pretty much remember everything, in minute detail."

"I guess that helps with archaeology, eh?" Matt commented.

Taryn nodded, folding the towel. "We'd better get going, or Ross and Jenna will start to get nervous," she said, smiling at him.

Matt looked up at Taryn, with her newly tanned skin, smiling white teeth, and perfectly shaped eyebrows. This girl wasn't Taryn anymore. The old Taryn was the Gilley Monster. This new Taryn had confidence, shiny hair, and perfectly glossed lips.

Matt suddenly felt strange, almost shy. "Yeah, you're probably right," he said, standing up. He motioned for her to go through the door first, and she stepped in front of him, nearly tripping on her sandals. He caught her deftly and set her right.

"Sorry, I'm a klutz," she admitted ruefully. She seemed so small next to him. Small . . . and clumsy.

Well, one part of her is still the same, he thought, amused, as she pushed the door open.

26

"MAN, WE ALL LOOK LIKE MISSIONARIES!" ROSS COM-plained loudly as Matt entered the tent behind Taryn.

Everyone burst into laughter. It was true. All of the guys, with the exception of Mitchell, had short missionary-like haircuts.

Ben entered the tent with Manny, Jared, and Nan in tow, all wearing rain slickers. He looked around at all the newly shorn heads. "Have I entered the MTC tent?" he joked, and everyone laughed—except Matt, who leaned in to Jenna.

"MTC tent?" he repeated.

Jenna looked at him strangely. "Yeah, you know, *Missionary Training Center*," she prompted.

Matt immediately felt stupid. But Jenna leaned into him and whispered in his ear. "I think your hair looks sexy." She smiled at him and bit off the end of her carrot stick.

Matt had to admit, it *felt* a lot better having his old short haircut back. He didn't feel so hot and scratchy.

They ate and talked and joked, and after people were mostly finished, Ben clapped his hands to get everyone's attention.

"I have an announcement to make, as a sort of treat for everyone," he said loudly over the sound of the rain. "This rain is supposed to clear up in a few hours, and we thought we'd bus everyone in to Cholula to take in the sights and have dinner."

The tent erupted in loud cheers, whistles, applause.

"We've had a degree of success on this dig that we weren't expecting," Ben continued. "You've all been working hard, and as a thank-you for your efforts, we wanted to give you a night off. Within limits, of course. Even outside the dig grounds, the same standards and rules apply."

"Yeah, *Mitchell*!" Jack yelled. Mitchell, seated next to Claudia, dropped her hand as if it was a hot potato, and everyone sniggered.

Jenna leaned in and whispered in Matt's ear. "I guess that means we have to behave," she said smoothly, her sweet breath tickling his ear. Matt smiled at her and caught Taryn's eye across the table. Ross was busy whispering in her ear too, and she quickly looked away, blushing, as Matt's eyes met hers.

After lunch, they all went their separate ways, and Matt kissed Jenna quickly in front of her barrack, feeling silly. He didn't like public displays of affection; it wasn't his style. He watched her go inside and noticed a lot of the students had paired up. Claudia and Mitchell were right behind them, and following them were Ross and Taryn, and Andy and Candace. Jack walked behind everyone, alone, his hands shoved deep in his pockets. His new short haircut made him look like he was twelve.

Poor Jack, Matt thought.

When he entered the barrack, Jared was seated on one of the beds in the middle of the room, relating football stories to some of the guys, who were staring at him worshipfully. It was really the first time Jared had hung out in the barrack with them; he was usually in the trailer or the lab or at the dig site.

Matt pulled up a chair, and Ross and Andy pulled chairs up too as they all gathered around Jared.

"But you don't have regrets?" the newly bald Dan asked, a curious look on his face. "I mean, you were at the peak of your game. They were talking about it on ESPN for months."

"Believe me, I know," Jared answered. "But it was a personal decision. One that I couldn't very well talk about publicly."

"What do you mean?" Ross asked. "It was splashed all over the news. It was pretty public."

Jared nodded. "Yes, the story I *wanted* them to know."

There was a murmur through the crowd of boys, and Jared continued. "The story the media got was that I had a head injury, got nervous, and decided to retire and teach."

"It happens," Jack said. "Look at Steve Young."

"Yes," Jared agreed. "You get enough injuries, and you start to get nervous. I wanted to be around for my wife—and my family. But that wasn't the true reason. I would have kept playing."

Everyone was silent as he looked down at his heavily muscled, folded arms. "The reason people don't know, and I would like you guys to keep this quiet, was I had a son who needed me."

Matt was stunned. "What do you mean?" he asked.

"My son was diagnosed with acute lymphoblastic leukemia," Jared replied. Some of the guys gasped in shock. This was something that *definitely* hadn't made it into the news. "They caught it early," Jared continued. "And the cancer's in remission now, but at the time, I realized I wasn't spending much time with my family. I was always training, always playing, and always tucking my kids in at night over the phone. I only saw my family once every few weeks."

"But you were a god in the sports community," Jack insisted. "Not to mention the money."

Jared grinned. "Yeah, the money was definitely a motivator. But I've always had this little bookmark that my mom cross-stitched for me when I was a newlywed. It says, 'No amount of success can compensate for failure in the home.'"

"David O. McKay," Ross volunteered.

"You're right, Mr. West," Jared said. "A wise man. And wise of my mom to give me that bookmark. It was always in my scriptures, and every night—or rather on the nights I wasn't too tired from getting my body smashed by two-ton guys," he amended as everyone chuckled, "when I read my scriptures, I looked at that bookmark. I thought of my wife, all alone raising our kids while I was tossing a football around. And when Zach was diagnosed, that was it for me. I knew I had to be there for my wife and for him."

Everyone in the room was quiet, contemplating the news.

"And now, teaching has been quite rewarding because I was a language major in college, and I've always loved the history and study of languages," Jared continued. "And I get to go home at night to my family. Unless Ben Staubach drags me with him on one of his summer digs," he joked, and the boys laughed.

Matt sat with a smile on his face, but inside he was conflicted. He had questions. Questions that wouldn't wait.

As Jared started telling the boys about his Super Bowl experience, Matt discreetly slipped from the room and out into the rain.

He hurried to the trailer, several yards away, and opened

the door. Ben sat at one of the tables with a map of the dig site spread out in front of him, where he'd marked their finds. Otherwise, he was alone.

"Hello, son, what can I do for you?" he asked as Matt came in and sat down.

"Well, I want to talk to you," Matt said. He half expected his dad to put him off, to say he was busy and for Matt to come back later, but to his surprise, Ben set down his pencil and removed his glasses.

"Sure, son, what is it?"

Matt didn't know where to start, so he decided to start with the truth. "You know, I didn't decide to come here on my own."

"I suspected as much," Ben replied sincerely. "Taryn had a hand in it, didn't she?"

Matt smiled to himself. "She bribed me, actually."

Ben grinned and shook his head. "That girl is something else."

"Yes, she is," Matt agreed. "But my point is I didn't want to come. I wasn't interested in your work." Ben didn't say anything, only nodded. Matt pushed on. "And then we started finding all this cool stuff, and people told me about the process. I just . . . well, I guess I understand a little about what you do." He paused. "But what I don't understand is why your work is more important to you than your family is sometimes."

Ben looked at Matt with a look he'd never seen before. He seemed surprised, but there was a look of sadness too. He sighed heavily and folded his arms.

"I figured we'd be having this talk sooner or later," Ben began. "But I'm glad it's sooner. I could tell you weren't 'into' my work when you came up here. But I've also seen your face at the discoveries we've made, and that day when you found the stela, I thought you might understand then. It's a rush, isn't it?"

"Yes, it is," Matt agreed.

"Well, I guess you could call me a bit of an 'adrenaline junkie,'" Ben continued. "I always feel important when I find things . . ." he trailed off, looking at Matt, when suddenly his voice broke, and he rubbed his eyes. "Mattie, I'm not athletic. I was the nerdy kid who always lived in the library and had his nose buried in books. I have zero interest in sports. And you were always so into them—you get that from your mom, you know." Matt nodded. "So," Ben continued, "I figured sports would be your thing, and archaeology—well, it's just my thing. It's the only thing I'm good at."

"But I'm your *son*," Matt countered. Feelings of suppressed disappointment over the years were spilling into his voice, making it crack. "You could have *pretended* to be interested in my sports, because I'm your son. But you never made the effort!"

"You're right," Ben said quietly. "I made the mistake of thinking that having your mother at your games was good enough. I'm not perfect, Matt. Heaven knows I'm not a perfect father. I figured you just saw me as a big nerd who liked to live at the lab and dig up things. So I tried harder to be a better archaeologist, so I could make bigger discoveries, so you might . . ." He stopped and wiped his nose with a tissue from a tissue box on the desk.

"So I might *what*?" Matt urged.

"I don't know—think of me less as a *nerd* and more of a cool dad," Ben admitted finally. "I have some pride too, you know. It hurts when your only son thinks you're dorky."

"You are dorky," Matt deadpanned.

"Yes, I guess I am. But then you stopped going to church, and I figured that was my fault too. You turned your back on the Church because of me."

Matt's eyebrows went up. "You knew that?"

Ben gave him a wan smile. "I don't have to be a psychologist to see your displaced anger issues. You started resenting what I was doing, and the only way you could strike at me was to reject something important to me—the Church. But I fear the one who suffered the most was you."

"I'm reading the Book of Mormon," Matt blurted out.

Ben seemed surprised. "You . . . you are?"

"Yes," Matt admitted shyly. "I don't know why I'm telling you, but I'm reading."

Ben leaned forward. "Look, Matt, I know this isn't what you're used to, and I know that everything happens in baby steps—"

"Exactly. Baby steps," Matt agreed. "Dad, I'm just reading it. I want you to know I am because I want to know for myself. I've never read it before."

"But . . . seminary?" Ben asked. "I thought the Book of Mormon was required reading?"

"I lied," Matt smirked at his dad. "I never read it. I just wanted the pizza party at the end of the year, so I told Sister Jensen I read it."

Ben laughed to himself and scratched his ear. "So what happens next?"

"You could say you're sorry," Matt said simply.

Ben reached over the table and clasped Matt's hands in his. "Son, you have no idea how sorry I am for these past few years. Now that I have you here with me, I feel like we have a lot of making up to do. Rather, *I* have a lot to make up for. I wasn't there for you, and I feel awful about it. I think I've worked even harder because you never believed in me. I wanted you to, more than anything."

He released Matt's hands and sat back as tears streamed down his face. "Can you forgive me for being a dork?"

Matt looked at his dad for a moment, a lump forming in

his throat. "I guess," he replied. "I just need some time."

"You've got it," Ben said. "Take all the time you need. As long as you *do* forgive me in the end." He winked.

"Thanks, Dad," Matt replied, standing up. He felt awkward. He nodded at his dad and left the trailer, letting the door shut behind him.

It had stopped raining. The sun was out, and the air felt humid and heavy. Everything was new and dripping, and Matt felt . . . different. Like a large weight had been removed from his heart.

He suddenly realized that he could eventually forgive his dad. *I really can.*

27

AD 33

TEOM HATED THE ROBBERS' DEN—THE STINK OF IT AND THE constant shouting and chaos. Hagoram had his men keep a tight watch on Teom so he could never get away. Hagoram was always cordial, but cordial the way a cunning beast might be with its eventual prey.

The robbers certainly ate well; they were constantly glutting themselves on wine and tables of food, so Teom didn't go hungry, but he felt like a prisoner.

There were always men coming and going, meeting with Hagoram. Most of them were dressed in fine clothing. Teom recognized some of them as elites from the city, wealthy men who knew his father.

Teom and two other young men were always kept inside the walls of the former chief judge's house. By day, they were watched. At night, when the girls were brought in, the feasting and debauchery would begin.

Teom attempted to appear as if he enjoyed himself, but in his heart, he was sick at how everything had become.

Finally, after a few days, Hagoram announced that Teom and the two other inductees would be taking part in a "naming ceremony" that night.

"You will be one of us, Teom," Hagoram said proudly, loud enough so everyone could hear. "And you, Kib, and Mulok. You three will all be part of us. Come into my chamber. We have much to discuss."

The three of them followed Hagoram into the former chief judge's inner chamber, and Hagoram motioned for one of his women to pour wine for all of them. Teom accepted his cup along with the others, but he only sipped his wine. He would need a clear head tonight.

Hagoram seated himself in the large seat and commanded the young men to sit. They sat on mats, their legs folded underneath them. He told the woman and the others to leave them so that he was alone with the three of them.

"We have simple rules here," Hagoram began, taking a large sip of his own wine. "Secrecy is key. Outside these walls we are not who we claim to be inside them. We are faceless. Our power lies in numbers and tricks, and *we* control the fear of the people, and keep them at our mercy. We are the dictators who shape the people's minds, like potter's clay." He spread his arms wide. "Tonight, we increase our number. Tomorrow, King Jacob will come to the city and take his place as its rightful king." He closed his eyes, seeming to savor his triumph. "The City of Jacob. We will be rewarded for our efforts."

Teom felt fear in the pit of his stomach at these words. He hadn't seen his father in days. He knew the fate that awaited his father, because of Jahza's information. But he hadn't been able to get any messages out of the robbers' den or receive any either.

"Tonight you will join us and will swear to us, your brethren-to-be, that you will not betray our secrets to the outside world," Hagoram continued. "We require proof of your dedication . . . a blood sacrifice, so that we may believe your intentions are true to our purpose."

Teom flinched at these words, but it was not a surprise. These robbers had their secret ways and secret signs and combinations, and he knew some sort of sacrifice would be involved. He lifted his head up and stared at Hagoram, his face stern, not betraying the fear he felt.

The young man sitting next to him, Kib, had turned a slight green color. Suddenly two men entered, one with a large clay bowl, the other with something wrapped in a finely spun cloth.

They set these items down before Hagoram, who rose and gestured for the young men to rise as well.

Hagoram motioned to the man with the bundle, and he leaned forward and opened the cloth to reveal a large number of knives with gold hilts. Mulok gasped. Teom's eyes grew wide as well. The common blade he wore at his side was nothing compared to such workmanship.

"These," Hagoram announced, taking one of the knives and holding them up so the men might see it better, "came with King Jacob when he came from the land southward. They were made there, and only members of our band may possess them. They are a symbol of our power and our strength. We are the Order of the Jaguar, to be feared and worshipped. The only way a man might receive one of these is if I bestow it upon him." He walked forward to Mulok and pointed the tip of the knife at his throat. Mulok held still, but Teom could see the blood of his veins pulsing rapidly in his neck as Hagoram pressed the knife lightly. Mulok looked as if he might faint; clearly he had not been made aware of this part of becoming a robber.

"Take my arm," Hagoram commanded, offering his fore-arm, and Mulok immediately grasped the man's arm with his right hand.

Hagoram took Mulok's limp left hand and smiled at him the way a father might smile at his own son. "Your right hand is your strong hand. We would want you to have the use of it." With a deft motion, he twisted Mulok's left arm and pinned his hand to the table. Before Teom knew what was happening, there was a flash of movement, and Hagoram drove the knife through the back of Mulok's hand into the wooden table.

Teom recoiled as Mulok screamed in pain, but Hagoram prevented him from moving.

"It is painful, yes?" he hissed in Mulok's ear.

"Y-yes," Mulok choked out, tears streaming down his face. Hagoram shoved him to his knees so that he knelt before his pinned hand.

"Do not move or your throat will be slit," Hagoram com-manded and then lunged at Kib, who was standing next to Teom. He screamed before Hagoram could even drive the knife, and a moment later Kib sunk to his knees, his right hand gruesomely pinned to the table as Mulok's had been.

Teom knew what was next. Hagoram took another one of the knives and held out his arm, that Teom might grasp it.

The taste of fear was a coppery tang in the back of Teom's throat, but instead of grabbing Hagoram's offered forearm, he knelt next to Kib and set his left hand out onto the table, his fingers splayed.

Hagoram seemed surprised, but he chuckled loudly as Teom closed his eyes, waiting for the pain to come. And it did, as Hagoram drove the knife nearly to the hilt into his waiting hand.

A hot wire of agony shot through his hand as sensitive nerves screamed in exquisite pain. Darkness fluttered behind Teom's eyelids, and he bit down on his tongue, willing himself not to lose consciousness. He looked at the handle of the knife protruding from the top of his hand as the symbol of the jaguar carved into the golden handle winked at him in the firelight. He gritted his teeth, keeping himself from moaning at the intense pain.

"This is your proof," Hagoram spat. He sounded out of breath from the exertion. "You will remain here in your pain, and even as you feel it, you must remember that it is nothing compared to the pain you would feel if you ever betrayed us to the outside world."

Blood was running freely from the three pierced hands and by now dripped from the table onto the stone floor. Teom looked down and realized with a jolt of nausea that the floor was stained brown, most likely from the blood of others. He remembered the bandage on Helam's hand. Helam had gone through this as well. Helam had survived what the robbers had done to him. So would Teom.

"You will remain here for as long as I deem necessary," Hagoram told them, his voice businesslike. If you wish to join with us, you will remain as I leave you. If you decide you no longer wish to join, you may simply remove the knife and leave. Only"—he motioned to the clay bowl—"drop the knife on your way out." He looked at Teom, his dark eyes piercing and cruel. "I know you suffer, but after the suffering comes great reward, if you are man enough to accept it." He drew his robe around himself, and with a sweeping gesture, left the room.

Mulok expelled his breath in a rush after Hagoram was

gone and looked at Teom. "Did you know of this?" he asked, his breath coming in ragged gasps.

Teom relaxed his left hand, willing the pain in his hand to lessen. "No, I did not."

Kib said nothing but wept, silent tears streaming down his cheeks.

"Be strong," Teom warned, "or we die. It is a test."

"It is proof of Hagoram's cruelty," Mulok hissed.

"You think he chose this way?" Teom asked them both. "Did you not see his own hand? He had a scar on his left hand. A scar just like we will have, after this is over. He suffered through this as well. It is the robbers' way."

"I want no part of it!" Kib wailed suddenly. And before anyone could stop him, he rose and tore the knife out of his hand with a mighty cry of pain, and immediately four men ran in, grabbed the hapless Kib by the arms and legs, and removed him, yelling and struggling, from the room. The knife fell to the floor with a clatter as they forced him through the doorway, and Teom lowered his head, listening to Kib's screams as they faded away until they were finally, abruptly, silenced.

"Is he dead?" Mulok whispered. "Did they kill him?"

Teom shook his head. "I do not know. I doubt they let him walk out."

Mulok shuddered and gasped at the pain in his hand. "I will stay here. Hagoram promised me many riches if I joined them."

Teom hadn't been promised riches or power. Hagoram had merely forced him to join by threatening his family. It was enough.

*   *   *

Minutes passed by as if they were hours. Teom's entire arm, all the way to his shoulder, throbbed with a dull pain, but his entire hand throbbed agonizingly as the foreign object stabbed through it reminded him of his precarious situation. But he had promised his father. He told him he would do whatever it took and he would become one of them.

Finally, just as Teom felt he could bear the pain no longer, Hagoram entered with three men wearing the pelts of jaguars on their arms and legs and heads. They were richly dressed in ceremonial jewels and clothing, and they carried more bowls and cloths with them.

Hagoram sat in his chair and motioned for the men to approach Teom and Mulok.

The third man, obviously intended for the unfortunate Kib, turned his bowl upside down, washing Kib's blood from the floor. The two other men bent down to the knives piercing Mulok and Teom's hands to the table, and, chanting, they yanked them out.

Teom grunted as fresh pain assaulted his hand, and the jaguar-clad man forced his hand into the bowl of cold water. It felt good at first, but something in the water made his hand start to sting, and he looked away, feeling nauseated as the water turned pink with his blood. The scent coming from the water was sharp with herbs, and it stung his nostrils.

Then the man, still chanting, took Teom's hand out of the bowl, wrapped strips of cloth tightly around it, and tied the ends together. "It must be tight," he told Teom, so your blood will no longer flow." He placed his hand on Teom's head and announced that Teom's new name would be "Teom Thunder Warrior." Grinning, he backed away, chanting in a language Teom wasn't familiar with.

Mulok was attended the same way, and when the jaguar-clad men departed, Hagoram motioned for Teom and Mulok to sit on fine cushions that had been brought in.

"I am proud of your bravery," he told them both as servants brought in wine and food. Soon many men entered as well and crowded around Teom and Mulok.

Hagoram stood up, and all the men were instantly silent. One of the men set the knives, which had been rinsed of blood, in Hagoram's hands. Hagoram stepped forward and placed his hand on Mulok's shoulder.

Teom noticed that the color had drained from Mulok's face. The bandage on his hand was already stained with blood. Hagoram held up the gold knife that moments before had been driven into Mulok's own flesh.

"This, Mulok, son of Neber, is a token of our brotherhood. Only we possess these tokens, for we have all earned them."

To Teom's surprise, all the men held up one hand, and shouted as a whole. He noticed that the hands they held up all bore scars identical to Hagoram's. He looked down at his own bandaged hand and winced.

"We welcome you into our fold as a brother. You have been named as one of us, and we will use our might to always defend and protect you, and in return, you will use your might to always defend and protect the brethren."

The men cheered again as Hagoram bestowed the knife into Mulok's good hand, and he held Mulok's fist up in the air, and the men continued to cheer and congratulate him.

Hagoram waved them all to be silent again, and he took the last knife and stood before Teom. "This, Teom, son of Ammaron, is a token of our brotherhood. Only we possess these tokens, for we have all earned them."

Teom noted that Hagoram spoke the exact words he had spoken to Mulok. All the men raised their hands and cheered in unity, and Teom hardly heard as Hagoram continued speaking. He was in a fog of pain and fatigue and cared little for anything at the moment. His entire left arm throbbed with intense pain, radiating from the wound in his hand.

Then the men cheered him, and the coolness of the knife slipped into his right hand. Teom took his old knife out of its girding and replaced it with the new knife. This was met with shouts of approval, and the men congratulated him and clapped him on the back.

Then they departed, and Mulok, Teom, and Hagoram were alone once more.

"Now, there is only one more part of your initiation into our band," Hagoram told them. "Mulok, you wait outside. I will tell Teom of his assignment, and you will come in after him."

After Mulok had left, Hagoram clapped Teom on the shoulder. "I am proud of you, Teom. Or shall I say, Thunder Warrior?"

Teom forced a grin. His hand hurt too badly to do much else.

"You showed exceptional bravery. I would have expected no less from you," Hagoram continued. "Now, I will give you your first task as one of the brethren, and it will be yours, and only yours."

Teom nodded. "Tell me what I must do, Hagoram, and I will do it," he said with all the strength he could muster. Hagoram nodded and put his arm around Teom's shoulder and then bent in to whisper in his ear. His breath was sour from the wine he'd been drinking.

"I want you to kill Helam."

28

WHEN MATT RETURNED TO THE BARRACK, ALL THE GUYS were busy getting ready for the night. When he walked in, he was nearly knocked over.

"Whoa, guys, what's the occasion?" he asked as a barrage of different colognes assaulted his nose. "It smells like the men's fragrance counter at Macy's in here."

Andy brushed past him, wearing a polo shirt, his hair freshly combed. "We figured tonight was going to be like a group date," he explained. All the guys were busy shaving, showering, or getting dressed.

Jack was seated on his bunk with a tiny handheld mirror, trying to pop a zit on his nose, because there wasn't room in the bathroom.

Matt smiled to himself and then whipped out a shirt with a collar and replaced his T-shirt.

Ross came out with his toothbrush. He'd changed as well. "Where'd you go?" he asked as he packed it into his travel kit.

"Just to see my dad," Matt replied as he grabbed his own toothbrush out.

*   *   *

Apparently the girls felt it was a group date as well, for when they all met between the boys' and girls' barracks, the girls were all wearing nice clothes and their hair and makeup were done a little more than usual. Matt caught sight of Taryn in a white blouse and olive-colored shorts, and he did a double take. She actually looked stunning.

Jenna, perfect as usual, came forward in—once again—short shorts and a tight shirt. Matt had the decency to be embarrassed over her lack of clothes. All the other girls were wearing longer shorts or capris that weren't going to be dangerous when they bent over.

Jenna was clearly confident about her body, but she stood out like a sore thumb against all the other modestly dressed girls.

She planted herself at Matt's side. "You ready to have some fun?" she asked as Ben walked up with Manny, Nan, and Jared.

"All right, everyone into the vans!" Ben announced, and the students trooped in. Matt and Jenna started walking, but Nan stepped forward, intercepting them so quickly she was mostly a blur.

"Miss Grayson, a word if you please," she said, leading Jenna away from the group.

Jenna shrugged her shoulders at Matt as Nan led her into the girls' barrack.

Soon everyone was in the van, and Matt stood outside waiting. A few minutes passed. Then Nan emerged from the girls' barrack alone, looking red in the face. Jenna didn't come out after her.

"Miss Grayson has decided to stay behind this evening," she announced to Matt as she walked past him and got into the van.

Matt, feeling extremely embarrassed, got into the other van and sat next to Andy.

The door shut, and they were on their way to Cholula.

*   *   *

Matt was really beginning to like the city. He'd only been a couple of times, but the city's narrow cobbled streets and huge stone plazas always seemed to have some sort of entertainment going on, and now, at dusk, there was a fireworks show gearing up.

They found a restaurant with local music blaring into the street, and they all gathered inside.

The smells of authentic food hit their noses, and a live band played in one corner of the restaurant, where a few couples danced.

The wait staff had been expecting them. There were several tables pulled together, and the adults sat at one, leaving the students to decide where to sit. Matt took a chair at a table with Ross and Taryn, Andy and Candace, and Claudia and Mitchell. With Jenna gone, he was the odd man out, but he shrugged it off and picked up a menu.

Taryn, sitting at Ross's left, was moving to the music in her chair as they studied their menus. Claudia and Mitchell were buried behind one menu, sharing it. Matt leaned over to

Candace, seated to his right. "What happened to Jenna?"

"You really want to know?" she asked, raising her voice over the din. Matt nodded, and she shrugged her shoulders. "Well, Nan said once they got inside the barrack, she asked Jenna to change into something more . . . *appropriate*, because we're all adhering to Church standards on the dig," she explained. "But Jenna refused, and I guess they got into a shouting match over it, and Jenna told Nan she was jealous because she could never look as pretty as her, or something like that. And she said she wasn't changing. So, Nan told her to stay behind."

Ross leaned in, grinning. "Got yourself a little spitfire, there, Staubach."

Matt shook his head. "I don't know about that," he said, feeling ungallant.

He was even more embarrassed to hear Jenna had said those things to Nan. Jenna was beautiful, but clearly, she was a bit of a brat. Matt was used to that type because he'd dated them in high school: the pretty girls who knew they were pretty and who looked down on everyone else. He seemed to attract those types the most.

Matt observed all the couples at his table, leaning together and whispering, and jealousy shot through him so furiously, it startled him. True to form, he'd picked the one girl on the dig who was beautiful but shallow to pair up with. *Typical Matt Staubach*. All the girls he'd dated the last few years had been just like Jenna: beautiful but with no substance. This revelation hit him like a freight train, and Ross leaned over once more.

"You feeling okay?" he asked. "You look like your dog just died."

"Just thinking about stuff," Matt answered back. It was a lame answer, but it was the only one he was ready to provide.

"What looks good?" he asked before Ross could inquire more.

"Oooh!" Claudia emitted a gasp. "They serve escamoles here!" Everyone at the table collectively shuddered.

"What's that?" Matt asked.

"Oh, just a little delicacy made up of seasoned ant larvae," Candace explained.

Matt scrunched his nose in disgust, and everyone around the table laughed. "Well, I won't be ordering that," he replied. The thought of eating ant maggots made him, actually, quite sick.

"Viva México!" Taryn said, raising her water bottle, and everyone around the table did the same.

*   *   *

The next morning, Matt woke to sun in his eyes. He had fallen into bed without brushing his teeth the night before, and his mouth tasted like garbage.

He stumbled into the bathroom, brushed his teeth, and came back out. Everyone was still asleep, so he pulled the scriptures out and began reading. He was in Mosiah—he'd just finished King Benjamin's speech to his people and was reading about Ammon's adventures. Ammon was a complete stud, and Matt enjoyed reading about him.

He found he was interested in the Nephites; they never seemed to quite get it. They were good, and then they became prideful, which led to being bad, and then they were chastised by God and became humble. Then they were good again, and after a while, pride started creeping in, and inevitably the cycle started all over again.

Matt thought about his own life. He had been raised to be good. But then he'd gotten prideful about his skills at basketball and his good looks, and he started thinking he was better than everyone. Including his dad. And then he'd fallen away from the good.

He felt all his past wrongs acutely as he read the book, and his conscience started to weigh on him as he read. These men—prophets of God who had written the book thousands of years before—were speaking to *him*. Speaking to him from the dust. It was a sobering thought. He had been especially struck by Nephi's descriptions of what he had been shown by the Lord in the first book of Nephi.

Nephi had seen the future. He had seen so many things, all shown to him by the Lord, and had written them down. And they had *all happened*. Yet he had lived and written his visions in 600 BC—centuries before.

Matt was beginning to understand what Ross had said about reading the book. There was no way this was made up by one man. The prophets all had distinctive voices, and the things they spoke about were sacred and special, and Matt felt the truth of their words as he read. It was a good feeling. His doubts and skepticism were melting away with every chapter, and he found he actually looked forward to reading—to see what happened next.

A loud alarm clock went off, startling Matt, and all the guys stirred in their beds. Matt didn't want to stop reading, but he did, tucking the scriptures underneath his covers as he got up and slung a towel over his shoulder to head to the showers.

*   *   *

Jenna wasn't in the breakfast tent. Matt figured she was too embarrassed to show her face after the scene with Nan yesterday. He sat down next to Andy with his plate full of food. More girls trooped into the tent, and soon Taryn arrived, her hair pulled into a ponytail.

After she got her food and sat down at their table, Matt leaned over. "Where's Jenna?" he asked quietly.

Taryn looked at him. "You haven't heard? She's going home."

"What?" Matt exclaimed. "They're sending her home over . . . her clothes?"

"No," Taryn continued, peeling the lid off her yogurt. "She asked to go home. She said this wasn't her thing. Apparently her dad forced her to come."

"Yeah, I knew that," Matt said flatly.

"So, you're probably going to want to go home too now?" Taryn asked bluntly.

Matt stared at her. "Why would you say that?" he demanded, an edge to his voice. He glanced over at Ross and Andy, who suddenly seemed very interested in their plates of food.

"Well, you two were close . . ." Taryn replied awkwardly, "so I thought . . ."

"You thought wrong," Matt said, stabbing his eggs with his fork. "I'm not going anywhere." He realized he'd lost his appetite. He stood up, pitched his plate into the large trash dumpster, and stalked off.

He ended up at the trailer. Just as he was about to step inside, Jenna came out, her hair pulled into a simple ponytail, her eyes red from crying.

"Don't look at me. I'm a mess," she said, wiping her nose with a tissue. "I'm leaving."

"I heard," Matt replied. "When?"

"As soon as I can," Jenna sniffled. "This just isn't my thing. The rules are too much. It isn't even a Church-sponsored dig.

Why do we have to adhere to Church standards?" she sulked.

"Well, my dad's in charge, and he felt it would be best, since we're all LDS, to enforce them. Makes sense to me," Matt answered.

"*You're* not LDS," she pointed out. "You don't like rules. You're not like everyone else."

"Maybe not," Matt agreed. "But that's not saying it's right to break the rule. And I *am* LDS. I was baptized when I was eight."

Jenna looked sheepish. "I just want to look nice," she muttered into her tissue. "I thought you'd like how I looked."

Matt sighed heavily. "Look, you're really pretty, but you don't need to dress like that to get my attention."

Jenna smirked. "Well, I *got it*, didn't I?" Then her mouth turned into a pout. "This is so stupid. Claudia is fat, and Taryn has all the charm of a wet sponge. But *they* landed boyfriends."

"What were you expecting, the *Love Dig*?" Matt retorted. "Because that's not why everyone is here."

"Well, you certainly weren't here to participate either!" Jenna snapped back. "In fact, if I remember correctly, someone had to bribe you to even consider coming here."

Matt didn't have a reply for her. She was right.

"Look," Jenna continued, her voice softer. "I don't want to fight, okay? Call me if you ever find yourself in Cali, all right?" She planted a quick kiss on his cheek. "Nice knowing you, Staubach." She gave him a dazzling smile and left him standing in front of the trailer.

To his surprise, Matt wasn't sad to see her go. He liked her, but his feelings had changed in the last week. In fact, aside from the physical attraction, they'd had very little in common to begin with.

Matt felt strange. So many things had happened in these last few days. He felt like his brain was one big jumble.

"It never would have worked out, you know." Taryn's voice brought him out of his thoughts.

"Why?" he asked, turning to look at her. She was on the path in front of him, alone.

"You would have gotten tired of her antics," Taryn answered. "Trust me. I've lived the past few weeks with her. She would drive even the most long-suffering Saint insane."

Matt laughed quietly and walked back toward the food tent, slipping his arm around Taryn's shoulders as she walked with him.

"Taryn, Taryn, what would I do without you?" he joked, releasing her after a few steps.

"You'd be back home, drunk on a beach somewhere," she replied curtly, and Matt laughed heartily as they entered the food tent.

He was so busy laughing, he barely noticed the blush that had crept into Taryn's cheeks as she darted back to Ross's side and sat down.

29

AD 33

TEOM FROZE, STARING INTO HAGORAM'S EYES, WHICH WERE only inches from his own.

"*Kill him*?" he uttered. "But, he is one of us! One of the . . . brethren!"

Hagoram scowled and took his arm from Teom's shoulder. He marched across the room, pacing as his robe swished with his catlike movements. "Helam is a fool and an embarrassment. He knows nothing of secrecy or concealment. He bungled the task we gave him to perform."

"What? The chief judge's murder?" Teom answered boldly. "The chief judge is dead. How did Helam fail?"

Hagoram froze, and his face twitched with anger. "He didn't kill the chief judge! He hesitated at the last moment! Another one of my men had to finish the job!" Hagoram's jaws snapped shut. Clearly Teom had forced him into admitting something he had not wished to reveal.

"Take care, Teom," Hagoram warned. "We were going to have him kill your sister, originally. Lucky for you the chief judge's death was a matter of some . . . urgency."

"My sister?" Teom managed. "Why?"

"Helam is in love with her," Hagoram spat. "A fool's love. We have no room for fancies and whims. Love has no place in our hearts." He stepped forward, a frightful zeal burning in his eyes. "We are warriors of Jacob."

"I see," Teom said evenly. "But why kill him? He is eager to please you."

Hagoram smiled wryly, counting off his fingers. "He flinches when I give him simple tasks, he didn't have the stomach to murder Gilgal, and he didn't even possess the strength to convince you to join us. I had to do that all myself! Everything he has attempted has been disappointing. You know what happens to men who *disappoint* me."

"All too well," Teom assured. A few moments went by in silence. "When do you want me to do it?"

"Tonight," Hagoram's voice took on a whispered tone once more. "King Jacob comes to the city tomorrow. He wants to meet you. The son of a chief judge is a prized commodity, and he will be pleased to have you with us." Hagoram narrowed his eyes. "Of course, he will wonder why you so willingly joined us, young Teom. You certainly weren't willing a week ago. What will your answer be?"

Teom knew this question was bound to be asked, and he was prepared for it. "I realized it was useless to fight such a formidable opponent," he said graciously, nodding to Hagoram. "I knew resistance was futile to such a powerful group. And then I realized that I too could be as powerful as you are."

Hagoram seemed pleased with his answer. He nodded.

"Take Helam from here. I want you to do it outside the city. Tell him he can meet your sister. Anything to get him out."

Teom nodded once and departed.

"Oh, and Teom," Hagoram called out behind him. Teom halted and turned around.

"Bring me his hand. The hand with the scar. We will burn it in the fires," Hagoram said almost casually.

Teom nodded again and left the room.

*   *   *

"Nuria wants to see me?"

Helam seemed shocked. He sat on the stone steps of the large inner room where all the robbers were making merry, one harlot on each side of him, his arms around both.

Teom gritted his teeth. "Yes. She wants to meet you at the place we used to play as children."

Helam squinted at Teom. "Why would I want to speak to her?"

Teom looked at him. "Perhaps she has had a change of heart?"

Helam looked doubtful but dragged his arms from around the ladies, who sighed, looking petulant. "When?"

"Right now," Teom said, looking around the room. "We need to go."

Helam moved quickly. He followed Teom out of the robbers' den. They walked in silence out of the city, and finally, out of breath, they arrived at the stone rocks.

There was no one else besides the two of them, and Helam turned to Teom.

"She isn't coming, is she?" Helam said matter-of-factly.

"No, my brother, she is not," Teom replied, unsheathing his newly acquired gold knife.

* * *

Jahza knew something was not right. Teom and Helam had left quickly—she had watched them from her throne of cushions as one of the smellier robbers tried to charm her. She had heard Seantum talking earlier about Helam and how he would be bothering them no more.

Now, she put the facts together and understood. Hagoram had commanded Teom to kill Helam. It was the only reason Teom would have spoken to Helam again.

Jahza rose from the cushions, and the smelly robber who had been trying desperately to get her attention for the last half hour groaned in disappointment.

"I shall fetch some more wine, and we may talk more," she reassured him and stepped away from him. To her relief, he smiled back at her . . . and passed out face-first onto the cushions.

Most of the robbers were drunk by now, and Seantum was with Hagoram in the antechamber. Jahza slipped from the chief judge's house wholly unnoticed, except for the tinkling of the jewelry on her feet and arms as she fled.

As she hurried out of the city, she looked upward at Kom, the great live mountain just beyond the city, as it belched smoke and fire into the night. The air had an electric feel to it, and the hairs of Jahza's neck stood up as she walked through the crowded streets. She had an idea of where Teom had taken him.

Teom is still good, she thought. *He would not lie with me, and he will not murder his friend.* But something in her gut told her otherwise, and she hurried onward to a fate of which she was unsure.

* * *

Alba looked out the window of her stone house, the same house she and Ammaron had shared since he had become a priest. It was a fine house and held many memories, including the birth of their children.

And now they were leaving. Ammaron had announced it to her that morning.

"We must flee, Alba," he had said. "It is no longer safe here for our family. Teom has gone and joined with the robbers, and he is lost to us."

Alba had spent the day packing what little they could carry and grieving the loss of her eldest son. Nuria and Chemish were hit the hardest. Nuria could not stop weeping, and Chemish had refused to believe it, watching at the door all day, staring out into the street the last few days as if he believed his older brother would come walking down the road to their door at the end of the day, like he always did. Only he never came.

They were going to leave in the night to go to a place the Lord had told Ammaron to go in a dream. Something bad was about to happen, and although Ammaron did not tell Alba what it was, she believed her husband and knew he would not lead them to danger. After all, Sariah, in times of old, had believed in her husband, Lehi, and left all their worldly possessions behind to journey to this land. Was she any better than Sariah? When Ammaron spoke of God, Alba always took it seriously.

They had spoken of Teom only rarely since he'd left. Alba could not understand how her righteous son could have turned on his family and his God so easily. It didn't make sense to her. She had spent a lot of the day praying as well as packing, and in the end, she had received little comfort. Her heart was broken. And now, they were leaving.

"What else is to happen?" she demanded of the darkening

sky as she baked bread for the last time in the stone oven behind the house. "What will become of us, Lord?"

The sky told her nothing, and a cold fear crept into her heart, draining her faith as swiftly as a cracked jar drains itself of water.

30

So, THERE'S A NEW CRACK?" MATT ASKED HIS DAD. THE students had finished breakfast and headed over to the dig site to see the stela, and Ben had surprised them with the news.

"Well, of sorts, yes," Ben replied, excitement in his voice. "The fissure must have run deeper, because there's another crevasse. When we cleared away the large boulders in the wall behind the stela, some of the rocks gave way, and we saw this . . ." He pointed up above the stela, and a few students gasped at what they saw.

At the top of the pile of boulders, there was indeed a narrow, cave-like opening. But it was too high up in the rock to see what was inside.

"The conclusion is," Ben continued, "that this stela tells

of a great leader or a king. If this is the case, they only placed monuments like these outside of *cities*."

"But where's the city?" Jack asked, perplexed.

"That's exactly the point. I'm wondering if maybe during a volcanic eruption the city was covered over," Ben answered, "not unlike the city of Pompeii." A murmur of assent passed through the crowd of students at these words. "If my assumptions and the core samples we retrieved are correct, we may have stumbled on evidence of a city that was destroyed in a massive volcanic eruption two thousand years ago," Ben concluded.

Everyone was silent. "This is way cool," Ross leaned in and whispered to Matt. "A lost city!"

Matt was silent, mulling everything over.

Taryn raised her hand. "Yes, Taryn?" Ben acknowledged.

"I'm wondering," she began, "if you read in Third Nephi, immediately following Christ's crucifixion, there was massive destruction on this continent. Cities were burned, cities were sunk into the ocean . . ."

"And cities were buried in the earth. Exactly," Ben finished for her.

"Well, considering the landscape, and the chain of volcanoes at close range, is it plausible we could be standing in the same place one of those cities once stood?" she asked, her voice a note higher from excitement.

"One can only hope," Ben replied, winking. "As you can imagine, I am in a frenzy to tear out those boulders and find out what is in that crevasse, but since they are too heavy for human hands, we've had to call in the big guns once more. We have another blasting team arriving first thing tomorrow."

"We're not going to take a look at it now?" Taryn objected. "It would be so easy to climb up there . . ."

"And get yourself killed. Yes, I know," Ben dismissed.

"We've already evaluated it. Those rocks are far too unstable. It's too dangerous."

"But—" Taryn began.

"Good things come to those who wait," Ben interrupted firmly. "Just be patient. By tomorrow afternoon, we'll be able to go in and see what we can see. So, is everyone as excited as Taryn here?"

A cheer erupted from the students crowded around him, and within a few minutes they had all settled to work on their grids.

Matt, however, slipped away unnoticed. He double-timed it back to the boys' barrack, where he flopped onto his bed and pulled the scriptures out from under his pillow.

He had all day to read, and that was what he wanted to do. Especially the part in Third Nephi Taryn had been talking about.

He wasn't sure why he wanted to read so much; he only knew that he did. After, glancing at the clock, he bent his head down to the open pages and began.

*　　*　　*

Lunchtime came and went in a blur. Matt didn't bother going to the food tent. He pulled out an apple he'd been hiding from his bag and ate it instead.

By three o'clock, he was in the book of Alma. At six, when the rest of the boys trooped in, dusty and tired and smelling of sweat and earth, Matt was still reading.

"I wondered where you were all day," Ross remarked as he sat down next to Matt, who closed the book and stretched.

"Man, my neck is killing me," Matt said, yawning and rubbing his shoulder.

"Have you been here the whole time reading?" Ross asked, a note of surprise in his voice.

"Yup," Matt answered quickly.

Ross grinned with joy. "That's awesome. You coming to dinner? Or do you want me to bring you something?"

"I'm in Third Nephi," Matt replied. "I'm almost done. If you want to bring me a plate, I'd appreciate it."

"I'll be right back," Ross said, and he nudged Andy out the door with the rest of the guys.

Several minutes later, he brought Matt back a plate loaded with tacos and a few cartons of milk.

"Everyone wants to know where you've been," Ross informed him as he handed the plate over.

Matt greedily bit into the first taco with a loud crunch. "What did you tell them?"

"That you had the squats," Ross deadpanned. Matt looked at him and realized he was kidding. "Actually, I told them you were sleeping. That better?"

"Much," Matt commented thickly. "Thanks, man. I'm really starved."

"Well, it was those or pulled pork. Taryn said you'd prefer the tacos." He grinned at Matt and left, the door swinging shut behind him.

With his stomach full, Matt was able to concentrate more clearly on the words as he sat back down to read.

*   *   *

Hours later, when the lights were out and all the boys snored and grunted in their beds, Matt finished the book of Moroni. He shut the scriptures, his heart pounding. He felt bad for Moroni. He had been the very last Nephite, and he had seen his entire people massacred and hunted until they were extinct, and he himself would be hunted the rest of his life. What a sad end, to die alone. But he accomplished what God had wanted him to do, and he hid the plates in a stone box so Joseph Smith could find them fourteen hundred years later and translate them.

Matt knew that now. He didn't need to even pray about the book. He just *knew*. Finally, he felt for himself the sweet warmth of the Spirit coursing through him, reassuring him that the book was true.

He snapped off his flashlight, and, aching all over from lying down for so long, he stretched and got underneath his covers to sleep.

*   *   *

Matt snapped awake to a familiar creaking noise. Someone had opened the door to the girls' barrack. The clock on the desk across the room read 1:17 a.m. in the darkness.

Who's sneaking out, and why?

Matt slid out of bed, put on a T-shirt, and stuck the flashlight in the pocket of his shorts as he slipped into his basketball shoes, which were lying by the bed.

He left the boys' barrack (luckily *his* door wasn't noisy) and looked around the camp. All was still. But in his peripheral vision, he saw a light disappear into the thick trees to the left along he path that led to the dig sites.

He jogged toward the light as it flickered in and out of the trees. Then it snapped off, and he couldn't see much in the faint moonlight. He continued down the path until he broke out and scanned the large field in front of him. He could barely make out the form of someone walking swiftly in the direction of the dig pit. The person wasn't using a light, and he or she wasn't making a sound.

He continued jogging to catch up, and as soon as he reached the pit, he clicked on the flashlight in his pocket and shone it down on the figure that had stopped by the stela, which stood ghostly in the moonlight.

The figure turned and gasped, shielding her eyes from the bright beam of light, and Matt gasped too.

"*Taryn*? What are you doing down here?" he asked sternly.

"Matt, you scared me!" she chided. "Do you mind lowering that thing?" Matt lowered the flashlight and walked down into the pit to join her.

"You didn't tell me what you're doing here," he asked.

"What, are you a DIG guard now?" Taryn retorted. She looked at him and sighed. "I lost my bracelet here today. I came back to find it."

"At one in the morning?" Matt asked. "Please, I'm not *that* dumb. You can't even see out here."

Taryn looked at him for a moment. "I just wanted to see something, okay?" she ejected rudely and started walking toward the large pile of boulders where the walls of the pit opened just above them.

"Oh, no you don't," Matt said matter-of-factly. "Dad said it was too dangerous."

"Who is the climbing expert here?" Taryn retorted. "I've already studied these boulders. My weight is too slight to move them. I'll be fine."

"Yeah, you're such a great climber, you didn't think of a rope?" Matt shot back.

Taryn whipped a coiled rope out of her pocket. "Now, you have two options," she said quickly. "You can either help me or beat it."

Matt came forward. "I like the third option best."

Taryn stopped and looked at him. "What's that?"

"The option where I sling you over my shoulder and take you back to camp by force," Matt threatened, taking a step closer to her. A look of panic crossed Taryn's face in the moonlight. He'd gotten her there. He was clearly too strong for her.

"Matt, please," she said. "Think about this—what if it was the day before Christmas, and you got this enormous present from someone you know would give you something amazing. It's just sitting there, waiting for you to open it. Would you open it right away or wait until Christmas?"

Matt stared at her. "I'd wait."

Taryn stared back. "Liar."

"Okay, maybe I would open it. But what does that have to do with this?"

"That cave is the present," Taryn told him, uncoiling her rope. "And I can't wait until Christmas."

"*But Christmas is tomorrow!*" Matt whispered harshly. "Dad even said they were coming to clear the boulders away tomorrow!"

"Then it will be a whole day," Taryn said quietly. "I can't wait. Are you going to help me or not? I just want a tiny peek."

Matt folded his arms and looked at her. "What if something happens to you?"

Taryn sighed. "Nothing will happen. I'm going to climb up, take a peek, climb down, and go back to bed. No harm done."

"You're totally crazy, you know that?" Matt scoffed as Taryn threw him a grin and tied a quick bowline knot in one end of the rope. She stepped into it and handed one end to Matt, who glared at her but took it anyway. She started to climb the boulders.

She sure is nimble. Matt had to give her that. Taryn sprang lightly up the first few boulders and leaned forward to climb to the top. Within less than a minute, she had reached the mouth of the cave, pulling out a large flashlight to investigate.

Matt couldn't help it. He was curious too. "What do you see?" he whispered loudly.

"There's a good drop here," Taryn said as she shone the flashlight into the cave. "But it keeps going!"

"How far?" Matt asked.

"I can't tell. After about ten feet it curves to the right, and I can only see a wall of rock." She leaned forward as far as she dared, trying to see the ground inside the cave.

"Well, there you go. Now you can get down," Matt said, tugging gently on the rope.

"Don't do that," Taryn warned. "I might—"

And then with a gasp and a low rumble of stones, she disappeared from sight into the mouth of the cave.

31

Taryn!" Matt hissed and ran forward to the base of the boulders. "Taryn? Are you okay?"

There was no answer. "*Taryn!*" he yelled this time.

"I'm fine," Taryn's muffled voice came to him from somewhere inside the cave. "I lost my footing. *Ouch.*"

Matt, without thinking, started climbing up the loose rocks. "I'm coming to pull you out," he told her as he ran up.

"NO, Matt! Go for help!" Taryn yelled back. "Don't worry about me. I'm fine!"

"But I've got the rope," Matt countered. He slipped as he reached the top but regained his balance. A small shower of rocks erupted from underneath his shoe and tumbled down onto the larger boulders. He peered into the cave. He couldn't see anything. "I'm here. Let me pull you up."

"No, just go get help. It would be better," Taryn said.

Matt pulled his flashlight out, shone it down into the mouth of the cave, and saw her, about three yards down, sitting on the ground. She was covered in dirt and bled from a cut over one eye. "Aw, *man*, are you sure you're not hurt?" he demanded.

"I just got the wind knocked out of me, that's all," Taryn reassured, looking up at him. She stood up, brushing herself off. "I'm fine, see? Now you need to go."

"But I can pull you up," Matt protested, showing her the rope. "All I need to do is brace myself against . . . *whoa!*" The rocks gave way underneath his shoes, and suddenly he was plunging forward into the blackness of the cave as the rocks tumbled down behind him. He landed on his feet and fell onto his side with a painful thud, and Taryn screamed next to him.

"*Matt!* Are you all right?"

Matt groaned and lay on his side. "I think . . . I just bruised my ribs," he managed. He sat up, woozy. "I need a moment to breathe."

"Serves you right!" Taryn yelled at him. "I told you to go get help! Now no one knows we're stuck down here!"

"Hold on a minute," Matt winced as he sat up. "We're stuck down here because *you* got the idiotic idea in your head to come look in this cave in the first place!"

"Well, you tugged on the rope and made me lose my balance!" Taryn threw at him.

"Well *you* shouldn't have been goofing around on loose boulders!" Matt grunted.

"Just . . . be quiet and let me think!" Taryn yelled back. She looked up at the cave opening. It was about fifteen feet to the lip. "Hand me the rope," she instructed. Matt grimaced as he pulled the rope out from under his rear end, where he'd fallen on it. He handed it to her. She rooted around with the flashlight until she found a small but long and jagged rock. She tied one end of the rope around the rock, and threw it up into the opening of the cave.

"What are you doing?" Matt barked, holding his ribs.

"If I can catch on something, we can pull ourselves out," she explained quickly. "My dad did it once. It worked for him." She pulled on the rope until the rock fell back down at them. She squealed, moving just as it landed where she'd been standing.

"Smooth," Matt commented wryly. "Bashing your own brains in seems like such a bright idea."

"Then stop being a dork and *help me*," she said, picking up the rock to throw it upward again. "You've got the strong basketball player arms, why don't *you* try?"

Matt heaved himself to his feet and took the rock from her. He hesitated as he held it in both hands, like he was about to sink a free throw. He pitched the rock up into the opening of the cave. He pulled slowly on the rope, feeling it give, and suddenly, the rope stopped. He tugged on it once, twice, and it held.

He looked at Taryn, who gave him a smug look. "Don't even say it," he warned her. "Now, I'll go up first and then pull you up."

He started to climb up the rope, hand over hand. *Don't break, don't break, don't break*, he thought frantically, but then he heard a loud scraping sound, and the rope gave, sending him backward falling backward . . . again. He fell on top of Taryn and she muttered a surprised *Oomph!* as he landed on her.

"*Get. Off. Me*," she managed.

"Sorry, it's not like I was aiming for you—" he began, but his words were cut short by a dull rumbling sound and Taryn screamed directly into his ear.

"The rocks! *Move!*"

Before Matt had time to register another thought, he rolled off Taryn and pulled her out of the way as boulders and rocks crashed down from the opening above them. Matt tripped blindly along the dusty earth, dragging Taryn away from the rocks and debris as they continued to rain down. He pulled her into a corner and covered her with his arms as the opening closed itself from above in a mighty shower of rocks and stones and earth.

Finally, after what seemed like an eternity, the rockslide stopped, and Taryn and Matt uncovered their heads and looked up, coughing heavily in the thick dust and dirt that hung in the air.

The only light was an eerie patch cast on the cavern wall from the flashlight Taryn had dropped. She broke Matt's grasp and crawled over to it, grabbing the flashlight and shining it upward.

"We're sealed in," she said, her voice cracking. "Look."

Matt rubbed his eyes and saw where the cave opening used to be. It was now a solid wall of rubble. "That's just great," he spluttered, coughing and getting to his knees. "Now they're never going to find us."

"And if they do, we'll be mummies," Taryn said flatly, shining her flashlight around. "We might be sealed in here pretty good. The air might run out. I can't tell." Then she doubled over, coughing.

"No, I feel fresh air," Matt told her, holding his hand out toward the darkness of the cave. He could feel it, a faint breeze on his outstretched palm.

After Taryn recovered from her coughing fit, she stepped forward and shined the light into the cave. "See? The cave keeps going."

Matt let out a big cough and spit dirt out of his mouth.

He could feel the grit on his teeth, and he spit again.

"Well, we could keep on going to see where it leads," Taryn suggested. "But it's not smart. The best chance we have of being found is if the workers come back, and we can shout.

"Shout?" Matt ejected. "And they're gonna hear us over their jackhammers and bulldozers?"

"I didn't say it was a *perfect* plan," Taryn retorted. "But I *do* think we should stay here for now."

"We can't really go anywhere," Matt shot back.

"So, what do you want to do?" Taryn yelled. "I'm thinking as hard as I can, and I'm not coming up with anything!"

Matt didn't have an answer. "I don't know," he told her, sinking down to the ground, favoring his sore ribs. "I need to think."

Taryn sighed and sat cross-legged on the ground next to Matt. "I'm going to turn off the flashlight, to save the batteries, okay?" She clicked it off, and they were immersed in a thick darkness. Matt instantly broke out in a cold sweat. He hated total darkness. Just like he hated dark water. It gave him the creeps.

"We need to figure out what happens next," Taryn's disembodied voice said next to him.

"I feel like we're playing 'Seven Minutes in Heaven'," Matt attempted to joke, reaching out in front of him, waving his hand. "I can't even see my own hand in front of my face." *Please let me not act like a total sissy down here in the dark. Not in front of her.*

"Well, then, we're in a really *big* closet," Taryn joked, but Matt wasn't listening. He was busy doing mental math.

"So, we have about five hours until the sun is up, and knowing my dad, he'll be up then too. It will probably take an hour or so to turn up missing . . ."

"Try thirty minutes," Taryn interrupted. "You don't

know Nan. She's way strict. Likes to have all her ducklings accounted for."

"Okay, so roughly six hours," Matt conceded. "You know my dad will figure it out," he reassured.

"Yeah, I'm not worried about that," Taryn replied. "I just hope they can find us quickly once they *have* figured it out.

"They will," Matt reassured. "They'll have helicopters, SWAT teams, and the Marines looking for us." He wiped his sweaty forehead with a shaky hand. He didn't like being immersed in such complete darkness. "Can't you turn the light back on?"

Taryn clicked the flashlight back on, and Matt held his hand out to take it. "I dropped my flashlight somewhere around here." She gave it to him, and he stood up, wincing as he straightened to his full height, and shined the flashlight all around. "There it is." He walked over and picked it up off the ground next to the wall of the cave, brushing it off. He tested it out.

"Good, it works." *If only I hadn't used it to read the Book of Mormon for a few hours last night.* "It probably doesn't have much juice left."

Then he noticed the rope, sticking out from under some rubble. He pulled it out. "Looks like I saved the rope."

"We probably should just find a place to wait," Taryn said as he shined the light around. "Over there, against the wall."

Taryn stood up and walked over to the smoother part of the cave wall. She pulled her jacket from round her middle and sat down, her back propped against the wall. "Should we try to get some sleep, then?" she asked.

"What else is there to do?" Matt said. "We'll just waste the lights looking for a way out, and if we go farther into the cave, our chances of getting out get slimmer. I say we stay right here and wait for my dad."

Taryn managed a weak smile. "Okay. I'm with you on that one."

Matt walked over and sat down next to her, taking care not to touch her, and handed her the light. She clicked it off, enveloping them in inky blackness again.

Matt leaned against the surface of the cold rock, tilting his head back, and sighed heavily.

"Matt?" Taryn whispered through the darkness.

"Yes?"

"I'm sorry."

"I know."

He could hear Taryn moving around, making herself comfortable—as comfortable as she could get in a dusty cave, anyway.

"Taryn?"

"Yeah, Matt?"

"There isn't anything . . . *alive* in here besides us, is there?"

"I don't think so. Whatever *was* in here was probably hermetically sealed in by ash and debris, and wouldn't have survived. At least, that's what I think. Why do you ask?"

"I was . . . worried about you. You don't like bugs much, right?"

Taryn smiled. "Not a lot. Night, Matt."

"Night."

*   *   *

At six fifteen the next morning, Jared burst into the operations trailer, his face flushed with excitement. Ben looked up from the computer he was typing at, a cell phone cradled under his ear. He motioned for Jared to wait.

"Yeah, the blasters arrived about half an hour ago," he spoke into the phone. Yes, they're getting ready to set the charges now. I see. Uh huh . . . yeah, we aren't letting the students go near there until later. No. Nan is going to give them a lesson on cleaning artifacts after breakfast."

"You want to see this," Jared whispered, pointing at a rolled up piece of paper he was carrying.

"Hey, Dee, can I call you back?" Ben asked. "Great, thanks. 'Bye." He hung up the phone and leaned forward. "What is it?"

Jared unrolled a large photo of the stela Matt had unearthed and pinned the edges down with staplers and his own cell phone.

"I was looking at these glyphs at the bottom and trying to figure out why they weren't finished. I mean, with the Olmec sculptures, someone tried to deface them, but this is different. It's like the workers were working on this thing, and something happened to prevent them from finishing it."

"Theories?" Ben asked.

"That's just it. The only explanation for not finishing something this important would be death. And if it was only one stonecutter, they'd simply replace him. But *no one* finished it. So, I began to think death—on a grand scale," Jared replied. "I looked through my notes on glyphs, compared them to everything we know exists, and they're way too difficult to decipher without some sort of codex. But then I looked in the Book of Mormon, and Taryn was right."

He brought out a tattered, leather-bound copy of the Book of Mormon and flipped it open easily to where he wanted to read. "I cross-referenced all the possible city sites and considered post-crucifixion destruction, and I found this. It's been here the whole time!" He read:

"And behold that great city, Jacobugath, which was inhabited by the people of king Jacob, have I caused to be burned with fire, because of their sins and their wickedness, which was above all the wickedness of the whole earth, because of their secret murders and combinations; for it was they that did destroy the peace of my people and the government of the land; therefore I caused them to be burned."

"Right," Ben concurred. "We know this."

"Wasn't the theory that Jacobugath was burned and then rebuilt? And centuries later Teotihuacan was built over it?" Jared asked.

"It's a theory," Ben agreed.

"Well, I found this as well," Jared continued:

"And behold the city of Gadiandi, and the city of Gadiomnah, and the city of Jacob . . . all these have I caused to be sunk, and made hills and valleys in the places thereof; and the inhabitants thereof have I buried up in the depths of the earth, to hide their wickedness and abominations from before my face, that the blood of the prophets and the saints should not come up any more unto me against them."

Ben was silent and looked at him. "What are you thinking?"

"Well, look at this figure," Jared prompted, pointing at the picture of the stela. "He's clearly a king. Look at what he's wearing. And if you look at his knife, there's a little spot in the hilt—it looks exactly like the one we found at the site."

"Yes, I saw that too," Ben agreed.

Jared pointed to the picture. "I theorize that this was being made for a city, a city that fell victim to the catastrophic activity after Christ's death. A city that was sunk. We know specifically from the Book of Mormon that in this geographic area, four cities were sunk in the earth, Gadiandi, Gadiomnah, Gimgimno, and . . . *Jacob*."

"Oh my gosh," Ben breathed, not moving.

Jared grinned triumphantly. "If you considered yourself a

great king and had a city named after you, wouldn't you put a big old poster of yourself on it, so people would know it was your city? I know this is a stretch . . . but *this*," he said, pointing to the man on the stela, "could be Jacob, the same robber king who came over from the land southward. He infiltrated these cities. He destroyed the existing governments. Only a pompous, arrogant robber would proclaim himself king in such a way." Jared was speaking fast now. "The timeline is right, Ben. Nan dated the samples. They're from the time period. The geography definitely makes sense. The knife, the secret society, it all fits." Jared took a deep breath. "You know what this means if I'm right, don't you?"

"That we've stumbled onto the City of Jacob," Ben said simply, staring at the picture.

"It all makes sense—everyone was buried and killed before this stela could be finished," Jared finished. "We wondered what force could be strong enough to knock the stela over—a whirlwind or tempest, or *pyroclastic blast* sounds about right. It has to be true, Ben. It *has* to be."

Both men simply stared at each other, with large grins on their faces. Then Manny and Nan burst into the trailer, breaking the spell.

Manny glanced around the trailer. "He's not here either. Have you seen Matt?" he asked quickly.

Ben tore his eyes reluctantly from the picture. "Um, no," he said absentmindedly. "Haven't seen him since yesterday. Why?"

"Well, he wasn't in the barrack this morning when the students woke up," Manny reported.

Ben looked at his friend. "So, he's probably somewhere around."

Manny shook his head. "We've already checked, and the vehicles are all accounted for."

"Well, of course they'd be. We had the perimeter alarms armed all night," Ben said quickly. "He'll turn up."

Nan stepped forward. "Taryn wasn't in her bed this morning either."

Now they had Ben's full attention. He stood up. "Taryn too?"

"Do you think they would run off somewhere for . . . *romance* maybe?" Manny asked.

Ben leaned against the table. "No way, not Matt. No way." Then he thought a moment. "Well, I don't *think* so . . ." He thought some more. "Gosh, I hope not . . ." He was silent for a moment, deep in thought, and he looked up. "Okay, let's go look for them."

He turned to Jared as they left. "Let's continue this conversation ASAP, okay Jared?" he asked.

"I'm coming to look too," Jared said, setting his scriptures on the table.

32

AD 33

"THE TIME HAS COME," AMMARON TOLD THEM ALL.

Alba, Nuria, and Chemish had been sitting on the floor for hours since the sun had gone down, waiting silently for the city to quiet with sleep. Chemish had fallen asleep on his mother's shoulder, and what belongings they could carry were piled by the door, waiting for them. Ammaron had told them they would leave in darkness, but it already felt like the early hours of morning.

Alba choked back silent tears. They were really leaving. She would never see her eldest son again. The pain of this revelation wracked at her heart, and she held Chemish closer to her. "Can't we wait a little longer?" she asked.

"No, my wife," Ammaron said quietly. "All the houses have gone quiet. We must leave now. We'll have a few hours to get where we need to be before the daylight comes."

Alba nodded and looked at Nuria, who sat straight and tall, her mouth a tight line. She was afraid but trying hard not to show it.

"Come, Chem, it's time to go," Alba nudged her sleeping son, and he gave out a whimper and stretched against her.

Ammaron looked out the front door, watching the street, a strange expression on his face. He seemed anxious about something.

"What is it, husband?" Alba inquired. "Do we wait for someone?" Hope suddenly leaped up in her heart.

Ammaron looked at her for a moment but then looked back outside. "No," he said, his voice heavy. "We have waited long enough. It is past the time we should go. We must hurry, and quickly."

Alba stood and pulled Chemish silently to his feet, and he stumbled, whining softly. She bent down to him. "You must be strong and silent, little one," she told him, smoothing his curls. "I know you are sleepy. Will you be strong for us?"

Chemish nodded, rubbing his eyes. "Yes, Mother."

Then Ammaron gasped, taking in a large breath. The moonlight shining through the open doorway was blotted out, and suddenly large men were entering the house—men who smelled of rank and blood and filth. But one of the shapes was familiar. Alba gasped as Chemish yelled, "*Teom! Teom!*"

She threw herself at her surprised son, who caught her easily in his arms and held her close.

*   *   *

Teom *did* stink. But Alba didn't care. Her son had returned. And Helam was with him. And another girl she didn't know.

"Mother, this is Jahza, daughter of Nimrah," Teom explained. "She will be coming with us too."

Alba smiled at the girl, welcoming her, and broke the embrace, putting her hands on Teom's cheeks. "We thought you had deserted us and joined the robbers," she said softly.

Teom smiled at her. "I did, Mother."

She looked questioningly over at Ammaron. "He did it for us, my dear," her husband explained, walking forward. "We needed the robbers to believe he was intending to join them, to give us time."

"Time for what?" Nuria asked. Alba noticed her daughter staring at Helam with a large smile on her face.

"To leave, before the ceremony," Teom said hastily. "King Jacob is coming to the city today to claim it as his."

"How does that affect us?" Alba asked, drawing Chemish closer to her.

Teom looked at Ammaron, who nodded. "Hagoram was intending to have Father slain as a sacrifice to Jacob, to show the city that the reign of the chief judges is no more and that Jacob is their true king."

Alba looked at Teom with horror. "This is true?" she managed.

The girl named Jahza nodded. "I heard it myself. Hagoram was counting on the mob to rejoice in his death and worship Jacob as their new king."

"They've been carving monuments of him," Nuria added. "I noticed a new one when I went to draw water a week ago. Mekish the stonecutter has been working on it many hours every day. He told me it is because Jacob named the city after himself."

"And now we are the City of Jacob," Teom muttered. "Let him claim it. We will be gone before he arrives."

"Let us go, in haste," Ammaron said, lifting a bundle onto

his back. "Helam and Jahza, you are welcome to join us. God has showed me a place we will be safe if the robbers search for us."

Alba put a hand on Teom's arm and smiled at him, happy he was there. Her family was complete again. Then she noticed his hand.

"What has happened to your hand, my son?" she asked, gasping at the bloodstained bandage.

"I will have to tell you later," Teom said swiftly. "Do you still have the healing herbs?"

Alba nodded. "Yes, Nuria carries them."

"We must go now," Ammaron said, motioning to them. "We can tend to Teom's hand when we get there. It is a long journey of many hours. Will you be all right, son?"

Teom nodded. "Let's go."

They all took up their bundles, one by one, and disappeared into the night.

*   *   *

They stopped at the place of water first, and Nuria, who had been carrying the empty water jar, filled it with cool, sweet water for them to fill their water skins. Once they were all full, Nuria left the jar on the bank—it was too heavy to carry.

They walked again, and Teom suddenly remembered. He reached at his side and pulled out the knife of the robbers, with its sharp blade and golden hilt. He looked at Helam, who smiled at him. "I already threw mine away, after you told me Hagoram's plans," Helam said quietly. "When I realized there is no honor in these men."

Teom looked at the knife with the symbol of the jaguar and threw it away, into the brush. "That is what I think of them," he said, wincing at the pain in his hand.

"It only hurts for a few days," Helam told him, feeling the scar of his own hand. "If you have any brownroot, it helps with the pain." Helam looked down at the ground. "I'm sorry, Teom, for everything."

Teom managed a small smile. "You are a brother to me. All is forgiven. Now you must only make my sister happy." They both looked at Nuria, who walked several yards ahead of them with Jahza by her side.

Teom and Helam looked at each other, smiling, and walked swiftly to catch up with the others.

*   *   *

Morning came, and the sun shone hotly down, but they had been walking all night. They were journeying southward and had entered a land of trees that stood tall and lush, unscathed by the stonemason's blades.

"Is it much farther, Father?" Chemish lamented and was immediately shushed by his mother.

"Not too far, son," Ammaron replied, scanning the horizon. "By now Hagoram will have realized we are gone. We must keep going so that his men may not overtake us."

They walked a few hours more, taking sparing drinks of water and sharing cornmeal cakes Alba had brought.

They were still walking at midday. Teom had taken Alba's bundle onto his own back a few hours before, and Helam had taken Nuria's bundle so that they would be able to continue. Teom was surprised that he was not heavily fatigued. It was as if the strength of God Himself had poured into his own veins, to give him support. He walked with lightness of step, feeling the strength as it buoyed him up.

About an hour later, Ammaron stopped before the face of a large cliff and pointed to a small cave inside it. "This is where the Lord showed me to go," he announced, and everyone dropped their bundles lightly to the jungle floor, sighing as they stood up straight and stretched.

The cave was small, but it stretched far back into the rock, and it was clean. Ammaron instructed them to go all the way inside and bring everything with them. They unrolled blankets and laid them down, lighting a lamp to give them light. Ammaron instructed them to rest.

"We are to stay here," he told them solemnly. "Now I will tell you what I could not before. We may not leave this safe place. Something is going to happen. God showed me in a dream."

"What did he show you?" Alba asked, fear in her voice.

"Terrible things," Ammaron replied. "Cities burned, cities destroyed, and all their inhabitants slain. Jacobugath will be burned."

Helam gasped. "The great city?" he breathed. Ammaron nodded.

"And . . . our city?" Teom asked.

"All will be killed," Ammaron answered gravely. "Jacob, Hagoram, everyone within the city. God will smite them for their iniquities. They will be wiped from the face of the earth." He looked out toward the mouth of the cave. "It will not be long, now."

Helam wept for Izel, his mother, who would certainly be killed. Nuria put her arms around him and comforted him.

"We must pray to God and thank him for sparing us," Alba said after a long silence.

Teom nodded. "I will do it, Mother." They all bowed their heads as Teom prayed.

*   *   *

They quickly fell asleep afterwards since they were all exhausted from their journey. They had refilled their water skins earlier at a nearby stream, and Alba had packed food for three days, according to Ammaron's instruction. The inside of the cave was cool and pleasant, and a light breeze blew over them as they slept.

A sudden jolt woke them all. Chemish yelled out in fear, and the lamp went out. They huddled together in the darkness, clinging to each other, frightened, as the earth shook, and the mouth of the cave became blocked by falling rocks.

They could hear a terrible tempest howling outside, and feel the earth shaking and rumbling around them. The women wept, and Ammaron shouted above the chaos, telling them to be brave and not fear.

Teom held Chemish in his arms and closed his eyes as he felt the ground shake underneath them. There were terrible sounds outside—thunder, howling wind, the crashing of rocks. Utter destruction, as Ammaron had told them.

It went on and on for hours as they all held each other in the darkness of the cave, and then, suddenly, like a light being blown out, it ended, and all was still.

33

MATT AWOKE, DISORIENTED. HE WAS IN TOTAL DARKNESS, and his neck was sore. His arm had a heavy weight on it and had gone completely numb. Soon he realized the heavy weight was a lightly snoring Taryn, and then he happened to remember they were trapped in an underground cavern.

"Taryn, wake up," he said gruffly, nudging her off of him.

"Ow!" she said. "*What the . . . ?* Oh, yeah. I forgot. We're trapped."

"Did I ever tell you, you look fantastic in utter darkness?" Matt joked and felt Taryn hit his arm. *Hard*.

"Ouch! How did you know where I was?"

"Your voice, doofus," she said next to him. "I've lost my bearings. I'm going to turn on the flashlight."

He heard a rummaging sound and a click, and the bright light illuminated the cavern.

"Creepy," he muttered.

"Yes, it is," Taryn agreed. "Look, I bet your dad is going to come busting through these rocks, like, any second, so you stay here."

"And where are you going?" Matt demanded.

"I just want to walk a little way this way," Taryn motioned to the cleft in the rocks. "Just to see . . ."

"That's the same attitude that got us in here in the first place."

Taryn looked at him with doe eyes. "Pleeease? I won't go far at all, and I have light."

"Well," Matt said, getting to his feet. "I'm going with you. What if you run into a hungry bear or something?"

Taryn giggled. "Nice try. There aren't any bears in Central America, Matt."

Matt peered into the inky darkness ahead and stretched. His ribs creaked with soreness. He was sure his torso was covered with bruises from the fall. "There could be anything down here," he observed. Then he smirked an evil smirk. "Ladies first."

Taryn tied her sweatshirt around her waist again and started walking forward, with Matt following closely behind. The cleft in the rock was narrow. Taryn squeezed through easily, but Matt had to suck in his chest to get through. His bruised ribs smarted at the movement.

He stopped when Taryn stopped short in front of him with a large intake of breath.

"Matt! *Look!*"

"I can't see. Give me the flashlight," he said, taking it from her. He shined it straight ahead, and his jaw dropped open.

"*That* wasn't made by Mother Nature," he observed. Taryn said nothing. She just stared.

They had stopped in front of a stone wall covered with intricate carvings.

"What is it?" Matt breathed.

"It's a bas-relief," Taryn finally managed. She stepped forward and placed the tips of her fingers on the rough stone, touching the carved figures surrounded by scrolling shapes. "I think . . . I think this might be part of a wall or *building*, Matt. If we can just get around it . . ." Taryn walked to the left and held her hands out in the darkness before her, feeling her way until she disappeared around the corner.

"Wait, Taryn! You don't know what's in there!" Matt protested. He suddenly remembered all the Indiana Jones movies he'd seen growing up. Indiana Jones was always encountering trouble in ruins—the kind of trouble that could get you killed. Natives with poison darts. Passageways filled with death pits and spikes and *booby traps*.

"TARYN!" he yelled. He pushed and grunted through the slim passageway until he came out around the wall. Only it wasn't a wall.

He heard Taryn gasp for breath. "Oh my . . . *gosh*!"

Matt stepped out and stood beside her, hardly feeling as the flashlight slipped from his hands and fell to the earth with a clattering thud. They both stood, frozen, mouths agape.

About seventy feet up, a jagged crack opened up the ceiling of the cavern, where sunlight shone through in visible beams, revealing stone buildings that stood before them, ghostly and silent in the semidarkness.

It was a city. *A lost, ancient city.*

Matt hardly knew where to look first. Tall buildings, squat buildings—all covered in friezes carved with geometric patterns and shapes, perfectly preserved. It was as if the city had stood, frozen in time, waiting patiently for them to find it.

"Are you seeing this?" Taryn managed to whisper.

Matt nodded. "Uh-huh. Are those . . ." Matt breathed, still frozen.

"Yes," Taryn replied, her throat visibly working. She couldn't say anything else.

They both stared for a minute more. Or it could have been several minutes, or an hour. Time was immeasurable. At least until Taryn jumped in the air, letting out a whoop of triumph.

"YES! YES!" She threw both hands up and hugged Matt, surprising him, and releasing him just as quickly. She turned to face the city, put her hands on her cheeks, and continued jumping up and down, giggling hysterically. "We found it. *We found it! WOO-HOO!*"

She finally stopped jumping but continued to stare in awe at the sight before them. "I can't *believe* this, Matt! Can you?"

"It doesn't seem real," Matt managed. "Like out of a movie or something."

Taryn looked up at the crack in the cavern ceiling. "Yeah, it does seem surreal, doesn't it? Let's go further in."

Matt nodded silently and took Taryn's arm as they walked forward. He squinted at the dark doorways of the buildings, shuddering.

"What is it?" Taryn whispered.

"It's creepy," Matt whispered back. "Like something gross and unholy is going to come slithering out of those buildings or something."

"You've seen too many horror movies," Taryn chuckled as they made their way around chunks of broken stone and debris. "There won't be any zombies or gross, unholy—" Her words were cut off as she recoiled violently with a sharp intake of breath, staggering backward until she nearly fell into Matt.

"Ugh!" she exclaimed, and Matt steadied her, fighting the fear that rose in his throat at what he saw. Taryn whimpered and turned her head, burying her face in his chest as he shined the light ahead.

"Oh, *crap*," was all he could get out.

They were dead. Hundreds of them. Mummified skeletal remains piled at the base of a temple-like building, twisted and contorted in poses of agony, rotted clothing falling off their bodies.

Matt gulped. "They're all *dead*, right?"

Taryn regained her composure, releasing him. "Sorry. Yes, yes they are." She walked forward until she was standing right in front of them.

"Don't touch them!" Matt warned, grimacing. He shuddered as the light of the flashlight shined on rotted clothing, mummified flesh, and skeletal mouths frozen open in silent screams.

"I wouldn't dream of it," Taryn muttered, observing them. "Amazing."

"Are they mummies?" Matt asked as he walked forward, peering at the corpses. "Wow. The 'Hall of a Thousand Corpses' has nothing on this!" he remarked, remembering the grisly attraction that came to town every Halloween.

Taryn turned and looked at him. "They're not mummies, they're *mummified*," she corrected as she looked out over the vastness of the remains. "There's so many of them," she observed as she walked, sadness in her voice. She halted at the corpses of two small children, huddled together. She turned to look at Matt, eyes wide. "They were all trapped in here, Matt. They ran out of air."

"What a horrible way to go," Matt murmured, grimacing at the child-sized skeletons. He imagined being shut in complete blackness, unable to breathe, starving and suffocating to death. He shuddered again.

"You know what? I think this is one of the cities that was destroyed after Christ died," Taryn said quietly. "In the Book of Mormon—"

"I know, there were some cities that were sunk because of

their iniquities," Matt finished for her.

Taryn turned around and looked at him with surprise. "You finished it?"

Matt nodded. "Yep, I did. So, if we're right, these people were destroyed for a reason. They were all bad. Or at least *most* of them were," he amended, looking at the two little children again.

"Yep, they suffered an 'ignominious death,'" Taryn agreed. She looked again at the smaller skeletons. "And their children paid the price."

They were both silent for a moment, looking at all the dead.

"It looks like most of the survivors congregated here, at the base of this temple," Taryn observed. The structure, triangular in shape, rose up to the top of the cavern, where the flat top was concealed by black rock. "Who knows how long they lived, with their air supply dwindling, trapped in utter darkness," Taryn finished, looking down at one corpse whose jeweled bracelets and necklaces were still visible on its tattered clothing.

"Let's go farther in," Matt suggested, eager to get away from the dead.

"These are an amazing find," Taryn commented as they continued. "They'll give us insight into their everyday lives, their clothing and daily habits, everything."

"*Yippee,*" Matt retorted, dusting off his hands. "I'm more interested in the nonorganic stuff."

Taryn chuckled. "Of course you are. So, now that we've made a serious discovery, are you going to start appreciating what we do anytime soon?"

"I already do, Taryn," Matt reproved, looking around. "I don't need this to justify anything."

"You *don't?*" Taryn looked utterly nonplussed.

Matt looked at her. "No, I don't. You can rest easy."

Taryn didn't answer for a minute and then broke into a large smile and pretended to be interested in a sculpture of a snake on one of the buildings.

"To think, we were so close to this all night," Taryn mused as she looked upward at the light. "Oh my gosh, it can't be . . . you know what? I think that's the smaller fissure, at Dig Site B!"

Matt tore his gaze away from a pile of remains and looked up. "Are you serious?"

"Yeah," Taryn replied, chuckling to herself. "If we'd only investigated it first, we'd have found all this right away. But your dad went for the big fissure instead."

"Typical," Matt commented, amused.

"It's amazing," Taryn marveled, looking at the city and the cavern surrounding it. "It seems the city was trapped in an air pocket made by the volcanic debris and lava. It formed over part of the city and preserved it, intact. Do you realize what a find this is?" She gestured at the buildings. "We'll be able to get a snapshot of a way of life like never before! Not to mention ruins that are so perfectly preserved—they're almost *anti-ruins*."

"Un-ruined ruins," Matt suggested, smiling. "So, should we just climb up on that temple-looking building and scream into the fissure until someone hears us?"

"That's not a half-bad idea," Taryn replied, surveying the large building. "It looks like a climb, but I'm game." She thought a moment. "It might be easier with a rope. We left it where we slept, right?"

"Yeah," Matt replied, scratching his neck. "Want me to go get it?"

"No, I'll run back. I'm smaller," Taryn offered. "I noticed you had a rough time in the crevasse, back there."

"Okay, but if you're not back in ten minutes, I'm coming after you," Matt told her firmly.

Taryn grabbed an elastic band out of her pocket and whipped her hair into a ponytail. "I'll be right back." She winked and turned on the flashlight, disappearing around the side of the building.

When she had gone, Matt felt strange and a little anxious. Granted, he was standing in the middle of an underground tomb full of *corpses*, so the feeling was probably warranted. He liked Taryn's term "great archaeological find" better. It sounded less morbid.

He folded his arms and looked around. This was not a time to let his inherited irrational fear of dark places manifest itself. He should have gone back to get the rope. Then again, floundering in the dark would not be fun either. Taryn didn't seem to be afraid of anything. Ever.

Matt sat down on the base stone of a building and chuckled. *Taryn isn't afraid of anything.* Of course, her "bravery" had gotten them into this mess. *If only she'd stayed put and waited,* Matt thought. *I could be in my bed, sleeping in, because the blasters are going to blow up . . .* His eyes opened wide in horror and realization, and for a moment his heart stopped.

The blasters!

"Taryn!" he yelled with all his might, jumping up and sprinting toward the narrow opening she'd gone into a few minutes before. "Taryn! Come back! The blasters!"

But before he reached the opening, a large explosion rocked the cave, sending him sprawling, face-first into the dirt.

*   *   *

Nan, Manny, and Jared waited in front of the girls' barrack as Ben finished speaking to the DIG guards on his walkie-talkie.

"They combed through the trees, and they didn't find

either of them," Ben said, shaking his head. "It's strange. Where else would they have gone?"

Nan put her hands on her hips. "We've looked everywhere. Well, we haven't looked at the dig site, because of the blasting crew." Immediately after she spoke, a loud explosion shook the air, making them all jump.

"Wow, that's loud," Nan commented, sticking a finger in one ear and jiggling it. "So, anyway, short of flying over the fence, how else could they have gotten out? I'm pretty sure Taryn was up to something. She borrowed Claudia Phelps's flashlight."

"I still think they were meeting up for romance," Manny remarked. "Why else would she need the flashlight? They were sneaking out."

They were interrupted by Mark, head of the blasting crew, as he walked up to them, all dusty and wearing his hard hat.

"We had a good blast," he reported. "The cave you mentioned was sealed up—it looks like there was some sort of cave-in in the night. But we set the charges to clear away the boulders. It's wider now, but there was a secondary cave-in, and it's blocked with fresh rubble. Come see it and tell me what you think."

"Good, good," Ben replied, preoccupied. "I'll tell the . . . Hold up . . . did you say there was a cave-in?"

"Yeah," Mark answered. "We couldn't get inside to set the charges, 'cause there'd been a rockslide. Covered the mouth right up. So we set them in the . . . Hey, are you okay, Ben?"

Ben had frozen with a look of wide-eyed panic on his face. He looked at Nan, his mouth working soundlessly.

"*Flashlight*," he managed before breaking away from them and starting to run.

"*Oh my gosh*," Nan breathed, understanding immediately. "The *cave*!"

They all immediately ran after Ben.

*   *   *

Matt coughed violently, ejecting dirt from his mouth and lungs. He shook his head and tried to hoist himself to his knees, but he fell back down, dizzy.

"TARYN!" he yelled into the darkness of the tunnel. *There is no way she survived that*, his panicked brain told him. *She could be dead.*

No, she couldn't be! He staggered to his feet and stumbled into the darkness of the tunnel, calling her name hoarsely. He'd lost his flashlight and was running blind, his hands out in front of him, coughing and choking as he ran. Dust hung thick in the air, clogging up his lungs, but he pressed forward, tripping on a rock and falling down painfully onto one knee.

He stayed down for a moment, spasming into a coughing fit as hot tears squeezed out of his eyes. *She can't be dead. It's all wrong.*

"Taryn!" he yelled again with all his might, and his voice echoed through the thick blackness of the tunnel. He waited, holding his breath.

Nothing. Only silence.

34

BEN YELLED MATT'S NAME AS HE STUMBLED DOWN INTO the excavation pit, with Jared, Manny, and Nan running close behind.

He stopped, bent over with his hands on his knees, winded. He saw the gaping mouth of the tunnel as bulldozers worked to remove the rocks and debris. Jared and Manny caught up to him first, breathing heavily.

"My son," Ben managed, pointing at the cave opening.

Nan put a hand on his back. "They couldn't have been in there, Ben. They're somewhere else."

Ben shook his head as tears streamed down his face. "No. Taryn wanted to see that cave yesterday. She gave me a hard time about it. They snuck out to see it. I can feel it." He sobbed and ran toward the entrance, dodging boulders and barely escaping getting squashed by an oncoming bulldozer.

The operator stopped the machine and jumped from his seat, cursing at Ben as he ran.

"What are you doing, buddy? You freakin' crazy? This is a hard hat area!"

As the others ran past him after Ben, he threw his hands up in the air and stomped off.

Ben caught his breath at the mouth of the cave, cringing, afraid to look in case he saw any pieces of his son lying around. There was no way Matt could have survived a blast like that. The blast had caused another cave in, and the entrance, although widened, had been completely blocked once more.

Jared caught up to him. "Ben, be reasonable. They knew the blasters were coming. They wouldn't have gone in here."

"There was a rockslide!" Ben yelled at him. "They were trapped! They couldn't get out!" He collapsed against Jared as Nan burst into tears.

"Hey, what's goin' on here, Ben?" Mark walked up to them with the red-faced bulldozer operator at his side. "You guys know it isn't safe here."

Ben raised his head and looked at Mark. "My son was in that cave, Mark," he said simply.

Mark went white. "Are . . . are you sure? Because you said there wasn't anyone around, so we . . ."

"Look, we need you to clear away this rubble as fast as you can," Manny stepped in, taking charge. "They could still be alive in there, *comprende*?

Mark nodded furiously. "Yeah, you guys get back to a safe distance. I'll get more guys in here. Bill!" he yelled at the guy next to him. "Get all the guys in here now! Bring four hard hats!"

Bill took off running. Mark turned to Ben. "We'll get it cleared right away, Ben. Just sit tight." He looked at them all, and not knowing what else to say, he left.

"Let's go, Ben," Jared said, putting his arm around Ben's slumped shoulders. "Let's give them room to work. Don't give up yet."

Ben nodded mutely and allowed them to lead him away from the cave entrance.

*   *   *

Matt didn't know what to do. He'd yelled himself hoarse and worn himself out calling Taryn's name and stumbling over rocks, straining to hear any sound from her. But there was none. After a while, he gave up.

Taryn's dead.

He collapsed onto the floor of the tunnel, defeated and scared, feeling utterly alone. They'd been through so much together these last few hours. They'd kept each other safe. They'd made a huge discovery. And now she was gone.

Feelings he didn't realize he had bubbled to the surface, and Matt sank down to his knees, his body heaving in great wracking sobs. He was alone in the dark, and Taryn was dead. It was the worst feeling he'd felt in his entire life. He stretched out in the dirt, his body wracked with pain as he sobbed— sobbed for a friendship that could have been and never would be. For a girl he hardly knew but had known all his life. For a young life snuffed out too soon. Taryn would never again hit him on the arm in mock indignation or call him a dummy or ask him those uncomfortable questions that made him rethink things. He was *here* because of Taryn. He had reconnected with his dad because of her. And now, she was gone.

"*Please, Heavenly Father,*" he begged, clasping his hands in front of him. "Please let her be okay. Please help me." He let out one last sob, and buried his face in his arms.

Slowly, a warm, peaceful feeling spread over him, surprising him. Matt lifted his head, wiped a grimy hand over his eyes, and sat up in the darkness, as the warmth spread through his veins and gave him strength. "Thank you, Father," he uttered, closing his eyes in gratitude. "*Thank you.*"

He could go on now. Taryn might be gone, but *he was still alive.* He was going to find the rope and somehow get back to the fissure and yell through it with all his might. He put his arms out and found the wall of the cave. Thick blackness pressed in on him as he walked forward, keeping a hand to the cave wall to steady himself. The rough wall scraped his hands, but he was too anguished to care.

Then he heard something. His heart flopped over in his chest and his head snapped up as he strained to hear. It was a small sound, like someone coughing.

"Taryn?" he asked into the blackness, hardly daring to hope.

The coughing sound came again, faint and far away. *Taryn.*

"Taryn!" Matt lurched forward, stumbling and sliding with his hands out in front of him.

He tripped on her body, sprawled underneath a bunch of rubble, and fell over her, missing her by inches.

"Ow!" she protested. "What happened?" She coughed as Matt sank down next to her, shaking with elation and relief.

"You're alive," he managed. "I thought . . . I thought . . ."

"I was running back, and I got knocked out," she interrupted. She could barely choke out the words, and she broke down into a fit of coughing.

Matt felt in the darkness for her, found her face with his hands, and slipped his hands down to her shoulders. "I'm *so* glad you're okay," he said, fully meaning it. "Can you stand?"

"Yes, I think so," Taryn managed, and he helped her up.

"I'm covered in dirt." She tried to laugh, and it turned into another fit of coughing. Matt steadied her as she coughed and spat dirt out onto the cave floor. "I guess it wouldn't be a normal day if I didn't need to wash my hair!" She laughed again, and Matt laughed with her and crushed her to him in ia bear hug in the darkness.

"I thought you were dead," he told her, his voice serious.

"That makes two of us," she replied, her voice muffled by his shirt. "I forgot about the blasters."

"Me too." He released her.

"Here, I still have the flashlight," she said, turning it on.

"Wow, you *are* covered in dirt," Matt observed, in awe.

"So are you," she remarked. "Look," she pointed past his shoulder. "The wall. This is where the tunnel turned, remember? The wall must have protected me." She turned to face him. "Kinda scary, huh? Just a few less feet and I would have been—"

But she didn't get any more out because Matt put his arms around her and covered her mouth with his.

*   *   *

Some time later, they broke apart and looked at each other. Matt grinned down at her, bringing his hands up to her smudged face. "Don't ever scare me like that again, okay?"

Taryn blinked. "Uh . . . *okay*." For once she seemed unable to say anything else.

"Look, we'd better get away from here," Matt said suddenly. "What if they decide to blast again?"

"Smart thinking," Taryn agreed, and she welcomed his strong, warm hand over hers as they broke into a run back toward the ruins.

The ruins of the city, bathed in shards of sunlight from above, were a welcome sight. They walked past the remains and settled down on the same base stone Matt had sat on before, sitting together closely, shoulders touching.

"Well, at least we know they'll be unblocking the cave soon," Taryn said after a moment. "So, it's a waiting game. Man, I'm thirsty. I didn't plan very well, did I?"

Matt laughed, stroking her hair and making dirt fall out of it. "Nope. I'm thirsty too. But most of all . . . I have to pee."

"So, pee," Taryn said matter-of-factly. "But go do it in the tunnel. I won't have you desecrating our archaeological find."

"Yes, ma'am," Matt retorted, jumping down.

Taryn glanced around after he'd left. "Man, I wish I had more eyes. This is too amazing!"

*   *   *

They waited and waited. And waited some more. They fell asleep at one point, leaning against each other. But they were both jostled awake by a loud crashing noise and voices far away, calling their names.

*   *   *

"Matt! Taryn!" Ben yelled into the darkness of the cave.

Jared entered behind him and cupped both hands to his mouth, shouting their names as well.

"Look how far back this goes," he pointed out. "They probably weren't even here when the blast went off."

Ben peered into the blackness, the light on his hard hat shining brightly into the dust and rubble of the cave. Hope rose within him. He had spent the last hour on his knees behind a large rock, praying to God they'd be unharmed.

Then, to his great joy, a familiar voice came out of the darkness.

"Hi, Dad."

Ben cried out, unable to speak, as Matt and Taryn stumbled into view, shielding their eyes from the bright lights. They were both black with dust and dirt, and crusted with blood from assorted cuts and gashes.

"Oh, son, you're alive—both of you, I'm so sorry, I had no idea . . ."

"Dad, we're okay," Matt reassured, and Ben caught him up in a hug.

"My son," he wept. "You're safe." He grabbed Taryn as well and hugged them both to him. "I thought I'd lost you."

"Well, you found me," Matt said happily, hugging him back.

After a long while, Ben released them and glared at Matt. "I should turn you over my knee and spank your rear end," he chided, regaining his composure. "You scared the crap out of me! Out of all of us!"

Matt pointed his finger at Taryn. "It was *her idea*," he blamed.

Taryn put her hands on her hips. "*Traitor*," she hissed, grinning at him. "But I think you'll forgive us, very soon," she said, stepping forward and taking Ben's hand. "There's something we need to show you."

"What is it?" Ben asked, his eyes brightening.

"Just come and see, Dad," Matt answered, taking his father's other hand. He looked at the workers gathered around them. "Can we have some lights? We need a bunch." The workers scrambled out of the cave opening and returned a few seconds later carrying heavy-duty industrial lights and passed them all around.

"What did you find?" Ben asked as Jared handed him a flashlight.

Matt grinned his thousand-watt grin. "We can't describe it to you, Dad—you just need to see it for yourself."

And they disappeared into the tunnel of the cave, followed by everyone else.

EPILOGUE

AD 33

THE ROCKS COVERING THE CAVE OPENING FELL OUTWARD, and Teom and Helam emerged into the dusky, ash-filled air.

"I can't believe it," Helam uttered, surveying the landscape.

"Nor I," Teom agreed, his eyes wide.

They had been in the cave for three days, and now everything was different. It was as if a great storm had come and leveled the earth in places, as far as the eye could see. The trees and vegetation were destroyed, and where hills had once stood, there was flat, rocky earth. Where the ground had been flat, great jagged rocks pointed up toward the blackened sky. The land before them lay desolate and barren.

Kom, the great mountain, was completely obscured by a large cloud of blackness, as fire and smoke belched from its peak. The air was hot and stifling, and a thick gray haze hung over everything.

"Where is the great city?" Helam asked.

"It is gone," Teom marveled. "All of it."

Ammaron came out of the opening in the rocks behind them and stood surveying the destruction.

"It's all gone," Teom breathed.

"Yes, as God said it would be," Ammaron replied. "But look, here, the land has been spared."

"They looked to the south and saw that far in the distance, the land was relatively untouched in places.

"God has saved us," Ammaron said quietly. "We must bow down on our knees and thank him for his mercy."

Teom nodded. "Where will we go now?"

"South, where the land is unharmed," Ammaron answered. "There, we may settle and live again in peace."

Alba came out of the opening then, followed by Nuria and Jahza and, finally, Chemish. They stood in awe, looking out over the land that had once been so lush, so beautiful, with the grand city rising above everything. Now, it was all gone.

But they were *alive*. They had been spared.

They linked hands silently, not speaking, but looked to the land southward, filled with hope.

Hope for the future.

BOOK CLUB QUESTIONS

1. What do you think the similarities are between Matt and Teom's lives? How are they different?

2. The title of the book, *Unearthed*, implies that something was found. What do you think this could be, literally and figuratively?

3. What lessons do you think Matt learned from his time in Mexico?

4. What temptations did Matt and Teom face, respectively?

5. What would the Gadiantion robbers of Teom's time be likened to today? How are they even more dangerous now?

6. How do you think Alba felt as each chief judge was murdered, knowing her husband could one day be called to that position? Would you consider her a strong person or a weak person?

7. After reading Teom's story, do you think the people of the Book of Mormon faced the same basic problems, dilemmas, and temptations as we do today?

8. Did Teom make the right choice, pretending to join the robbers? Would you have chosen differently were you in his situation?

9. Taryn used bribery to get Matt to go to Mexico. What does this tell you about Taryn? How do you feel about her character, knowing the outcome of her choice to bribe Matt?

ABOUT THE AUTHOR

A LIFELONG MEMBER OF THE LDS CHURCH, LARA STAUFFER grew up wanting to write. A voracious reader, she loved the escape a good read would always provide. Her writing has been shaped by a deep love of the things of the past, and *Unearthed* is the result of her fascination with history and the people of the Book of Mormon.

Lara is the author of the blogs *Ramblings of a Suburban Soccer Mom* and *The Potted Pen,* and she can be found on Facebook and Twitter. She currently lives with her husband and four children (and a maltipoo named Maggie) in North Carolina.